Yonders, Illinois

By Dennis Noyes

ISBN: 978-84-09-54291-8
Spanish Legal Deposit: B-17263-2023

Cover design:
Trebol Editions

Layout:
Amelia Fernández Valledor

Printing:
Publikum d.o.o.

Publishing house:
Trebol Editions (treboleditions.com)

To my grandmother, Bessie Lee Swisher, the little girl from Iowa who loved the sounds of the night.

October 2, 1959

The Dixie Flyer, running an hour late out of Chicago, came down hard from the north on the day of the night of the murders. The blue and gold streamliner called out for the graveyard crossing at the county line and cannoned past the white, gabled Wyatt farmhouse set back from the dirt road, stark amid the sweetcorn stubble.

Rachel, her yellow summer dress golden in the sunlight, ran barefoot the length of the lawn, both arms thrown high to the mile-a-minute train. The engineer gave a short blast of the whistle and waved from the high, rocking cab. Old man Wyatt looked up from the hunting rifle he was cleaning on the back porch to see that moron girl of his chasing the train again, like an old dog that still runs after corn wagons.

The Flyer, bound for Georgia and high-balling to make up time, set off the crossing bells at the north end of Yonders just as the two-minute whistle blew at the Illiana Canning Factory. The whole town could hear the big diesels churning past the grain elevators, raising dust in the lot out back of the old icehouse.

The kid, on his way back to work, heard the clanging of the crossing bells only a couple of blocks behind and floored his black '50 Ford, racing for the downtown gates, but the train was already rattling the dishes in the cupboards along First Street and scattering the sparrows up from the trees.

The Korean War hero, playing solitaire eight ball at Brownie's, felt the rumble in the floor, drawing his gaze from his shot and out the back screen door. From beneath the trees back of Jessup's Auto Repair, the tremendous locomotive broke into the sunlight hauling a dozen shining cars south in pounding staccato clatter over the Nickel Plate crossing. A ragged man in overalls, sitting noonday drunk on a rotting cable spool back of the power plant in the shadows along the roadbed, saw her pass and looked after the boat-tailed bar car with Indian summer longing.

The little Ford, tires squealing, turned onto Main. Rookie cop Buster Lawton, parked in the alley between the liquor store and the tracks, reached for the ignition, watching the kid's front tire skim the white line. Buster knew him, that Putnam kid, flirting with another reckless driving ticket. But the kid held his lane and the young cop's hand returned to the wheel.

Keelan Putnam saw the gates already down, and he slid to a whopper-jawed stop. He could have made it with a bit to spare, but now he was going to be late again. He could see the flag flying over the factory only two blocks away as the Flyer, shrieking and shaking the world, streamed across his path. It made him so goddamn mad that he wanted to kill somebody.

Above, coal-black crows gyred and played in the winds over Yonders, and the columns of smoke from the tall brick stacks of the Illiana and American Pride angled south following the Dixie Flyer on her way.

PART ONE

1959–1998

Chapter 1

1998
Thirty-Nine Years Ago Tomorrow

Police Chief Buster Lawton and Keelan Putnam sat alone in their houses only five blocks apart, both watching thc Cubs-Braves National League playoff game down in Atlanta while Buster's wife was attending a teachers conference at the University of Illinois, and Keelan's was in a jug on the bookshelf.

Even after thirty-nine years, Buster and Keelan had known each other at first sight. Keelan, walking along Main the day after his return, spotted Buster driving by in his green pickup. Keelan didn't need to see Buster in the police car to recognize him, and Buster saw through the years to the same Keelan, his prime suspect in the Wyatt murders, a case that was solved, closed and, to most, long forgotten. Keelan nodded and his grin was so slight that only Buster could have seen it.

"If he so much as spits on the sidewalk," Buster told Night Captain Murdock that evening. And Murdock got him, got his license anyway, for drunken driving, though he wasn't even driving.

Buster's house, the same house he grew up in from the age of eight, was a single-story, GI-Bill prefab that his dad, just back from the Pacific, bought in 1945. He gradually built onto it over the years, adding two rooms and extending it toward the now ragged and weedy right of way of the Nickel Plate Road that once carried the fury of black steam engines so close to the house that they shook the floor. The east-west branch of the Nickel Plate went derelict in the late 1980s and then, while Buster's parents were still alive, the tracks were taken up, leaving in their place only an overgrown space and the lost echoes of other times.

Keelan's rented shotgun shack was set close to the bank of the north-south C&EI that once carried passengers from Chicago to Evansville, Indiana, with transfer to Atlanta, New Orleans and Jacksonville, Florida. Many old Yonders folks said what they missed when they went out of town was the sound of the trains, especially the moaning whistles that blended with dreams.

The two railroads had other names when they intersected in 1872 on a section of open prairie known back then as "the lost forty." That crossing was the reason for Yonders, once sitting just off a major highway but now a town bypassed and isolated at the hub of a triangle of Interstates, none within twenty miles, as far away as close can be.

Buster was hopeful. There was nobody on and nobody out, Cubs holding a 1-0 lead, the Braves coming to bat in the bottom of the ninth and he was letting himself half-way believe this might be the year. It was his dad who was the big Cub fan. Buster and his dad used to listen to the games on the radio and now he watched them on TV whenever he didn't have anything else to do. Sometimes he almost felt his dad was there with him and, Lord! his dad would have been on the edge of his chair for this one. The umpire was dusting off the plate to start the bottom of the inning when the phone rang.

"One run won't be enough, Buster. Cubs won't hold them." It was a familiar voice, starting right in with no hello. Ira Cockrell, former Marigold County Chief Sheriff's Investigator.

As soon as he recognized his old friend's voice, he remembered that he was supposed to call him about trying to schedule a basketball game for the Yonders High School team. This had to be something else, and it had to be pretty important or Cockrell wouldn't be calling him during the game.

"Cockrell! I hear you're cheating the government out of retirement money since you took that high-paying job as athletic director with the high school," said Buster.

"I wish," said Cockrell. "I just try and make sure we don't schedule two games on the same night. They barely pay my gas to the games."

"What's on your mind, Ira?"

"It's what ought to be on yours I'm calling about. That boy that confessed to your triple homicide back in '59 just suddenly remembered the other day that he killed somebody else altogether and got confused during questioning and took credit for the wrong crime. Your old chief must be sitting straight up in his grave now, head up out of the ground, grass in his hair, looking around telling everybody he was right all along."

Finally, the call he had been half expecting since that day in the winter of '60 when old Judge Otto Rutledge—they called him "Sparky" due to his preference for the electric chair—sentenced a skinny Black kid from Blunt to a term only Methuselah could serve. The *Chicago Tribune* called the sentence, ninety-nine to one hundred and fifty years, "theatrical." Chief Warry went down to the one-day trial. When he returned, he told Buster, fresh out of the Army, just twenty-three years old and in his first year on the force, "This ain't right. Makes no goddamned sense."

"Let me turn this down," said Buster. "Lane something, wasn't it?"

"Freeman Lane, his name is. It seems the young man was confused at the time of the confession, but you'd think he'd have noticed the difference between one man in an alley and a farmer and his family in their house. Those old pre-Miranda interrogations befuddled a lot of folks back then. Anyhow, after studying it for about forty years, he finally figured out that he'd been mistaken about who he killed and how many there was of them. Maybe all white folks do look alike to them."

Buster imagined Cockrell sitting at the kitchen table down in Damascus thinking he was funny.

"You still there, Buster?" said Cockrell.

"You got my full-goddamned-undivided attention."

“Seems the old boy, less than a third of the way into his hundred-and-fifty-year sentence, told the prison preacher a story and this preacher started asking questions and called a lawyer out east with an outfit called the Innocence Project. That was a new one on me. You heard of it?”

“I have. Go on.”

“Well, whatever he told the preacher and the preacher told the lawyer made enough sense to cause the lawyer out east to call some lawyer in Springfield to go after the transcripts of the old trial. He called a reporter from the *Herald* too.”

“A reporter named Wolf-something?”

“So, why am I calling you if you already know everything?”

Klesko lifted a flyball to short right and Sosa was there to take it for the first out.

“I’m just starting to put it together,” said Buster. “He came to see me a couple of weeks back writing something on the Wyatt murders of ‘59. I drove him out to where the old gate posts used to stand. Place stood empty for years and burnt down back in the seventies. Who does the convict think he killed instead of the Wyatts?”

“You’ll remember a couple of weeks after your farmers got killed we had a Damascus big shot turn up with his throat cut in an alley down on Jackson Street. Crawford, his name was. He would have been heir to Crawford Real Estate. Lane recalls now that he killed Jack Crawford. I think you’ll be reading about all this real soon.”

“You mean in the paper from this Wolf guy of yours?”

“Andy Wolfden. He’s the one wrote all that on meth

dealers in high school. You do get our paper up there, don't you?"

"Yeah, and a bit of your meth too. I'll be looking forward to tomorrow's paper. But, you know, it's funny you calling me because I been meaning to call you about a basketball matter. You home tomorrow? I got a big meeting down your way with the Sheriff that will probably run till after five. I'm going to get something to eat downtown and I could drop by after supper and take up this basketball matter with you."

"That'd work just fine if you could drop by around six, but I'm betting it won't be just to talk about no basketball."

"I should be able to make that and be home in time for…" and then, under his breath he said "Shit!" watching the ball fall into the fifth or sixth row beyond the left field wall down in Atlanta. Tie game.

"Home run!" said Cockrell. "What'd I tell you? Your damn Cubs is cursed."

The Braves All-Star catcher was doing his home run trot and Tapani, on the mound, was looking like his dog died. "Since when do you watch the Cubs, Ira?"

"When there's no other comedies on."

The fans were carrying on. The hot-shot kid that hit it was high-fiving the batboy and the Atlanta fans were tomahawking and chanting. Buster looked away from the TV and out the front window to the old football field across the street. "You still live in the same place, Ira?"

By the time Cockrell finished explaining in too much detail how to avoid some roadwork on the way to his new house, the Cubs had men on first and third with one out, still tied 1-1 in the top of the tenth.

"I'll be seeing you tomorrow," said Cockrell. "I'll let you get back to enjoying your ballgame."

Damn! Double play. Typical Cubs, but it didn't even make him mad, because he was way back in 1959 and remembering how Chief Warry returned from the trial in Damascus shaking his head, saying there was no way that Black kid ever killed anybody in Yonders, saying the kid had probably never set foot in Yonders.

Bottom of the tenth. Buster went to the kitchen to get a Black Label. He saw through the kitchen window that he'd left the mower out. He opened the bottle and stepped out. The night was fresh and clean in the moonlight and he heard a freight train coming down from the north, wailing faintly over the fields, still miles off, probably half way down from Willows. Sounds carry on windless nights. He stood for a minute listening before putting the mower in the garage. Fat moon, waxing. He went back in to watch the rest of the game, but it was already over.

The Braves were all jumping around and the Cubs were walking off, hanging their heads. Buster didn't know what happened and he didn't want to. Game three, the announcer said, was in Chicago, October 3, the day after tomorrow.

That's when it hit him. The next day, Friday, was October 2, the day in 1959 when all hell broke loose, sirens yowling, red lights flashing. The night dispatcher called and said get out there quick. He remembered the bodies, all three long-buried out on Floral Hill just east of the tracks. That's why the Damascus reporter came to see him. It made sense now. The big story would be in the morning paper. It all happened exactly thirty-nine years ago tomorrow.

He put on a jacket and went out on the porch. Across the street the old moonlit football field took him back, as it always did, to memories of the good times running on that grass. The old high school didn't have a field back then, so Buster played his home games at the grade school, right across the street from his own house. Now they played at the new high school and Wishing Well Field was used for soccer, but his mind's eye re-chalked the yard lines and hash marks of the old gridiron.

From the north of town, he heard the freight train again, a lot closer now, whistling for the Double Aught crossing and a little later calling out for Johnson Avenue.

Chief Warry was sure from the day it happened that the murderer was either Keelan Putnam or Clive Barber, sure of it till his dying day. "It'll all come out some day." And now it had, some of it anyway. Buster never believed a word of Freeman Lane's confession, but he'd never seen Barber as the killer either. It was Keelan he'd been thinking about all these years and now that killer was sitting over there along the tracks probably watching the same ball game, both of them hearing the same train whistles.

▪▪▪

Keelan Putnam, in his little house by the C&EI tracks, didn't really give a damn whether the Cubs won or lost. There was nothing else on and watching the Cubs lose took his mind off the crazy talk he'd heard just that day when he was having lunch downtown. Somebody talking about the ghost of Running Rachel. He was just starting in on his Belly-Buster Special at the front window nook of the Two Spot Cafe when some old fool, a northsider by his Kentucky way of talking, was saying some old lady was claiming she'd seen Rachel. And right then Buster came cruising past on Main Street in his shiny, new police car. It was just a glance but, even from halfway across Main and at twenty miles per hour, he saw Buster looking right at him, still out to get him, and for what? For crimes some Black kid confessed to and was serving life for.

The rest of the day, doing yard work and painting a doghouse for Mrs. Spencer over on Indiana Road, he tried to put Buster out of his mind, but that man had it in for him, always had. Everybody thought that stocky little bastard was some kind of hero just because he knocked people around on the football field forever ago, and now he was the big chief with nothing better to do than spend his time poking around in what was dead and gone.

Keelan's TV was yelling. Last time he paid any attention, the Cubs and Braves were tied 1-1 with the Braves coming up in the bottom of the tenth and the announcer was carrying on about the Cubs winning and going to the World Series. And now the game was over. Look away for a minute and everything changes. The announcer was saying the Cubs needed to win two in a row to keep their faint hopes alive. They just needed their luck to change, the announcer said. That's about all anybody needed.

"Here's to good luck," Keelan said aloud, holding up his can of Bud and looking up at his wife on the bookshelf in her little blue jug with the yellow butterfly on the side. She didn't answer, but sometimes she almost did if he listened hard enough.

All in all, he'd been a pretty lucky man, and all he had reason to fear had been left a half a country away. Except for Buster. He was only a few blocks away and he just didn't know how to quit.

Out back on the C&EI, a long freight train was passing, whistling to wake the dead, if the dead could wake. He looked out the window and there was enough moonlight to see the scrawling on the boxcars and containers—gang writing you couldn't make heads or tails of even if the train was stopped. The white cross on a maroon Santa Fe boxcar reminded him of the crucifix on the back wall at the God Behind Bars services at Nevada State Prison.

When the last of the cars passed, he sat looking a while longer at the tracks in the moonlight. There was no ghost in a yellow dress running by.

Chapter 2

1998
Like the Day Before Yesterday

Buster sat in the swing with his beer listening to the whistle of the southbound freight and looking across the street to the old football field. In 1955, his senior year, he was the captain of the Yonders Harvesters, number 60, leading the shouting, fired-up team, cleat-clattering up the echoing stairway from the basement locker room and out the double doors into the fresh November night, crunching gravel at a quick jog to the field and sprinting out to the shouting and applause from the home grandstand—twenty boys under the floodlights in their home whites, stopping in a cluster at midfield to salute the crowd as the horns and drums piped and rattled out the fight song and schoolmates, parents, neighbors and townsfolk cheered. He was All-County, offence and defense, guard and linebacker, young and fleet, without a care, raring to go, ready to rip.

That Homecoming Game seemed like the day before yesterday, and he made the tackle, a hard one, on the opening kick-off. His mom never went with his dad to the games. They scared her, but she sat out on the porch where he sat now, her sight of the field blocked by the brown canvas that covered the perimeter fence on game nights. She said it always made her happy to hear her boy´s name over the loudspeakers: "Tackle by number 60, Buster Lawton." Buster could hear it too, usually just as he got back to his feet. Right across the street. Like the day before yesterday.

Tomorrow would be a busy day, starting with the Action Group breakfast at the Dixie Diner at eight and later the drug bust planning meeting with Sheriff McIntyre set for 1 p.m. down in Damascus. Operation Marigold North. They made it sound like Desert Storm. These were not just some punk meth-cookers like last year. This time there was a Mexican from Old Mexico whose last name was O, Geronimo de la O—hell of a name—and another boy from up north. There was a local boy too.

He´d just about have time to stop off at Cockrell's and still get to the witch meeting at the First Church of Christ by eight. Witches! Every year there was more silly shit to be dealt with. When the city council decided to eliminate the position of dogcatcher, who did they think folks were going to call every time a stray lifted a leg? And then there was old lady Holt claiming people were sneaking into her house and watching her TV, playing her piano and looking at themselves in her bedroom mirror when she was out shopping. She said she knew they had been there because they always put things back exactly as they had been. Bruno Murdock, who went over to her place the first time she reported whatever it was she reported, asked her how she knew others had been looking at themselves in her mirror. "A lady knows," she said.

He'd stop by Cockrell's after the drug bust coordination meeting, but he had to allow for enough time to get back for the Neighborhood Watch meeting that everybody in town was calling the witch meeting, set for eight so the folks who ate late suppers could make it. It was Mayor Tom Wellington's big idea. Ellen called it a mixer. Easy for her, off in Champaign, but he'd have to be there in uniform with badge and gun to keep the peace in the basement of The First Church of Christ and prevent the Christians and the witches from getting out of hand and embarrassing the town in the Damascus paper and maybe even the *Chicago Tribune*. Towns like Yonders only made the papers when there were fires, murders or some silliness. This was Nat Hook's doing, leasing the old township building to a coven, a coven for Christ's sake, of goddamned witches. That stuff was OK for the movies or California maybe, but not for Yonders.

Old Ira Cockrell's call had knocked 1998 in the head and taken him back to 1959, to the thing that wasn't settled, that wasn't right. Down in Damascus everything was different, bigger, louder, but Yonders was just older and smaller. And a lot of those kids in the leather jackets with the old, loud cars, kids Buster grew up with, were still around. They graduated or didn't, joined the service or got drafted, too young for the war in Korea, but the ones a few years younger than Buster were just right for Vietnam. Most of them came back and got married to somebody they went to high school with, got jobs in the factories, had kids, drank at Sniders' or Turk's and went to the high school games to cheer for their kids, their grandkids now. They were either already retired or about to retire when the factory stacks stopped smoking and the town started to shrink and turn in on itself.

Warry only had one question back in '59: Was it Clive Barber or Keelan Putnam? If the old chief could have settled on one or the other, he'd have figured how to make an arrest, but then the county stopped him in his tracks by hanging the whole thing on some kid from Blunt who probably couldn't find Yonders on a map.

To Buster it seemed too much of a coincidence that Keelan was fired the same day as the murders and that he ran off when the investigation was still going on, especially right after Warry, bluffing to try and get one of his suspects to show his hand, told the paper that he had it narrowed down to a single suspect and expected to make an arrest shortly. No more than a couple of days after that story came out, Keelan headed off out west, running off in the night leaving a pregnant wife, but Warry was still hard set on Barber being his murderer, even after the Black kid confessed and was sentenced. To the day he died, Warry kept to the notion that it was Barber who killed the Wyatts.

Warry didn't like Barber's looks. He said he was just another Sugar Bowl hood with his collar turned up, trying to look like one of those California kids in the movies, but Buster saw it differently. If Clive looked like James Dean, it was because Dean looked like him. Dean was just a Hoosier kid from over in Fairmont, two hours due east of town. The puny, little lost kid and the girl in that old movie could be from California, but one look at Dean and you saw home, water tower, cornfields and that sweet '49 Mercury of his. Besides, no kids from Fairmont or Yonders or any other little town from those days would get themselves talked into playing chicken with a cliff above the ocean, even if they had a cliff to drive off of and an ocean to drown in, and Buster doubted even kids out in California were that stupid.

Well before the Wyatt murders, Warry had his eye on Clive because he was from out of town and because he didn't work cornpack. Keelan worked first at Pride and then at Illiana—they both fired him—but Clive worked at Cannon's Speed Shop in Damascus. That explained not only how good his Merc looked, but also how well it sounded and ran. Mike Murphy, who pumped gas out at Four Corners, said he got a glimpse under the hood when Clive was checking his oil. He always checked it himself. The motor, Mike said, was shiny and clean enough to eat off of, with finned aluminum cylinder heads, chrome head bolts and three deuces with chrome air filters. Buster wasn't a car guy but he knew what all that meant. Clive Barber's Merc was sweet to the ears.

The northside kids used to cruise out Main to the Dixie, on south to Indiana Road and loop back east onto Iroquois and then to Main and around again, breaking away now and then to make a little highway run, blowing the cobs out they said, and then back to the loop, flipping cigarette butts out the window, listening to the belting rock on WLS 890 or country on Yonders' own little station. Whenever Clive drove by, Buster and every man and boy in town, the northsiders anyway, looked up at the bark and growl of those pipes and, if they said anything, they said, "That sure is a nice car." When folks remembered Clive driving by, they likely as not saw pretty Jezzie sitting close at his side.

When Keelan drove by nobody much noticed.

Buster sipped his beer in the quiet. The summer nights were noisy and busy in town back then, especially during pack. At dusk the cicadas would give over to the crickets and katydids, whippoorwills and nightingales, the lonesome mockingbirds and the hoot owls. All during the hot August nights of cornpack, there was the hum and rattle of the factories, the whistles of the night trains and switch engines and the crashing of the couplings of the boxcars at the loading docks.

Then, in March of 1960, long after Freeman Lane flabbergasted Chief Warry by confessing to a crime Warry would have bet his soul the kid didn't commit, Barber left town too.

With both Barber and Putnam gone and a man found guilty, the case was about as closed as a case can be. Clive Barber went to California and on to Vietnam, missing and presumed dead, the Army said. Keelan Putnam never made it past Nevada before his first prison term. After Warry retired, Buster kept track of Keelan's arrests and convictions and his releases. He served three stretches in the Nevada prison system and, in early June, showed up back in town, walking down Main one evening.

That's when Buster thought of Harold Dresher, Mrs. Dresher's boy, an old man now, living all alone in the big house on Swisher Avenue. Warry always said the only possible clue to which of those boys killed the Wyatts was rattling around lost inside Harold Dresher's head.

Back then Harold was working down in Louisville. Drove up to see his mom and crashed his new car into the graveyard gate just across the tracks from the Wyatt farmhouse on the very night of the murders. Sheriff Foster questioned him as a possible suspect at the hospital in Damascus, but anybody who knew the terrain knew a man crashing into that gate would have been going the wrong way to be fleeing, and anybody who knew Harold Dresher knew he didn't go around killing people, at least not in peace time. Warry talked to him several times, asking if he'd seen anything that night, but all Harold remembered was a car jumping out at him off Double Aught Road. Warry said all he needed to know was whether that car was a Mercury or a Ford. That'd do it for him, he said, but Harold couldn't say. The doctors said Harold might yet recall some of it someday. He seemed to still be in his right mind and he was keeping himself fit too with his long evening walks, sometimes all the way downtown to the C&EI tracks, stepping out briskly for a man of his years and sometimes quietly talking to himself.

Buster finished his beer, went inside and set the alarm for seven. Lately, since he had started thinking about retirement, he found himself waking long before his alarm sounded. The bedside clock, a ticking, glow-in-the-dark wind-up that lost a minute every hour, had been his mom's. Ellen said he should get an electric one, but sometimes the power went out. Each night he wound it and put back the lost minutes.

Buster heard a southbound freight calling in the night from out north by the graveyard. They were running them close tonight. His mom loved hearing the trains day or night, especially the fast passenger trains on the C&EI—through town in two minutes—rattle-banging over the Nickel Plate crossing and gone in no time. The freights, slower, heavier, had their own sound. It had been years since they'd run passenger trains through town, but Buster remembered. His mom loved those mile-a-minute streamliners with names everybody knew, trains that only stopped to pick up or put down long-haul passengers: the Meadowlark, the Humming Bird, the Georgian, the Whippoorwill and the Dixie Flyer. She would look up from whatever she was doing and name the train. One of these days, his mom used to say, smiling, she might just hop on one of those fast trains and ride it all the way down to the Florida sunshine. She never did, but she listened for them every day: "Ten-ten," she'd say, squinting at the clock, "Dixie Flyer, right on time and she's not stopping this morning."

And what was it his mom used to say at the end of a day? His grandmother said it too. Something about God and the Devil and heaven and corn, all mixed up together.

Chapter 3

1959
Stacking Boxes

Seconds after the silver, streamlined bar car of the Dixie Flyer flashed by, Keelan accelerated hard under the rising gate, grazing it with the antenna, but out of the corner of his eye he saw the police car hunched trackside in the shadow of the liquor store. Wouldn't you know it! Nothing better to do than torment a man just for trying to get to the damn timeclock before the ink turns red.

He couldn't afford to be late again, but he couldn't afford another ticket either. He slowed and rolled down Main at 25 mph. Just take it steady, Keelan, he told himself. That's just Buster. If he stays put you'll be out of his sight once you get past the newspaper office. But in the mirror he saw Buster pull out from the alley in the black and white Fairlane Interceptor and tuck in behind him.

Buster eased up on Keelan's bumper and Keelan made a hand signal to turn left. His fist went out the window like a punch. Buster passed on the right. Their eyes, Keelan's glaring, Buster's steady, met for an instant and the rookie policeman carried on west out Main past American Pride. Once he was clear of Buster, Keelan floored it. As he pulled in the employee lot, he saw Buck standing half in shadow in the employee entrance, sucking on that damn cigar. The starting whistle blew and all over town folks checked their clocks and watches.

He punched in two minutes late. The time, 1:02, printed out in red on his time card. Buck was standing in his office door now, smiling that smile of his. Keelan walked past him looking straight ahead, stopped at the water fountain, bent and slowly drank the cold water. His line was running but there wasn't a single box on the belt. His two minutes in the red hadn't cost the Illiana a nickel.

Old Hobie, his stacking partner, usually the first back from lunch, was already there, looking up to the square maw at the top of the high wall where the conveyer belt from the main factory dumped the cases out onto the banked ramp of rollers that curved down to the stackers on the warehouse floor at the end of the line. Hobie was in his place, shifting back and forth from one foot to the other, his arms hanging straight down, opening and closing his hands, anxious to get stacking. Keelan thought stacking was the worst job in the warehouse. No way of knowing when there would be an avalanche of cases. Line goes light, boxes dribbling over, and a man wanders off to have a smoke on the dock or take a piss or get a coffee at the machine outside Buck's office and, all of a sudden, the line's backed up and Hobie's yelling for help. And the worst was working the long hours during pack. All you knew was that the two stackers and the last forklift driver, never Buck's boy, would be the last three sons of bitches in the warehouse to go home. When the line went quiet you'd step out on the dock and look over at the main factory and if the main chimney was still smoking you knew you had, at very least, two hours to go. When the white smoke finally broke and quit, you knew that the last batch was canned and cooked, but it still had to be labeled, cased and dumped on the belt. During the heaviest weeks of pack he'd get home between midnight and 2 a.m. after sixteen to eighteen hours stacking boxes, almost too tired to reheat the supper of hamburger and dried-out potatoes left for him on the stove, easing into bed beside Mae, still seeing boxes on the line when he closed his eyes, and then up at seven-thirty, with barely time to say good morning to his mom over bacon, eggs and coffee in the kitchen, Mae still sleeping, his dad already off to work. Punching in just on time, eyes stinging from the light, dog-tired, back at the line with grinning Hobie waiting for the morning's first run of boxes.

But cornpack was running down. Back on lazy eight and ten-hour days. He'd be looking at a fall, winter and spring of steady work and steady paychecks. Hobie liked stacking off the line, said it left his mind free to wander in the realms of the Lord. He could quote the Bible to beat the band, and he was always happy to tell you whatever he thought you needed to know about the awaiting glory in the golden streets of Heaven where every day was a spring Sunday and folks spent their forevers sitting in the porch swing, singing gospels at some little church in an East Kentucky heaven, cutting up around the supper table with the grandfolks, uncles and aunts, kin and old friends, all reunited in the happy homecoming of death. That was the same heaven Keelan had been taught, but he'd lost it somewhere along the way.

It was all quiet as the afternoon started that day, except for the hum of the empty belt, but from deeper in the warehouse amid the high stacks of cases of canned goods, came the sound of the forklifts groaning up to fetch down pallets and lowering them until the clink of the forks on the cement floor and then the whining of the propane-powered lifters and squeezers, hustling the cases to the railroad docks where the loading crews waited by the boxcars.

The lone marker case came off the belt and down the line: 24 number 303 cans to the box. Hobie grabbed it, gave it a couple of shakes and said, "'sparagus." He'd been stacking so many years he claimed he could feel the difference between a case of sweetcorn, beets, asparagus and butterbeans. Peas and corn felt about the same, he said. Keelan pulled up the flap of the next case and checked. Asparagus. The first run of the afternoon came down thick and heavy, fresh cooked, cases still warm with some of the flaps standing up like rabbit ears, but that often happened until they got the glue right.

Hobie dropped the first box onto the pallet, and for the next hour he and Keelan stacked without a break until the end marker box came down. Hobie rolled a cigarette and Keelan stepped out into the fresh air of the First Street truck dock. He could see his Ford at the end of the worker's lot. He'd be trading in one of these days on a '55 Chevy V8 if the bastards at the bank would grant him credit.

The bosses had their own parking lot and didn't have to punch in, just wandered in as they pleased, paid five times more for sitting on their asses all day than he was for busting his. Keelan knew he'd never be a boss, but he didn't want to end up like Hobie, stacking his life away in a rail-side warehouse. They said Hobie'd never been late since he got back from the big war. They said he was right in the thick of it, but he never talked about the war except to say that the Lord had watched over him through the Valley of the Shadow of Death.

Nobody knew much else about Hobie except that he could piss over a boxcar. Not from ground level—no man could do that—but from the loading dock with a lot of strutting around first and then a run halfway across the dock, stopping quick and letting go, arcing over the boxcar roof out to the mainline. Once during pack Keelan saw Hobie clear a rust-red boxcar on the south dock. He'd heard about it, but he didn't believe it until he saw it. Clear over the roof. Keelan doubted he'd ever see anything to top that if he lived a hundred years.

The other men laughed at Hobie, almost to his face, and Keelan knew they were talking about him too, behind his back, but one day when he was loading boxcars on the dock, Athol Fox leaned down from the forklift and asked him, right in front of the other men, if he didn't have to carry the Kentucky marriage certificate when he went out with his wife. "You be wanting to keep that handy, or old

Warry'll have you for contributing to the delinquency of a minor."

Keelan kept stacking cases; didn't even look at him. Athol leaned down a little farther and said, "You must be getting a good education with the little wife of yours. I mean, you must be helping her with her homework. What grade's she in now? Third or fourth? What's the stickin' age down in Kentucky, ten or twelve? I forget."

She would have been a freshman if she'd stayed in school and they knew it, but he just kept on stacking. He thought maybe they'd just forget and decide to torment somebody else, but the next day he was headed for the toilet and had to pass Athol, down off his lift truck and going over something with Buck on a clipboard in the door of Buck's office. Athol looked up and said something. Keelan heard his name and Buck laughed. Keelan slowed and looked over. Athol took a slow step towards him. "You got a problem, Putnam?" Athol was a brick shithouse of a man. A couple of men on the way to the coffee machine stopped to watch Athol back Keelan down. There's times a man has to eat a ration of shit and he never forgets the taste.

If Keelan was ever standing behind that big bastard—just the two of them out on the dock when they were coupling freight cars out on the line—he'd wait till the last instant and shove his ass on the tracks. He once heard about a young switchman over in Lafayette cut clean in two, the top half of him propped against the banking, his buddy giving him water and the water running out with his blood and guts, and his legs still twitching between the rails, they said.

That's what he'd like to see, Athol Fox cut clean in two and dying slow, his legs twitching their last on the tracks.

The whole factory and probably half the north side knew he backed down. There were lots of men working at the Illiana who wouldn't have stood up for a second to Athol. He could see some of them felt sorry for him and that made it worse. It would take time, a long time, but he could live it down if he kept working, kept taking home his paychecks and carrying his load.

He had to make sure he was never late again, never stepped out of line. He worked hard that last afternoon shift, slamming down cases, doing more than his share. About an hour before he punched out of what would be his last shift at the Illiana, he walked out onto the railroad dock for a smoke. He'd heard the Meadowlark's whistle and he got out there just in time to watch her storm past, coming up from down south and from places he'd never been. He was full of hope, standing in the warm breeze smoking a Camel, watching the Meadowlark till she was out of sight, hearing her whistling for Johnson Avenue and then for the Double Aught crossing, past the cemetery and the Wyatts' farmhouse, heading for Chicago.

It was the last day of his old life back when everything that could have been still could have been. He was so close to happy. He had a good job, a pretty little wife and it was payday. He'd have another fifty bucks and change in his bank account by Monday and every Monday after that until the overtime started again with next year's pack. He'd buy a better car, and move out of his folks' house and into his own place where what he said meant something. He'd do right and be a good man, putting food on the table, presents under the tree, drinking downtown on Saturday night like everybody, a man who was listened to when he had something to say and quiet when he didn't, a man who knew about guns and cars. A man nobody gave any shit to if they knew what was good for them.

He couldn't remember if he guessed what was coming when he joined the short punch-out line and saw Buck, square-faced and mean-eyed, waiting for him just outside the door in the evening sunlight. If he could have walked out the door past Buck with just a see-you-Monday nod, everything would have been different. But no, he wasn't allowed that. At least Buck didn't yell it; he said it soft and easy. "Putnam, we're cutting back a bit and we won't be needing you for a while."

They never tell a man he's laid off until the old boys in the offices get the last eight hours of sweat out of him. Keelan didn't even raise his voice to Buck. "I'd expect you'll be keeping your own boy on. I worked with him out at the Mexican Camp last week. Mostly I worked without him."

"You'd be advised to watch your mouth, Putnam," said Buck, speaking softly, leaning slightly forward. He was bigger than Keelan, not as big as Athol, but he was the foreman.

Keelan knew better than to say another word, but he heard himself talking anyway. "All I'm saying is he spends most of his time smoking out on the loading docks, knowing he can do as he pleases 'cause he's got his old daddy to cover for him."

"Did I say you was laid off? I misspoke. Your ass is fired. And I'll tell you something for your goddamn personal edification, Putnam. I was all set to lay off the hobo we hired out of a boxcar and keep you on, you being from here and all, but you punched in late again. You're a screw up, Putnam, and worse than that, you can't stop your own mouth to save your soul." And Buck turned away and walked back inside, out of the sunshine, nodding and joking with the men who were punching out.

Buck had said it plain the day Keelan was late his third day on the job. "I know they fired you over at Pride and I've heard it was for loafing. A man comes from Pride to Illiana knows he's gonna work a lot harder for a lot less, but a man fired at Illiana has got no place to go in this town."

Fired for the second time and it wasn't fair either time. At American Pride they'd had him poking cans high in the 110-degree loft with Davey Cooper, whose dad was a full-time Pride worker, and Davey was hung over and off in the toilet throwing up when a big run of cans came down. The only way one man working alone could keep the trough from backing up was to start forking cans onto the floor. The run finally stopped, cans all over the place. And, wouldn't you know it! Davey wanders back to the line just as old Spencer comes by, a boss working long past retirement age with nothing better to do than roam the lofts looking to make trouble. Keelan had been working his ass off and was sitting down to rest when Spencer comes in glaring and yelling about cans on the floor. Davey starts scrambling to pick them up and put them on the line and Keelan, slow to stir, said something—he didn't remember what, but the wrong thing. And, sure enough, when he punched out, Andy was waiting by the clock to tell him he was done, that old Spencer had shitcanned him. And now, for being two minutes late, Buck had left him nowhere to go.

Keelan stood for a moment looking at Buck's back until he went into his office. Keelan, fired, turned away, counting 1,2,3,4. It was a cloudless fall sky, all gold and orange out west, the kind of sky he remembered from his days as a kid playing along the tracks, counting boxcars and seeing how far he could tightrope walk the rails.

And there was Buck's red and white Oldsmobile sitting in the foreman's slot, clean whitewalls and a chrome spotlight on the driver's door too, like he thought he was a damn cop. The Ford started on the second try and Keelan drove slowly over the loose gravel to the head of the row. The Olds was in a perfect spot. He lined it up behind him and tromped the gas, flinging a spray of pea gravel on the hood of the two-tone Rocket V8. His dad taught him: "There's three things you don't fuck with: a man's house, a man's woman and a man's car." What else is there? There was a fourth thing. His damn life! Buck was getting off easy for now, thought Keelan, as he accelerated, spinning and fishtailing, out of the parking lot.

He was still in second gear and foot to the floor when he passed the Donut Shop. Somebody said, "Who's that damn fool?" Somebody answered him. "That's Etna Putnam's boy, a Tucker if ever there was one."

But he didn't run the stop sign onto Main. He got ahold of himself and counted his way home and, as he was counting, he slowed to a crawl through downtown. Looking out for that damned Buster Lawton. The train couldn't help making him late, but Buster could have just looked the other way. They'd left him no choice.

Stealing was easy to start and hard to quit. His mom caught him the first time. She took him over her knee and whipped him hard with her sewing ruler, whipped him till she broke it. He was old enough to go by himself to the store on the corner and buy candy. A nickel would buy a bottle of Coke, a Baby Ruth, or, when they were in, a Turkish Taffy stick. Keelan didn't have an allowance, but sometimes his mom used to give him a nickel.

One day he asked for a nickel and his mom said he'd have to wait till payday, but he knew she kept the milk money in a blue hanky in the top drawer of the sewing machine, and he stole it. The whipping he got was not for stealing; all kids do some stealing. It wasn't for lying; all kids lie. It was for lying to his mom, for stealing out of his own home. It wasn't just a whipping either, it was the whipping of his life. She slapped him hard on both cheeks before she turned him over her knee.

"I'll teach you to lie and steal," she said. And when the whipping stopped, she stood him up straight and shook him like a ragdoll. "Don't you never steal from your own and don't you never, never lie to your mother. A boy that lies to his mother and steals from his own people will grow up to be a man that ain't worth shootin'."

She dried his tears on her apron and then bent down and put her face so close to his that her eyes were all he saw. "You got the Tucker blood in you and you'll be fighting it all your days. You got to fight it! When you feel it in you, you got to count to ten, to a hundred, to the end of numbers, or the old Devil will come and drag you off to the hot place. Now here's what you stole from your own—a nickel your pa sweated for. I can tell when you lie. Are you gonna promise me that you'll never lie to me again?" He mumbled yes and reached for the nickel, but she closed it tight in her fist and said, "I mean promise me, promise me on your life." And he never forgot; he promised on his life. "Now you go and buy yourself something sweet from me and your dad and remember your promise always. Go on, git!"

He didn't want to go back to stealing, but now they'd left him no choice. There wasn't a shop or store on Main Street he hadn't considered and rejected, one by one. A man would be a fool to try and break into the clothing store or the coffee shop or the hardware store without knowing for a fact that there was cash money on the place and that there wasn't some loud burglar alarm with flashing lights waiting to bring the cops from two blocks away, but there was one place out on its lonesome with a cigar box full of money just waiting for him and he had it cased, just in case. As long as he was working, that box could stay put in its drawer, but if it ever came down to it, if they left him no way out, he'd do it on a Friday evening when the woman and the idiot girl would be at the show leaving the old man out there all alone with his box of money.

One day, standing by the empty line, Hobie said, just saying whatever came to him, "The day of the Lord will come like a thief in the night." That sounded right to Keelan as he slowly drove the red-brick, tree-tunneled street that led home, just over a country mile from the farmhouse standing alone out at the end of Iroquois across the tracks from the graveyard.

He parked out front so nobody could block him in the driveway in case he had to go somewhere after supper. He checked the gas gauge. His dad was in the garage bent over the fender of the Chevy, tinkering under the hood. Through the living room window, he saw his mom sitting by Mae on the davenport, their backs to the street, watching TV, and he saw his little sister Jezzie appear behind the screen door. She looked out whenever she heard slow driving. Jezzie, looking to see if that Clive Barber of hers was cruising by.

Chapter 4

1959 –1998
Something in the Air

Jezzie was wiping down the counters and the booths, getting ready for the breakfast shift at the Dixie Diner when something, a glint off the glass, the scent of approaching rain, took her back there, forty years ago. Lately it happened more often. Must be something in the air. No harm in it, and it was still ten minutes till opening time.

▪▪▪

She was just a freshman, getting a drink out of the fountain down on Iroquois and Main one spring day when she heard the Merc rumbling behind her at the curb. She knew that car and that boy. She took another swallow and let the water run, cool water against her chin, but the rumble stayed put.

"Hey there!"

Margie whispered. "Jezzie, Jezzie! He's talking to you!"

Jezzie turned, wiping her mouth with her wrist and hiding her smile, and saw him in the window of his low, black Merc, white tee shirt, black DA rolled up in front.

"Come on over here a minute. Unless you're scared," he said, smiling a tricky smile.

"Jezzie, don't go!" Margie clutched at her elbow.

"I ain't scared," Jezzie said, walking right over to the window.

"How old are you, anyhow?"

"Old enough to know better," she said.

"Here's a dime," he said, "Give me a call when you turn fifteen." And he drove off, smiling back, straight pipes rumbling. Everybody said he was bad. She slipped the little dime into her red wallet and dropped it into her purse.

▪▪▪

She could almost hear the open exhaust of Clive's Merc easing away, but then Ruth spoke her name from the arched kitchen window. "Jezzie, honey, can you put the Reserved sign on the corner booth. Buster and the boys are having another one of their Action Group meetings."

"Lord help us," said Jezzie.

The Dixie Diner sat alongside Buddy Bowman's Marathon Station. Gasoline and coffee and food and oil and bathrooms, just what folks needed, and the parking lot of the Dixie Diner joined with the forecourt of the gas station.

Lisa Riggs wrote in her "News and Views on Main Street" column that the town, at one time back in the fifties, had twelve filling stations, rail service north to Chicago and south all the way to Florida, and a population over 6,000. That was before the factories closed. Twelve gas stations and, by Jezzie's recollection, a dozen churches, five bars, four factories, two undertakers and one town fool. That was back when all the stores and shops were open on Main Street and when there were passenger trains running on the C&EI, stopping to pick up and put down passengers. Now the signs at the city limits read 5,208 and Yonders was down to two factories, three bars and four service stations, and the last town fool, poor Timmy, wandering the snowy fields south of town, got himself killed on a winter night in '61, mowed down by the northbound Humming Bird. There hadn't been any passenger trains running through town, let alone stopping, since the early seventies, but there were still a dozen churches, thirteen if you counted the Universalist Unitarians that is, and both undertakers were doing just fine.

Sometimes when she saw little, bandy-legged Buddy hustling out to the pumps and back, she thought of that night, the happiest of her life.

▪▪▪

Nobody expected to see Buddy come off the bench against Damascus in the Marigold County Championship Final in March of '60. Yonders had never beaten Damascus in anything and everybody knew it would take a miracle to beat them in the county final. Yet Yonders was still leading by one point with five seconds to go when the blond Damascus star—the one who went on to play for Purdue—was fouled in the act of shooting by big Tom Wellington, his fifth and the third Yonders starter to foul out. There was nobody left on the Yonders bench except the kid who never got into games.

Ross Harrison, who would have gotten the call, was in the locker room soaking his sprained ankle in a bucket, but Coach Jessup confessed later that if Ross had been on the bench he would have sent him in anyway, even if he was hopping on one foot.

When the Damascus coach saw Buddy, looking dazed, heading for the scorers' table, he called time to reset the defense for the final seconds. The blond boy hit both free throws to put Yonders one point behind with no time outs left. Damascus threw on a full-court press and Terry Savage, who owns the bowling alley now, was double-teamed and trapped at midcourt, but he managed to heave the ball to the only man open, the one player Damascus wasn't worried about. Buddy was standing scared and flat-footed, off catty-cornered to the right about eighteen feet out, unguarded because his defender was helping smother Savage.

Jezzie and the other Harvester cheerleaders in their blue and white outfits were kneeling at courtside. Since the tipoff they had been yelling, stomping, clapping, and jumping. Jezzie could walk on her hands and she did at the end of some of the cheers. Across court the Damascus cheerleaders, dressed in devil red, had their fans counting down the seconds. Everyone who was there that night remembers seeing Buddy catch the ball on a head-high bounce and heave up a two-handed prayer. It was off the backboard and in just as the buzzer sounded, and the Happ Hopkins Gymnasium went hog wild. The other four Yonders players leapt in the air again and again like little kids, and Buddy stood frozen amid it all watching the bouncing ball that nobody wanted anymore because the game was over. The Yonders Harvesters had beaten the Damascus Bulldogs and Buddy Bowman was a hero…

▪▪▪

…and he still is. Jezzie, so many years later, smiled to remember it all. People who weren't even born the day of Buddy's last-second shot knew of that game by the black-and-white picture, snapped by Lloyd Miles Sr. just after the buzzer. It ran on the front page of the *Chronicle* and is still enshrined behind the glass of the high school trophy case for all to see over the years, the Damascus players slumped and crumbled and the Yonders boys jumping high, hands over their heads, not a one of them touching wood but little Buddy, smiling the smile he still smiled now and then, his buzzer-beating smile that lasts a lifetime. The caption read, "Senior Harvester hero Buddy Bowman smiles as cheerleader Jezzie Putnam cartwheels in the joy of Yonders' miracle win over the mighty Damascus Bulldogs."

▪▪▪

A big cattle truck, airbrakes making a racket, pulled into the station, and Ruth was banging around in the kitchen, getting ready. The Coca Cola clock said five to seven, five minutes to opening time.

■■■

Clive was there the night of the big game, up in the high, back row where he always sat. Clive Barber, her demon lover. Her friend Margie called him that, from a poem they read at school. They warned Jezzie that she would be kicked off the cheerleading team if she was ever seen with him on school grounds, but they couldn't stop him from coming to the games. She didn't dare speak to him or even come close to him at the gym. It was a scandal that a fifteen-year-old cheerleader was going steady with a juvenile delinquent who was four years older, but it was the last home game of the season and Yonders had beaten Damascus for the Marigold County Championship and she just didn't give a damn what the principal said. She jostled her way through the rowdy, happy crowd to Clive. Principal or no principal, school board or no school board, she and Clive walked out of that gym holding hands, leaving the cheering behind. It wasn't until they reached the gravel parking lot that she realized she was barefoot.

They told her to keep her shoes on when she was cheerleading—those were the school rules—but she learned to cartwheel barefoot as a kid and she never remembered kicking off her shoes that night.

After the game, Jezzie rode proud and happy with Clive in the black Merc, cruising in the slow line of cars and pickups honking up and down Main Street. Later they parked out by the gravel pit and kissed and schemed. And they made love—went all the way, kids said back then—for the first time. He told her, "I'm getting out of here as soon as I get a couple of paychecks ahead. When I get me to California, I'll get a job and I'll make something of myself. You wait for me, Jez, and don't never believe nothing bad they tell you about me. I'll come back for you. I promise it on my life."

"When?" was all she asked. "When are you coming back?"

"As soon as I can," he said. "I won't let nothing stop me."

He called often at first, telling her he'd seen the Pacific Ocean and that he had a job, but the calls became less frequent, and sometimes neither one of them knew what to say. He called on Christmas eve, but there was music and laughter in the background and he seemed to be in a hurry.

Then, after months with no word, Clive phoned in the early spring to say he was in bad trouble but the judge said he wouldn't have to go to jail if he joined the Army. "I did something real stupid," he said, "but I'll make it up to you." He enlisted for three years. He never wrote or called again. But he promised on his life.

She couldn't find out anything. Clive's grandmother had moved away and no one in town knew anything about him. She kept cheerleading and was captain of the squad her senior year. Nobody but her mom and her best friend Margie knew she hadn't quit waiting and hoping. She went to her junior and senior year proms with a nice northside boy, John

Baker, whose dad worked with her dad at the Food Equipment Corporation factory.

John was sweet. He proposed twice, the second time during the summer after graduation. He was hired on steady at Food Equipment Corporation and her dad said he was a nice boy, solid and hard-working. After that second proposal—he offered a ring, but she said she had to think—she called the VA in Damascus, but they wouldn't tell her anything. She wasn't kin.

By the time she learned Corporal Clive Barber was missing in action—it was public information in a registry of Illinois MIAs printed in the *Chicago Tribune*—she was Mrs. John Baker, a married lady with a baby on the way. When she found Clive's name near the top of the alphabetical list, she realized she had still been waiting for a letter, hoping and fearing it would come.

But maybe he was still alive, hiding somewhere in the jungle. She watched the news on TV, looking for him in black and white and then in color. Someone missing could always be found. She didn't know what she'd do if Clive Barber drove into town one day, except she was afraid she really did know and it scared her. She continued to check the POW lists, but it wasn't until the seventies that they changed his classification from "Missing" to "Missing with presumptive finding of death."

Then came the happy years, busy times that flew by, raising kids, buying a house, tending a garden, working here and there after the kids were bigger and after they were gone off to live their own lives. But poor John, the picture of health, fell sick with pancreatic cancer and was gone only a few months after the prognosis. And then she was living alone. Sure, her mom lived close by and most of her old friends were still in town. John had taken out good life insurance and she had a job waiting tables anywhere she wanted, but often found herself remembering. Sometimes she'd almost see him driving by and hear that old Merc rumble and maybe the radio playing low, maybe poor Richie Valens singing that song of theirs. It did no harm to anyone else and, even though it was pure foolishness, it almost made her happy sometimes. Sad too.

"I won't let nothing stop me," he said. She still had his dime.

■■■

Jezzie turned the sign in the window to OPEN and soon the breakfast rush was on. Double sausage and eggs for a big old trucker in an Atlanta Braves hat. Poor thing. Wrasslin' that wheel day and night. She took the trucker's order and gave him his smile.

"Didn't nobody tell you this was Cubs country?" she said.

He looked puzzled at first, like he'd been far off, then he touched the brim of his ball cap and smiled back, "I'd wish y'all luck but I don't think it'd do y'all no good against our boys after what happened last night and what's gonna happen to y'all's Cubbies tomorrow."

She liked that. Three y'alls in the first words that man had most likely said to a living soul that morning. She'd never been to the South or anywhere else to speak of. She'd never even set foot in Kentucky, but in Yonders you didn't need to go to Kentucky to be a Kentuckian. Maybe someday she'd make the drive down to Regret that her mom was always talking about. Enough time had passed and it was the men who had to worry. Besides, that was all far away in blood and time.

The Dixie was nearly full. Just two booths empty and one of them reserved for the chief, Mayor Wellington and the other two Action Group boys for another one of their breakfast meetings. Looking around the diner, she saw everybody was taken care of for the moment, all the orders served, all the cups refilled. Richard, the Hoosier from the company over in Kokomo that was installing equipment at the Illiana, was in the little side booth, smiling at her way too much just because she'd gone to the show up in Jericho with him a couple of weeks back. He was pestering her to go again. She probably would, but not just yet. Nice fella, and it was fun to eat popcorn out of the same box with someone at the movies after so many years.

Most of the folks she could name, the rest she could place except for the trucker with the Atlanta hat and a thin, proper old lady who was just having coffee and toast and whose grey Pontiac Tempest had Iowa plates. Whichever direction she was coming from, there was no place except McDonalds to stop for breakfast at Four Corners and she'd have seen the sign with the big red finger pointing north. "You can't go wrong at the Dixie Diner"

Jezzie liked working at the Dixie a lot more than the other places she had waitressed downtown. There were only two others that served breakfast: The Two Spot and The Depot and they both wanted her back, but you couldn't please everybody. She'd see people at the Dixie that she'd never seen before and she'd never see again, folks in off the highway who'd never drive into town. Was that Iowa lady coming back from a funeral or going to one? Maybe she was going back home after a life somewhere else, her husband dead, her kids gone off, and one day she goes down to the bank and draws out some traveling money and locks up the house, leaves a note for the milkman—no, there ain't no milkman no more—tells her neighbors, an old couple she'd known since she was a spring bride, to watch the place, said she was going to visit a cousin in Ohio or Indiana or Illinois. Why, Bess—that'd be her name—Bess, they'd say, you never said nothing about no cousin over there. OK, she just moved there from out west or back east, but there was no cousin, she was going home after fifty years. Nobody waiting back there for her but ghosts and old shadows at street corners. But she wouldn't tell her neighbors she was going home to nobody.

There you go again, Jezzie Putnam Baker, she thought. Head in the clouds, her mom used to say. OK, maybe she killed her husband and managed to stuff him in the trunk and was hauling him to the only place she could think of—a little pond she used to swim in when she was a girl. Maybe she was taking him to dump him, weighted down with a couple of concrete blocks that used to prop open the back door in summertime, taking him to dump him in the swimming hole down in Milton. Jezzie imagined walking over to the table and saying, softly, Ma'am, it's all built up with fancy houses around the pond over there now. They'd see you for sure, but if you can wait till after I get off, I'll lead you out to the gravel pit and we can dump him there.

"Boo! A penny for your thoughts." Cotton Kramer, coming back in from the men's room, snuck right up on her.

"You got me dead to rights. I was planning how to run off with you without your wife finding out about it," said Jezzie.

"Don't you give it a thought," said Cotton's wife from the nearest booth. "You're more than welcome to him."

There was laughter from the closer booths. The lady from Iowa looked up surprised at the hubbub and she seemed to Jezzie to look straight at the trunk of her car.

"Here come Hook and Ladder," said Jezzie, gesturing toward the highway. Nat Hook and Rusty Rhodes were wheeling in from opposite directions, Hook in his white van that had Reddy Kilowatt with his red, lightning-bolt body and light bulb nose painted on the sides under the words Hook Electrics. Rhodes drove his big, red Ram pickup with the tool chest behind the cab and ladders in the bed racks. The two parked, in perfect sync, side-by-side under the tin roof that once sheltered summertime carhops in short shorts from sun and rain as they toted window trays of burgers and fries and cokes and milkshakes out to the kids in the cars, mostly driven by northside boys with their wet-combed DAs, some with a cigarette pack rolled tight into t-shirt sleeves, on their hopeful, nightly prowls in their old Fords and Chevys.

The first row of silver Orda-Phone speakers was still out there, the talk boxes hung on the posts between the parking slots. They were still connected but most folks from Yonders had quit using them. Once in a while someone driving through on the Dixie, often only joking, would push the button and be surprised by Ruth's voice saying "Can I take your order?" Whenever that happened, Jezzie was happy to be a carhop again. Lisa Riggs wrote in one of her columns that the Dixie was an historical monument and that it was a good thing those old speakers, listening all those years outside every driver's window, could keep a secret.

▪▪▪

It was Jezzie's first night carhopping and it was just after sundown on a warm, sweet summer night when she saw the one she was waiting for.

"Here comes trouble," Margie said. The low, black '49 Merc floated in with Clive Barber at the wheel, elbow resting in the window, a cigarette glowing between his fingers. Jezzie was on that boy before he could reach out the window for the order speaker.

"I was gonna use that dime to call you," she said, standing tall and looking down into his twinkly, tricky eyes, "but here you are and, guess what."

"You turned fifteen," said Clive.

"Yep, you want your old dime back?"

"Nah, you keep it."

"Well, you wasn't getting it back nohow."

Summertime car-hopping on Saturday nights, car radios playing loud and, as she passed from car to car, she'd hear all of those songs: country and rock and rockabilly. Jezzie and Clive's favorite was Richie Valens, who died so young. They played "Donna" all summer long in 1959, her only summer with Clive.

Everybody warned her about Clive. Nobody knew his people. He was what they called "bad," but that was better than "no good," a lot better. Jezzie never heard anybody say Clive was no good and she wasn't scared of bad Clive Barber. She was a Tucker girl, granddaughter of Demon Luke Tucker, and she wasn't scared of much of anything, except, at first anyway, of having to tote trays out to Creepy Calhoun in that green Kaiser Dragon of his, always parked alone at the last speaker way out back at the end of the lot by the alley. Had to walk his order all the way out there and he, smiling at her, whispering words under his breath that sounded dirty if she listened too close. None of the other girls would go out there alone, used to go out in pairs, except for Jezzie. Mel, who owned the Dixie back then, got mad and said that was silliness, that the poor old man couldn't help it if he looked like the Devil incarnate and had the mumbles. Mel said it was dirty minds thinking that old man was saying things he'd never dream of, but one night when Jezzie wasn't on, Mel himself had to carry the tray out to the Dragon. When he came back, he said he could understand how the girls might feel Calhoun was a little peculiar. Jezzie said she wasn't scared, but she was. That's why she carried his trays out to the dark end of the lot. She knew it's what you hide from that makes you imagine awful things in the shadows.

One night she looked Creepy Calhoun square in the eye and asked him why he always parked way out back and he said, "It suits me better, Sweetheart. You're name's Jezebel. I've never known a little girl named Jezebel."

"I ain't little and you still don't," said Jezzie, looking at him hard and straight. His eyes reminded her some of Keelan's, but she stuck a piece of tape over the keyhole of her bedroom door.

Then one day Creepy Calhoun was just as gone as if he'd never been. Left the farmhouse he was renting and never came back and nobody sorry to see him go. The word around town was Warry just ran him off. Gave him twenty-four hours to get out of the county and warned him never to come back, folks said. There must have been a reason. She heard her dad and mom talking about Creepy and heard her mom say, "Shooting would be too good for him." Now Keelan had come back, but Buster couldn't suddenly make people be gone the way Chief Warry just vanished Creepy back then.

▪▪▪

By a quarter after eight, the breakfast rush had slowed to refills. Everybody had ordered except Hook and Rhodes in their corner booth. They were waiting, Jezzie knew, for Wellington and Buster. Mayor Wellington, an estate lawyer who worked out of the family farmhouse just shy of the state line, was often late but Buster was usually right on time.

"The Chief must be busy arresting people," said Jezzie, topping up the mugs for Hook and Rhodes.

With everyone served, she had a moment's peace and looked out over the highway to Scooter Keen Park. Just from looking, she thought, it would be hard to know if it was now or back then or any time in between.

Chapter 5

1959
Treed

The day before he was fired at the Illiana, Keelan spent a quiet evening at home. Mae had turned fifteen and that seemed to sit better with folks. The marriage was legal and all down in Kentucky, but even Keelan thought fourteen sounded a little too young for a wife up in Yonders. Mae would have been a freshman if she'd stayed in school. That sounded better than her being an eighth grader. Jezzie was about to turn sixteen and she was a sophomore.

Mae fell asleep on the davenport in the living room watching a singing and dancing show that nobody liked while he and his dad were out tinkering in the garage and while his mom and Jezzie were doing dishes. The days were still warm but getting shorter; streetlights coming on just after six.

Things were working out a lot better than he thought they would back in July when Mae's mom told his mom that he'd gotten Mae pregnant. He only found out a couple of days after Mae got back from riding the bus down to Damascus with her mom to see a doctor.

Keelan first noticed Mae in the lot at the Dixie Diner in the early spring. He couldn't remember ever seeing her before. Girls change so much from one year to the other when they're just busting out. He'd probably been seeing her for years, skipping rope or walking around with her friends, just another skinny little girl like sister Jezzie used to be, but he paid her no mind till the day she was riding shotgun with her older sister and a couple of girlfriends. They parked next speaker to him. Mae said Hi! with a big smile, flirting window to window, '53 Chevy to '50 Ford. He didn't even know her name until she said who she was. He started to say who he was and she said, "You're Keelan, Jezzie Putnam's big brother." Behind Mae, her sister was shaking her head at him. What was he doing? Just talking. But when the Cokes arrived, Mae grabbed hers, hopped out, ran around and jumped in with Keelan, and when her sister yelled at her to get back in her car, he put his tray on the ground and drove off leaving Mae's sister honking at his taillights.

Just over three months later, Mae's mother walked, stone-faced, the three blocks over to the Putnam house to talk to Etna while the men were working their morning shifts, Mae's dad at Pride, Keelan at the Illiana and his dad at Food Equipment.

Hattie Rowan, wearing a print, summer dress, rapped twice on the frame of the screen door and Etna saw in her eyes what had come to pass, unless it was something worse. Hattie was barely over the threshold when she said, "Your boy has got my little girl in trouble."

Etna was relieved. There was always something worse even if you couldn't imagine what it was. Standing a half foot taller than Hattie Rowen, she said, "If she's in trouble, she ain't that little. How old is she at this very moment and who all knows about this?"

"She's two months shy of being fifteen and your boy, me and you are the only ones to know."

"And I expect your girl knows too, unless you think Keelan had his way without her noticing," said Etna, her back turned now as she led Hattie into the kitchen.

The two women, born in neighboring counties of East Kentucky, fifty-odd miles from county seat to county seat, didn't know each other except to say How do you do? But it was as if they had known each other all their lives, as if they were their own mothers or grandmothers facing troubles as old as the hills. Etna understood why the mother of this foolish girl was scared, scared Keelan would just say the baby had nothing to do with him, scared Etna would say her daughter's problems were no skin off her nose, but also scared of mixing with Tuckers, although it was a little late for that. Etna knew that most Yonders folks from the old counties gave the Tuckers a wide berth. Most northsiders, especially those with bonds to Kentucky, knew Etna was a niece to Amos, the brawling gravedigger of Floral Hill, a cousin to Amos' dangerous, carousing boys and a daughter of the murderer they called Demon Luke down in Regret. Everybody in a dozen counties back down home in Kentucky knew the name of Demon Luke Tucker and knew the devilment he had done.

The Rowans, Etna knew, were tame folks—God-fearing, hard-working country Baptists, peaceful as cows. Wouldn't say boo if you stepped on their foot. They came up from Owsley County just after the war to work in the canning factories, and Etna imagined that one of the first warnings they got when they arrived was to steer clear of the Tuckers of Fugate Hill. They must have given the same warning to Mae, for all the good that did.

The first inkling Etna had of trouble was when Jezzie told her that Keelan was running around with "that little eighth grader, Mae Rowan, a year younger than me and flighty as a feather. Too young for what Keelan's up to."

Things went the way Etna expected them to go and she saw marriage as the best way of protecting her man's good Putnam name. If Keelan reneged, everybody would believe the little pregnant thing and they'd be right. Besides, a wife and baby might just settle that boy. Before she and Hattie sat down at the kitchen table, Etna had already worked out what had to be done and where, and she was already hoping for a girl. The Tucker blood was too wild for men to stand. Her pa proved that, and so did her uncle and her cousins, and now, although he wasn't as wild, Keelan was a worry because of his sideways ways. He had rage in him, but behind it he was guileful. The Tucker men up on Fugate Hill, Amos and his wild boys, Keelan's Kentucky cousins, were fierce and dangerous, getting in fights, getting in trouble, going to jail, but Keelan was a lone wolf, or maybe not so much a wolf as just lone.

"Whatever can we do?" said Hattie, sitting at the kitchen table where Etna had put her. Etna poured the warmed-up breakfast coffee and took her time before she spoke.

"There's only one thing to do. The age of marriage with parent's consent is fourteen down home just like here, but doing it up here would cause a lot of commotion. I'm guessing you or your man have kin who can set up a wedding before a justice of the peace on short notice and get the blood tests or get around them. Nobody here needs to know nothing. We just say they run off and got married back in April. Eloped without our knowing. Your only problem is to get your man through whatever fussing he'll do when he first learns about this and make sure that girl of yours keeps her lips shut as tight as she ought to have kept her knees."

Hattie blinked a couple of times—this was not the way the ladies spoke at church, but she heard home and the old folks in Etna's words—and finally she said, "Why cain't your people arrange it?"

Etna looked steadily over her coffee cup at Hattie, whose daddy never killed anybody. "There's reasons no Tucker man can yet set foot in Regret. But none of that is neither here nor there. What needs doing now is for you and your man to make your telephone calls to your people and get your man to drive the kids down and back as soon as you got your justice of the peace, licenses, witnesses and whatever needs lining up. Keelan, Mae, you and your man will make the trip. Vernon and I will stay back and watch over the houses."

What Etna wanted done was done as she wanted it done. Mae's dad shared the driving with Keelan. The four of them set off after work on Friday and were in the old county just after midnight and back in Yonders just before dark on Sunday. Mae's dad was at work on time Monday morning, but Keelan, only in his second week at the Illiana after getting fired at Pride, was hard to wake and punched in in the red. Mae's dad hauled Mae's things over to the Putnam house and that was that, and nobody who heard the story of the elopement back in the spring had any reason to doubt it, whether they believed it or not.

Mae, a little scared of her in-laws at first, was quickly adopted by Jezzie, less than a year older. The two were soon best of friends, though Jezzie was almost never seen with Mae when Keelan was present.

It was all working out for Keelan now that it looked like the Illiana would be keeping him on, and it was the night for *Zane Grey Theater* on Channel 3, the only channel folks could get without a rotating antenna. There was even a new show to look forward to: *Johnny Ringo*, about a gunfighter lawman who carried a seven-shot revolver with six .45 caliber bullets and a separate barrel that fired a .410-shotgun shell. Keelan's dad, who read magazines on firearms and owned two rifles, a shotgun and a revolver, said that there never had been such a thing, but it didn't matter whether there had ever been such a seven-shooter or not because Johnny Ringo would have one every Thursday night. Everybody was looking forward to it.

Keelan's best memories as a boy were of going shooting, but, mixed in those recollections was an image of a tan dog, almost a puppy, that somebody shot dead on the tracks right in front of him. He could remember the sound of a rifle shot fading over the spring corn. Was that real or something out of a movie? Maybe it was something someone told him about. A little tan dog. Who would do such a thing? He could almost remember a name.

His dad took him shooting at the gravel pit and took him turkey and duck hunting as soon as he was big enough to tote a rifle. He still had a couple of his old Daisy BB guns, his favorite toys, and, as far as his dad knew, only one hunting rifle, a Winchester 308. But, wrapped in an old blanket and shoved behind the spare tire in the trunk of the Ford, he still had the best gun he'd ever stolen, a Browning over-and-under 12-gauge.

He did a lot of stealing and window peeping when he was a kid and only got caught once when he was barely twelve. Chief Warry showed up at the Putnam's door and told his folks what their boy had been up to. Mr. Fletcher had seen him window peeping across the street at the Tyler place. Warry suspected him of breaking into the widow Lynch's grocery store and he was right, but he couldn't prove it. He got a whipping from his dad and a cussing from his mom, but it was what Warry told him that scared him. "Just keep it up, Putnam, and I'll have you off to reform school in Vandalia. They'll make a man of you or kill you trying." It made him more careful, but not careful enough though because two years later he was treed and scared half to death. He was thirteen

Thirteen, eighth grader, and in trouble at school. He broke into two houses on the same block in the same month. He was a damn fool, robbing too close to home from houses too close together. The stealing had him back then. He could hardly sleep for wanting to get out in the sweet night air and prowl the alleys, and that's what he was doing the summer night they almost got him. He saw the house on the corner, the Scotts' place, with no lights and no car in the drive, but he had no more than leaned on the back screen door when all hell broke loose.

Somebody yelled, "There he is!" and he heard them tromping around the house. Maybe they had been waiting for him. But he was fast and lucky too because the streetlight at the alley corner was out. He could hear them coming and cussing after him, wasting their breath because he was faster. He thought he was in the clear, but he heard a car race past parallel to him on Wilhelm Avenue, turn on Sixth Street and then turn into the same alley he was running. They were coming on foot behind him, and the car, its lights falling just short of him, had headed him off. There were closed garages, sheds and fences on both sides of the alley trapping him. Then he saw a crazy face suddenly appear in the scissoring flashlight beams. A big Indian with a feather sticking up, taller than a tall man, looking at him big-eyed from behind the garbage cans. It stopped him cold in his tracks until he saw it was just something crazy, something that wasn't quite real. What was real was the men coming hard behind him and the car coming at him from the other way, but that thing, whatever it was, Indian or just him going nuts, was standing by a narrow garden path between an outbuilding and a row of bushes. A way out. He turned up the backyard path, running hard, straight for the back door of the house. There was a garage just to the right and, between the house and the garage, a gap to the driveway out to the street. If he could just get off the path before they saw him, but the lights were close behind, playing off the house and the garage.

"There's the son of a bitch!" But he was in the clear again, out the driveway, across Swisher Avenue and through somebody's yard to the next alley. He wanted to keep running north, all the way to the fields if he had to, but he was thinking as fast as he was running. The next street over, McBride, had less trees and he'd be easy to see under the street lights. He could hear the men coming fast, not cussing now, their feet pounding the bricks of Swisher Avenue. And where was the damn car? Circling around for sure, maybe already ahead of him on McBride. They'd have had him if he hadn't still been enough of a kid to think of climbing a tree, and there was a sugar maple shade tree by a back shed with a limb low enough to jump up and get ahold of. He was up that tree like a cat, up and up till the limbs were almost too weak to hold him. There he stayed, hanging on, barely breathing. Down below he saw the searching beams knifing up backyard walks and scouring behind garbage cans, and he heard the men cussing him out. "I'll kill the little bastard if I ever get my hands on him," one said.

If they had thought to point a light up the tree they'd have seen his white All Stars. Last time he'd go robbing with white sneakers. Then Keelan saw the car stopped out on McBride, just like he thought. A nice '48 Ford, belonged to that Ferris guy who worked at the bowling alley, the guy he stole the portable radio from two weeks before. They had been waiting for him.

The two men with flashlights, still cussing him, walked through a vacant lot out to McBride where Ferris' Ford sat. He heard the doors slam and the car drive away, its single taillight glowing red. It might be a trick, so he stayed up the tree. The windless night was quiet except for a dog barking at the moon way off on Fugate Hill, and not much moon to bark at, just a sliver up there in the black starry night, a good night for stealing. Clutching the skinny trunk of that sugar maple, he promised himself that he'd quit, and if he ever did go back to it, he'd do his stealing far from home and with black goddamn shoes. Robbing was never as much fun again after getting treed. He still thanked his lucky stars for that big redskin, but who the devil would set a cigar store Indian, or whatever the hell that was, out by the alley?

It was Mae who sent him back to stealing at eighteen because he needed money to take her to the show and buy her Cokes and burgers, but he was smarter by then. He only broke in when he knew there was nobody home and, unless he just found a wad of money in a drawer, he only stole guns because he had a ready buyer. That buyer was Earl Wyatt. The old retired farmer had sold off his land but still lived in the farmhouse out by the graveyard with his wife and his feeble-minded daughter. He was a gunsmith and Keelan had traded with him before, but when he offered to sell Wyatt the Remington .470 that he stole from Wilber Blakey's house, the old man scared him.

"You stole this from Blakey," he said.

Seeing Keelan's face, Wyatt said, "But I got no way of knowing that, do I? I just got your word that it's yours to sell, but I wouldn't be trying to sell that around here to just anybody. I can take it off your hands but a gun stolen local ain't hardly worth the trouble it'll take me to sell it." And he smiled, the only time Keelan ever saw him smile.

Wyatt paid him only $40 for a $130 rifle, but he got careless and took Keelan through the living room into his office to pay him out of a yellow cigar box in the drawer of his desk. Keelan got a quick look and never forgot seeing Wyatt peel two twenties off a fat stack of bills and there were more stacks in there. Showing his money like that as if he thought Keelan wasn't dangerous. From that night on, Keelan started taking an interest in the Wyatts' habits. Wyatt hardly ever went anywhere except to the gun shows or to the bank to cash his monthly government check.

Since the night Keelan saw that stack of twenty-dollar bills, he watched the Wyatts with the thought of maybe, someday, taking that money, if it ever came to that.

The Wyatts had an old, red Ford pickup that the woman used for shopping and a blue '56 Ford Fairlane that only the old man drove. The pickup was always left out and the car was always kept in the garage. The woman always took the girl with her whenever she went out. He'd see them downtown sometimes on weekends or on his way to and from work. When Wyatt was out with the Fairlane, the garage door was left open. Keelan could usually see all that driving out Iroquois to Floral Hill, but to see if the truck was parked in the drive when the corn was high, he had to drive past on the dirt road, Double Aught. They called it Double Aught because the county line ran right up the middle—Rural Route 0 for both Marigold and Jericho counties.

Stalking the Wyatts was a game he played, no harm in it, unless it came to that. Besides, how could he know that Wyatt always had so much money in the house? Maybe it was just that one time. He wondered about that until the day he was working on the docks, loading boxcars with Bill Hawthorn and a new man who was looking to sell a shotgun. Hawthorn told the man to go out and see Wyatt. "He'll buy it off you on the spot if it's any good, but he'll jew you down. One thing, though. He won't keep you waiting for your money. He keeps a shitpot full of cash on the place. Cashes his government checks at the bank and makes them give him all twenties. My niece told me that. She clerks there."

He knew he'd have to kill old man Wyatt to get at that money, but he didn't want to kill women, so if it ever came down to it, he'd need to go out there when the woman and the girl were gone and were going to stay gone long enough for him to get in and get out. He made it his business to drive by the Little Lorraine on Friday nights just before the kiddie show started. The red pickup was almost always there, and that meant the old man was home alone with his cigar box. Something to think about. Thousands of dollars waiting for him in a big house out in the cornfields just across the tracks from the graveyard and not a neighbor for a mile around. Even if somebody heard a gunshot, Wyatt was always testing guns out there, even after dark.

The old man did more than just buy stolen guns. The night Keelan saw the money, Wyatt walked him to the door and out on the porch. After shutting the door behind him, he said, talking low, that a man had told him the other day that he'd heard Fred Watson had been seen shooting cans at the gravel pit with a brand-new Browning over-and-under 12-gauge. He even told Keelan where the Watson's place was out at the end of Johnson, all alone and set back from the road. He couldn´t have said it much plainer without just saying it. A week later Keelan was at Wyatt's door again and told him that he had Watson's Browning over-and-under in the trunk of his car, worth $300 if it was worth a dime, but instead of thanking him and paying up, Wyatt said to just hang onto it until October, until right before the Indianapolis gun show. He said he refused to keep such easily identifiable and freshly stolen property in his house.

"Suppose I sell it to somebody else?" Keelan said.

Wyatt just looked at him, a big man in bib overalls standing in the door of his big farmhouse, standing no more than thirty feet from a cigar box full of money. "You just go ahead and start announcing that you've got such a gun and you'll have Fred Watson or Chief Warry, more than likely both of them, on your doorstep," he told Keelan. "You come see me first week of October and I'll give you what I think it's worth. The man who buys picks the time and names the price and don't you forget it, Putnam." And he closed the door in Keelan's face.

Watson's Browning over-and-under was the last thing Keelan stole before he started working pack. It would be the last time, he promised himself. He was done with robbing. Besides, if it ever got down to it, it'd be easier to just go out to Wyatt's one night when the woman and the girl were gone and just shoot Wyatt and take the box.

He'd read in one of his dad's gun magazines that rhino hunters in Africa keep two shells jammed between their knuckles so they can break and reload quickly if the first two loads don't stop the charging monster, and that gave him an idea. He went out to the gravel pit one evening when there was nobody around and tried breaking the action and jamming in two shells and getting off a shot. It took four or five tries to get the hang of it. He couldn't get both shells in at the same time with an over-and-under, and he doubted rhino hunters could either, but if Wyatt turned his back, there'd be time enough to load both shells, one at a time.

Some nights to help get to sleep, Keelan went over the details, like counting sheep. But if he could stay on for the winter at the Illiana, he figured his robbing days would be over. He had a job and a wife now, and he had his eye on a little apartment above a garage on the other side of the Nickel Plate tracks, catty-cornered across from the library. He and Mae would be southsiders—the baby too. Just barely, by the width of the Nickel Plate Road. That made him smile.

Keelan felt good sitting on the davenport between his mom and Mae watching the brand-new *Johnny Ringo* show, Jezzie lying on the rug with a cushion behind her head, his dad leaning forward in his chair whenever there was a gunfight. It was a good show and it made Thursday, with *Zane Grey* and then *Johnny Ringo*, a real cowboy night, something to look forward to over the steady, long winter that was coming. It'd be easy working forty-hour weeks and coming home to nice, warm TV evenings. *Rawhide*, *Zane Gray*, *Johnny Ringo* and *Gunsmoke* till summertime came back again. He went to sleep halfway hopeful.

Chapter 6

1959
FIRE MUSIC

Keelan's last day at the Illiana started with a kiss and ended with three murders and a car wreck. He hit the alarm as soon as he heard it so as not to wake Mae, curled up, hugging her pillow. He quietly gathered his work clothes off the chair and pulled his new, hard-toed work boots from under the bed, but he rattled the handle on the dresser drawer when he went for fresh socks, and Mae fussed and mumbled half awake. He went back, straightened the covers and pulled them up under her chin. "Go back to sleep," he whispered into her ear and she turned to him, smiled and gave him a sleepy kiss.

Nearly nine hours later, fired and madder than he'd ever been, it came to him just as he was cresting the hump of the Nickel Plate crossing. He already had the over-and-under in the trunk, ready to take out to Wyatt. This was the perfect time to snatch that little yellow box of twenties waiting for him in Wyatt's drawer. The woman and the girl would be at the Friday night kids' movies, and there was nothing Buck or any of the rest of them the rest of them could do to stop him.

"How'd work go?" his dad said, looking up from the TV.

"Not so bad," said Keelan.

"Hi!" said Mae from the davenport, one foot up on the footstool, toilet paper between her toes and Jezzie doing her toenails. Jezzie didn't look up.

He was quiet at supper. His mom was watching him and even his dad noticed. "Something on your mind?" his dad said.

Yeah, I'm thinking about killing me a rhino. "Nothing special."

After supper, Jezzie helped with the dishes. Mae was in the living room watching whatever was on and Keelan went out to watch his dad set the points on the Chevy. His dad was talking about the new 283-inch, 230 horse-power V-8 Impala that he'd seen downtown with some southsider driving it. He said he might just get one of them in a few years when they were second-hand.

"Vernon! Keelan!" Etna yelled from the kitchen door. "Your program'll be starting up directly."

They were in their usual places when it began. Lightning bolts and thunder spooked the herd and Gil Favor was talking about the danger of a stampede toward the cliffs. Jezzie watched, stretched out on her belly as close to the TV as you could be without getting shot or kissed, as Etna used to say. Etna and Mae shared the davenport leaving room for Keelan in the middle. He loved *Rawhide*, but not on this night.

"Where you going, Hon?" said Mae.

"I'm out of smokes," he said. "I'm just running out to the Four Corners to get some. I might stop at the Sugar Bowl and shoot a game or two. I need to do something after standing at that line all day."

His dad looked up and said, "If you do go by the Sugar Bowl, get me a couple of cold RCs."

"Sure," said Keelan. He felt his mom's eyes on his back as he went out the door. His hand trembled slightly as he put the key in the ignition. If the engine was cool after sitting for an hour or more it needed a touch of choke, but too much choke would flood it. Maybe if the engine hadn't started…but it did. Clutch in, he pulled the shifter back and down and felt first gear engage and his feet worked together on the clutch and gas and his hands on the wheel chose the direction.

It was ten after seven when he drove past the Little Lorraine. They were showing a double feature, *Bambi* and *Lady and the Tramp*. Mrs. Wyatt's red pickup was parked across the street. He turned around at the depot and drove back by the show, moving his lips as he read the show times behind the glass:

Kids' Nite Double Feature

Bambi 7:00 *Lady and the Tramp* 8:25 Ends 9:30.

Wyatt would see the 12-gauge was unloaded. He would carry it over his left forearm, the action broken and his right hand at his side with the shells tucked between his knuckles and hidden behind his leg. He had practiced it in front of his mom's dresser mirror once when nobody was home, smiling a friendly smile at the man he was going to kill, except that it was himself he was smiling at.

It was black night beyond the last streetlight at the city limits. A mile farther north he turned off the pavement onto the dirt of Double Aught at the graveyard corner. As he approached the entrance to the Wyatts' place, he knew he could just drive by. He almost did, but his foot came up off the gas, he shifted down and his hands turned the wheel. He was looking up the drive at the big farmhouse, lights on in the living room and the yellow bug light lit over the front door, but pitch dark all around. He cut his lights and rolled slowly up the long drive and turned off the engine. He could hear the TV. Loud talking, a shoot-up and then the *Rawhide* music. He sat a bit in the car. Wyatt must not have heard him pull in. He wouldn't hear him leave either.

He left the key in the ignition and got out, his work boots crunching the gravel. He put his gloves in his back pocket. He'd put them on after he did it. He went to the trunk, pulled the over-and-under out from behind the spare, unwrapped it and laid it gently on the blanket while he fitted the two red and gold shells between the knuckles of his right hand. Even if Wyatt was watching out one of the dark windows, he wouldn't be able to see what Keelan was doing behind the open trunk lid and wouldn't be surprised to see him carrying the gun. In fact, he'd be expecting him. The Indy gun show was just a week off. The old man would be offering forty or fifty bucks for a piece worth a lot more, but this time he wasn't the one naming the price. Keelan's left hand held the gun just in front of the trigger guard, the barrels pointed down to the side, action broken, breach exposed and empty. He looked for the moon but the stars still had the night to themselves, and so did he. It was only a few paces to the porch. He stopped for a moment at the foot of the steps listening to the voices and music of *Rawhide* and imagined himself sitting on the davenport watching with Mae, but then he was at the door. He knocked and felt the killer's smile come over his face. He'd seen it in his mom's mirror. The volume of the TV lowered and Keelan heard footsteps. The curtain moved aside and he saw Wyatt squinting down at him through the door window, his eyes quickly settling on the shotgun. Keelan smiled. Open the door, old man. Give somebody else a chance. Wyatt hesitated, looked up from the shotgun to Keelan's face before opening the main door. He glanced behind Keelan up the drive and finally held open the screen door. "Carrying it out in plain sight. Are you stupid, boy?"

And then he did it. He turned his back and started to lead Keelan across the living room. "Come on back to the office," he said. Maybe he managed another word that Keelan didn't hear in the big blast that filled the room, so big it took all the sound away. Keelan didn't remember taking one step into the living room and slipping in the shells. The old man must have heard the action close just before the blast tore into the back of his head and sent him lunging forward as if he were running away, except his feet trailed out behind him as he fell face-down in the door of the little office with its racks of rifles and shotguns and its yellow cigar box.

Keelan stood still, his ears ringing. Wyatt was dead. He turned his back. Turned his back on a man with a gun. Are you stupid, boy? he said. Not as stupid as you, old man. Come on back to the office, he said and he turned his back. Turned his back and said Come on back to the office. Turned his back on a man with a gun. Who's stupid now?

Keelan thought he had time, but it was already too late for him because Bambi was amid the flames.

With the shot still ringing in the room, he stepped over the blasted head and over the big hands. He knew the hands couldn't grab him, but he stepped quickly over the strangling fingers and went to the office and to the drawer where the cigar box was. There was even more than he remembered. He picked up one fat stack and then another. He put them back in the box. Maybe there was more money. He looked in the upper side drawer and found a Colt .38 Special, loaded. He'd always wanted a gun like that. He put it on the desk by the cigar box. And there were rifles and shotguns on the wall racks. He took one down, a beauty, and then another, but he had to be smart. He put them back and looked at his watch. 7:45. What did that mean? The movie let out at what? 9:30. And they had to drive home. He thought he still had time, but he didn't because Rachel was screaming.

"Taking a girl like that to a show like this!" someone yelled in the fiery dark.

"Hush, Honey Baby!" said Mrs. Wyatt, and the other parents and kids turned in their seats, away from Bambi. "Hush, it's just a show."

Only Rachel watched Bambi fleeing the fires. Everyone else watched Rachel, hearing her scream over the sound of the fire and the fire music.

"Come on, Rachel, we're going," Mrs. Wyatt said, but Rachel's yell was one long howling now. The hellfire was coming and the little creatures scurried before the flames. Great Prince was leading Bambi through the fire into the stream, but still not safe, and only Rachel was watching Bambi. All the kids and parents in the Little Lorraine were standing now, looking at Rachel, sitting, her face twisted in the light of the screen's fire, her mouth open wide making that noise over the loud music. Mrs. Wyatt was standing by her, saying "Hush, Baby. We're going home." The waterfall carried Great Prince and Bambi down into the gentle water below and the music softened and the fire was far away. Rachel was quiet now as her mother led her up the aisle and into the warm night, a grown woman in a yellow dress crying a child's tears past gawking kids and their parents. Her mom told her Bambi was safe now as they drove past the stores and under the trees, safe under the streetlights and into the night, past the grain elevators and home.

There was a strange car parked off to the side of the drive.

"Wonder who that is?" said Mrs. Wyatt. Rachel, her tears dry, hung back to look up at all the twinkling stars.

Keelan, crouched, the cigar box snug inside his jacket, was ransacking the bottom side drawer of the desk. He didn't see the lights coming up the drive and couldn't hear the truck tires on the gravel or Mrs. Wyatt say Wonder who that is? He couldn't hear the footsteps on the porch, but he sensed movement in the doorway. It was the woman. Her scream was faint to his ringing ears. He stood quickly, grabbed the over-and-under and fired, looking into her eyes. He saw her face jolt back and scramble, not a face anymore, and she went back and down.

Rachel was still among the stars when she heard the blast and saw her mother fallen in the doorway. Keelan saw the girl in her yellow dress appear and stoop over her mother, faceless on her back. He watched, crouching now behind the sprawl of Earl Wyatt, as Rachel slowly raised her head and gaped at him across the living room. Suddenly, her eyes fixed on his, she was running straight for him across the wide living room, her hands outstretched, her fingers like claws. He barely heard her screaming. He dropped the shotgun and grabbed the .38 from the desktop and fired two shots, faint pops quiet to his blasted ears, almost as quiet as his old BB gun. The first one stopped her and the second one dropped her to her knees, and she fell back against the davenport as if watching the TV, but her gaze was fixed on him and her eyes were still alive and in them he saw the hatred he knew deep inside but had never seen. Her mouth was open wide, but he didn't know if she was still making a noise. One more shot, aimed carefully at her brow, not looking again into those eyes, but looking into them forever.

His gaze wandered to the TV where a man was standing in an empty street looking lost and forsaken and there was a faint tinkling music. He felt something was wrong. What? His hands! He hadn't put on the damn gloves.

He couldn't remember which guns he had handled. His fingerprints must be everywhere, but he had time, lots of time. There was nobody left to come home now. There'd be dish rags in the kitchen. He saw the fridge and he was thirsty. He opened the door and found a Coke and three bottles of RC. There was a bottle opener hanging on a string from the fridge door. He drank the cold Coke in gulps and started to feel calm. He was doing fine. His dad wanted him to pick up a couple of RCs, so he stuck one in each pocket and zipped the pockets up to the protruding bottle necks. He patted the cigar box zipped tight under his jacket and went back to the office with the dish rag and carefully wiped any prints from the two guns he had used, then he wiped the doorknob and the drawer handles and all the guns he remembered touching and a few he wasn't sure about. He stood a second thinking. What else? The handle of the fridge and the opener and the empty Coke bottle. He returned to the kitchen, wiped each carefully and went back to the living room. He didn't want to look at the girl but he did and her eyes did something. They moved. No, they focused on him, and he saw the curse in those dead eyes. A jolt of cold fear shot through him and he looked away. On the TV that forsaken man still wandered alone.

Keelan had to get out of there. Counting, 1,2,3,4, he walked to the front door and stepped over the woman's body and shoved the screen door open. He used his forearm. No fingerprints. He hurried down the steps to the car, the RC bottles in his jacket pockets, cold against his sides.

He ground the starter for five seconds, pumped the gas and quit. Flooded! But still enough battery. He pressed the gas pedal to the floor and held it there as he counted to sixty. He lifted his foot, hit the starter and gave the carb just a nibble of gas, and she caught, quit, caught again and he revved it hard. He gave a sudden, last look back toward the house but the girl in the yellow dress wasn't running at him.

He turned the car around, careful not to roll off the gravel and leave a tire print in the dirt. At the end of the drive, he turned east on Double Aught and tromped the gas, throwing dirt, running fast with the lights off. The starlight was enough, but as he approached the turn onto Iroquois, he saw headlights coming out from town. He thought about stopping and pulling to the side, but what if whoever was coming turned west on Double Aught? There he'd be, parked at the side of the road just down from the Wyatt farmhouse. There were probably a dozen black Fords like his in town, but Warry would come straight after him. He flicked on the lights just as he swept onto Iroquois, off the dirt onto the pavement, running a little too fast and too wide but expecting that the damn fool would be on his own side of the road. And, wouldn't you know it! The car, a late model of some kind with four headlights, was right smack in the middle of the road, blinding him with its brights. It was a Chevy, leaving him no room, but the fool saw him just in time, swerved and missed him. Seconds later, he heard the crash and saw in the mirror the red, cat-eyed taillights stopped at the graveyard gates. He figured the crazy bastard, driving like that, must be bad hurt. He couldn't have seen much anyway. A head-on might have killed them both. Dead, it wouldn't have mattered, but alive they would have had him, old Wyatt's cigar box tucked in his jacket and, he suddenly thought, dead folks' blood on his boots!

He drove slowly into town and parked in front of his house. He shut off the lights and the engine. The porch light was on for him and the living room window dark except for the flickering of the TV. He unzipped his jacket and took the cigar box out and looked inside. Still there, all of it. He couldn't get it up to his room without carrying it past everybody. They'd see its shape tucked under his jacket. He got out, careful to close the door gently, and opened the trunk. He slipped the yellow box behind the spare tire where the over-and-under had been, covered it with the old blanket and then sat on the floor of the open trunk. His ears were ringing less, and he could hear the crickets in the grass. He looked at the soles of his boots. He took a dirty rag from the trunk and gave the soles a hard rubbing but the stain wouldn't wipe completely away. Even if he washed and boiled them, there'd still be some speck of blood somewhere. That's how they catch them on TV, with sniffing dogs and microscopes. He'd get rid of them in the morning. He threw the rag back in the trunk, closed the lid softly and started for the house, but stopped and went back to lock the trunk and both doors.

"Did you stop at the Sugar Bowl?" his dad said, without looking up from the TV.

"No," he said. That would be too easy to check. He handed both RCs to his dad.

"One's enough. Can you fetch me the opener?" his dad said, still not looking up, leaning toward the TV. He handed one RC back to Keelan. The bottle was not as cold now as when he first took hold of it in the Wyatts' kitchen.

"God," Jezzie said, "there's no hope for him now. He's gonna be all alone forever."

Keelan, startled, looked at Jezzie, but she was watching the wandering man, all alone on the TV screen. He sat down beside Mae on the davenport and she smiled and laid her hand on his knee. His mom came back from the kitchen with the bottle opener and handed it to his dad. Keelan felt her take the other RC bottle from his hand. She was looking at him, about to say something when they heard a siren passing fast on Iroquois. The kiddie movies weren't even over yet, but time didn't matter anymore. They all looked out the window as the police car, lights flashing, disappeared down Iroquois, headed out toward the graveyard, and then they heard another siren coming from downtown. The dogs were howling up on Fugate Hill when the second Yonders police car wailed by. It's the wreck, Keelan thought. No reason for anybody to be poking around the Wyatts' quite yet.

"What the hell?" said his dad, heading for the door. Keelan was last out of the house. Jezzie and his dad were at the curb watching after the flashing lights to the north and his mom and Mae stood in the lawn.

"I'll bet some fool ran into the cemetery gate again," said his dad. "That'd be about the third one in the last five years." That was what Keelan would have guessed too, if he'd had to guess.

The next-door neighbor woman said in a loud voice from her porch, "Linda Clark just called me from out on Johnson and said her man was the one to call it in. He saw a brand-new car crashed up against the gate and with a man in it knocked out or worse."

"Didn't I say so?" said his dad. "Somebody's gonna get killed out there one of these days." Keelan almost smiled.

The faint flashing lights a mile away pulsed the moonless sky at the county line, but his mom wasn't watching the sky; she was watching her boy. He knew his mom was already starting to figure something out, but she turned away when the third Yonders police car came shrieking past, red lights flashing under the trees. Mae's face, and his mom's too, were devilish red in the hullabaloo light. Keelan stepped in between his mom and Mae, draping his arm over Mae's shoulder. His mom, without looking at him, asked in a low, flat voice, "If you didn't go by the Sugar Bowl, wherever did you get them RCs at this hour?"

He started to say he got them out at the Four Corners Texaco station, but everybody knew the big RC bottles wouldn't fit in their Coke machine. Besides, she would have known it for a lie. He leaned away from Mae and close to his mom's ear, answering just as softly as her asking, "I got them out of a dead man's icebox."

Chapter 7

1959
Sugar Creek

Sitting alone hours later in the dark living room, Etna recalled her boy's words. "Out of a dead man's icebox." After the family had all gone up to bed, she pulled a chair to the open front window and sat looking through the screen out Iroquois toward the graveyard. A light breeze carried the scent of dry cornstalks in the night air and, after the Watson's dog finally quit its barking, she listened to the nightbirds. A freight train whistled from out beyond Floral Hill and came charging through town, calling out—long, long, short, long—over and over until it cleared the six crossings. She heard it once more, faintly, at the gravel road beyond the drive-in, half-way to Milton, heading south.

A few cars passed, kids with their loud radios, folks coming home after the bars closed at midnight, but it was mostly dead quiet until around one in the morning. A truck and a car came by fast, headed out toward the cemetery. A Yonders police car was tucked in behind Chief Warry's red pickup.

A few minutes later a big, fancy car came rolling by over the bricks. Not quite in a hurry. It was the doctor's car, Doc Kline's new Imperial. And not long after, the Yonders ambulance rushed by fast and silent, red lights flashing but no siren.

Over the long night Etna saw more vehicles pass. First a couple of sheriff's department cars up from Damascus. Then, just before dawn, a long, black van. She could just make out the first two words when it passed under the corner street light; Illinois State something or other.

Whatever Keelan had done was done and, just like what her pa did down in Regret, nothing on God's green earth could change it.

▪▪▪

It was August of '31 and Etna was only six the day Aunt Unity took her to the courthouse for her pa's sentencing. The courtroom had a high ceiling and tall windows that showed a blue Kentucky sky. The judge in his black robes was up in his high place like a king on a throne, like the Lord in Aunt Unity's Illustrated Bible, and sometimes he beat on his desk with a little hammer. Her mom was dead by then, died bringing Purity, her namesake, into the world. Little Purity, who everybody would call Spite, was back at the cabin with Uncle Amos, who couldn't risk showing his face in town. The Corrothers were gunning for him, but they wouldn't shoot a woman or a little girl.

The defense lawyer said it might soften the judge's hard heart to see a little girl's face peeking over the polished wood rail behind the defendant's table when it came time to say what would become of Demon Luke Tucker on Earth. The judge even called him that, as if Demon was a Christian name. Aunt Unity told her the judge's words years later when Etna was old enough to understand: "Demon Luke Tucker, having been found guilty of the premeditated murder of Ukiah Corrothers, I sentence you to death by electrocution." And then, Aunt Unity told her, "the judge pounded his hammer to make it so."

When her pa heard that, standing tall and bearded, dressed in city clothes she had never seen him wear, a suit he was too big for, he seemed to grow even taller. The whole courthouse was quiet for a moment and then Demon Luke turned to his lawyer and, according to how Aunt Unity told it, he said, loud enough for all to hear, "Thank you for your efforts. I was scared I'd get life on this jailhouse food, but now it'll be steak and mashed taters in Heaven."

Etna didn't understand why everyone was laughing, but they laughed even harder, Aunt Unity said, when his lawyer replied, "I got you death, Demon Luke, but I didn't get you Heaven."

And when the laughing died down, Etna remembered that her pa turned to her, and the Sheriff's men let him reach over the railing and pick her up. He gave her a kiss and whispered, his whiskers tickling her cheek, "You take care of these poor Tuckers now, Etna Tucker."

Although Etna only lived her first six years in Regret, it seemed that half her memories were from down home in the woods and the hills before they took her pa off to the

Castle on the Cumberland at Eddyville, a place she only saw in pictures. Its real name was Kentucky State Penitentiary, but it looked like a castle.

A death sentence wasn't enough to please the Corrothers bunch. Uncle Amos, as guilty as her pa, was spared by the law, but not by the Corrothers. They swore blood vengeance. That got Aunt Unity on the telephone out front of the post office with her purse full of quarters, nickels and dimes for calling cousins and kin, and before she'd run out of coins, she talked to a Tucker blood cousin named Mort Tucker who had been up in Illinois for years and was custodian of the graveyard in a place called Yonders. He told Aunt Unity that there was plenty of field and factory work in the town for strong men.

They wasted no time, but they lost almost all they owned making the move. The Great Depression, as they called it in the papers, had hit and the real estate man told Amos the only folks buying were vultures paying nickels on the dollar for the houses and lands, and the bank would pay even less. Amos took what was offered for the two Tucker cabins. It was chicken feed, but at least they had some starting-out money. And they lit out, the six Tuckers: Uncle Amos and Aunt Unity, their two boys and Demon Luke's two girls, now without mother or father, and made it to Yonders in Demon Luke's Model T truck under a single August sun.

Cousin Mort arranged for Amos to rent an unpainted and rambling two-story place on Waylon Avenue out at the very north end of Yonders on Fugate Hill, but none of the Tuckers could see anything they'd call a real hill there or anywhere else in town or for miles around, except for the one at the graveyard. Amos started in jerking corn the same week he got to town and later, because he was a big man, they had him loading on the Illiana warehouse docks. When pack was done the first week of September, they let him go. They said they'd keep him in mind if they needed a man over the fall and winter, but he told Unity he'd rather clean outhouses than ever again set foot in the shade of a factory door.

"You won't never need to," Unity told him. "Cousin Mort run off the man who was working for him and he's taking you on as helper at the graveyard."

Amos took to the work of cutting grass in the summer, shoveling snow in the winter and digging graves whenever anybody had need of one. It was hard toil on hot days and harder with hard winter ground. When there was a burial, Amos took charge of rigging the ropes and lowering in the coffins. Before long, Amos was setting headstones and seeding and fertilizing fresh graves. He did everything but answer Mort's phone; he didn't like talking to folks he couldn't see.

The Tuckers settled in. Unity made friends with the neighbor ladies, and little Etna walked back and forth the six blocks to Wishing Well Grade School. She was put in first grade because she had no records from Regret, but before Christmas of 1931 she was moved up to second with her age group. Her teacher said she was "smart as a whip," but gave her a whipping for fighting a boy who said something she wasn't about to let pass. The boy's parents were angry at the teacher when their son came home with a black eye and a bloody nose, but when they learned that he had fought a girl, they shifted their anger to their boy for leaving out that part.

The families up from East Kentucky knew each other either personally or by reputation, and a few of the families from Regret and surrounding counties were what folks came to call "fightin' Kentuckians." Not a month after the Tuckers had moved in up on Fugate Hill, a man said the wrong thing to Amos at Sniders'. Amos got his name in the paper and spent a night in jail and the man who provoked him went to the doctor but made no complaint. Men didn't in those days, not northsider men. After that, the Tuckers of Fugate Hill were known to all as a family of fightin' Kentuckians, and Amos, who brought his fiddle north from Regret, made weekend music on the falling-down front porch and passed the jug to cousin Mort and to those of his neighbors that he chose to invite over and who dared to come. Prohibition was in its final years and the mayor of Yonders was a southsider, a Mason and a Prohibition Republican, but what a man did on his own front porch on the northside, especially up on Fugate Hill, was his own business.

Most of what Etna remembered of Regret was of the woods. She couldn't remember her mother's face at all, but she recalled her mother's voice and the touch of her hand as she led Etna down the shady path on a summer day to the secret, magic creek. Most of all, she remembered the birds, but her mother said there were critters too, watching. They talked, her mother said, whenever they were of a mind to. Her mother always told her about who lived here and who lived there, and once, when they came to a giant tree by the creek bank, her mother pointed up and said, "Mr. Owl sleeps all the day long up high in that tree and if you come a-wandering out here by night, he'll ask you your name. Who? he'll yell, and you best answer. Best say, I'm Etna Tucker and my pa is Demon Luke Tucker. Say that loud enough and every critter afoot, crawling and winged, will watch over you all your days and call your name back to you and remember it so that you're not forgot when your time comes to be taken up to your reward in the sweet bye and bye."

▪▪▪

Etna must have dozed off in her chair at the window because it was chilly sunrise when she woke still thinking of those old woods, but as soon as she opened her eyes, she remembered everything. She didn't fully know yet what she knew she'd soon know, but she prayed what she feared would never be. She combed her hair, dabbed some water on her face and made coffee. When she heard Vernon walking around upstairs and then Jezzie's radio playing softly, she started breakfast. Pack was over and nobody had to work Saturdays. Keelan was last to come down and he only wanted coffee and toast. He kept his eyes down. Vernon was cheerful, humming when he left after breakfast to drive downtown to the auto store. He came back excited and told about the murders at the Wyatt farm. Mae and

Jezzie looked scared and asked questions, but Keelan went to pour himself another cup of coffee. He seemed not to listen, but Etna saw he wasn't missing a word.

"They found them all dead, shot in their own living room, even that poor simple girl. Who would ever do such a thing?" said Vernon.

After Vernon finished telling all that he had heard, Keelan went upstairs and came back down carrying a brown grocery sack. Etna watched through the kitchen window blinds as Keelan went out to the alley. He looked around and dropped the sack into the garbage barrel. He then went straight to his car and drove off. Etna took her gardening bag to the alley. She saw the sack held Keelan's hard-toed work boots, his new ones. She put the sack in her bag and went back to the house, taking the spare car key from the nail in the kitchen. She backed out of the drive and stopped by Vernon who was still talking at the curb with the neighbor man, telling about the awful murders.

"I'm going out to tend Amos and Unity's graves," Etna said through the car window. "Be back in time to make lunch."

She could tell from his expression that he still didn't like her taking the car, but he smiled and waved. He'd learned to let her be. At first, when she passed her test and got her license at the age of thirty, he didn't like her driving places by herself, especially if he didn't know where or why. He even noted the mileage once and asked her where she went that took twenty-five miles to get there and back. She told him that she expected that would be the last time she'd ever hear such a question. Vernon was a good man, but he was a man all the same.

She sometimes drove out to visit her dead and, now and then, she strayed over the Indiana line where it was an hour later than in Illinois. Once she drove to Rankin and ate an ice cream cone in the park. She didn't know anybody there and nobody knew her. Her favorite drive on a nice day was the twelve miles up to Willows. She'd park by the bridge and walk down along the creek bank. She didn't do it often, but she did when she needed to. And that's where she drove with Keelan's murder boots, out Iroquois and onto Double Aught, past the Wyatt house. There were two Yonders police cars, a Sheriff's car and a big van parked in the Wyatts' drive. In the daylight, she could read the words on the van: Illinois State Crime Lab Springfield.

It was a nice drive up to Willows. The sweetcorn fields were all harvested, the soybeans were ready and Merry Sunshine was dancing off the red hood of the Chevy. At the Sugar Creek bridge, just shy of the Willows city limits, she pulled off and stopped where she always did. The creek was running deep after the rains up north. She took the bag and walked down the slope from the road into the shadow of the bridge. Her boy's work boots had stains on the soles. She gathered a few stones along the creek and packed them in. When she was satisfied they had enough heft, she pulled the laces up tight and tied the boots together. She remembered Keelan saying how much they cost, but saying he'd need them because he was staying on all winter. She heaved them out to the middle of the stream and hoped Sugar Creek could keep a secret too.

Etna lingered a moment by the fast-running water. The creek bank was in shadow and the trees were tall, like the woods of Regret, the woods her mom called secret, the woods with her mom's talking critters. It made her smile to remember how she thought she heard them talking to her so long ago when she was knee-high. She'd have sworn they called her by name.

Chapter 8

1998
The Twilight Zone Murderer

The morning after the call from Cockrell, Buster, on his own with Ellen off in Champaign, had a breakfast of coffee and toast and listened to WGN news. Chicago murder rate was on course to drop below seven hundred for the first time since '69. Sports guy going soft on the Cubs' manager for calling that attempted steal that took the Cubs out of the tenth. Their Gregg Maddox for Atlanta tomorrow against Chicago's Kerry Wood. Sunset start under the lights at Wrigley. Ellen would be home by then and they'd watch the game together.

Cockrell's call was a hell of a coincidence because Coach Dornfeld had been after him for a week to try and get a preseason basketball game with Damascus. Yonders had a transfer kid, a junior, a light-skinned Black kid with a funny name—he wrote it down, Whizdom Lahae—from one of the new witch families, a kid who had made varsity as a sophomore for some big upstate school. Coach couldn't believe his luck.

First time Buster ever saw a Black man in the flesh, he was a little kid in the car with his folks at the Main Street crossing with a streamliner stopped at the station. There in the doorway between the bar car and the diner, the lower half of the door closed but the big window folded back up against the roof, was a uniformed porter, smoking and leaning out, looking down Main. Buster would have said the same thing if it had been a cowboy, except he would have said cowboy instead. His mother said, "I ought to wash your mouth out with soap! Where did you hear that word?" He was about to say when he saw his dad's eyes in the mirror.

The only real minority in town when Buster was growing up was the Catholics. Some called them mackerel snappers, but not to their faces. There used to be three families of Jews headed up by two doctors and a scrap dealer. They were mostly gone. There were a few Mexican families—pickers and pack workers who came up from Texas for the harvest. They were seasonal, living out in what was the German POW camp during the war before it became the Mexican Camp in the fifties. Some stayed on and became part of the town. There was even a Hindu family of convenience store Indians. Then one day a Black kid showed up shooting baskets in the July sun at Scooter Keen Park, and it got around that his mom, a white woman, was part of a coven of witches, or whatever they said they were, coming down from Chicago to take over the Township Building.

Back in the twenties, the town had a chapter of the KKK. There were photographs of them marching down Main Street in robes and hoods, but everybody knew who they were. Buster's dad said he recognized some of them by their shoes. Now, outside of a couple of barstool loudmouths, there wasn't much of that anymore. When Buster was a kid, the teachers never talked much about that kind of thing; if they did, he didn't remember. Maybe he wasn't listening. It was like nuclear war. He remembered they showed in the Damascus paper that if an H-bomb went off over the county courthouse it would blow the hell out of Damascus and scald Blunt too, but the temperature would only go up twenty degrees in Yonders, which would be welcome if the Soviet Union attacked the county in winter. Everybody knew the Reds weren't going to H-bomb Damascus, so the teachers, in spite of what Springfield ordered, didn't make the kids practice crawling under their desks to avoid being vaporized. There were no Russians coming to bomb the town and no freedom riders coming to Yonders to stick up for people who weren't there to be stuck up for.

Buster remembered his dad said there was a Black family in Yonders once, but there had never been a Black kid in high school. Dornfeld said Buster had to drop by his Saturday shootaround and see this new kid. There were six players on the floor the day Buster stopped off. All but Whizdom were starters on the football team. Big Zeke Grandey and Cory Wilson were both a little gimpy from the weekend football game, a win down in Mariah. Whizdom, Buster thought, would have made a good pass receiver, maybe a halfback, maybe even a quarterback, but not everybody at the big-city schools went out for everything. The kid looked like he couldn't miss and even rattled the backboard with a dunk. If Buster hadn't seen Whizdom on court, he would have thought Dornfeld was crazy asking to play Damascus. Lahae was a hell of a long-range shooter and quick on his feet, but would the others take to him? They just might do some winning if they jelled.

When the Yonders football team went undefeated in his senior year, Buster was called up at the athletic banquet and given the Harvester Player of the Year award. They only gave one award a season back then. No Best Attitude, Most Improved or Never Give Up awards. "No surprise," old Coach Jessup said, when he handed him the little plaque. Player of the Year, 1955, Darrell "Buster" Lawton. Ellen found it in his trunk when she was looking for old clothes to donate to the poor, and she fixed a place for it on the living-room book shelf. That was nice of her.

Buster had been hearing praise all his life. It embarrassed him and it puzzled him because all he ever did was what was expected of him, what was expected of any person. "We're all lucky to have a man like Buster Lawton as police chief," Lisa Riggs wrote in the paper.

When he was having lunch at The Depot one day, he heard Paul Butler, the banker, talking to somebody in the next high-backed booth, say, "Chief Lawton is so damn honest you could shoot craps with him over the telephone." He was about to leave when he heard that, but he stayed a bit longer, until the two left, and he was glad they didn't see him.

Ellen laughed when he complained about people making too much of him for just doing his job. "It's your own fault," she told him. "What are people supposed to think about a policeman who gives himself a ticket?"

And they made too much of that too. The AP picked it up and it was in newspapers all over the country. "Cop Tickets Himself in Fender Bender" was the heading of the little piece in the *Los Angeles Times* that somebody sent to Mayor Wellington. It was sort of funny, but there wasn't any other right thing to do. He was tuning his radio, listening to a Bears game, and Bob Abram's wife—Elma was her name, dead now out on Floral Hill—suddenly hit the brakes when a squirrel ran out. He saw her brake lights too late. Buster wrote himself up right on the spot for "failure to avoid an accident." It cost the city the price of a little body work, some touch-up paint and the right-side, rocket-ship taillight assembly for a high-finned Ford Galaxy.

He was just starting out on the force then, and Chief Warry told him, "I wish I'd thought of that one! Be hard for a man to argue with an officer who'd give himself a ticket."

It was just going on seven-thirty when Buster parked his pickup in the slot marked Chief beside the new Crown Victoria Interceptor and the old Taurus Interceptor.

"You seen this? It just came," said Ronnie, his voice distorted over the speaker from his place in his wheelchair behind the bullet-resistant glass of the reception area. He handed Buster the *Damascus Herald*. "It's by that guy who came to see you last month."

Buster took the paper without looking at it. "What you got for me?"

"You want the new Interceptor or the old one? No, wait, the Taurus might need gas. Better take the Crown Vic."

Buster knew the Taurus would be full because Murdock had been on night duty with it and he always kept it tanked up, but he knew Ronnie wanted him to drive the new car now that they finally had one. He stopped to admire it after he came down the steps. It looked good sitting out front. No hood ornament, no Liberace grill or other general foolishness. Buster figured this would be his last brand new Interceptor.

Inside it still had the new-car smell and an instrument cluster like a space ship. He glanced at the front page of the *Herald* while the big V8 idled and white-smoked in the chilly morning air. Riots in Peru. A sixteen-year-old kid down in Mississippi beat his mother to death and then drove to the high school with a rifle and shot his ex-girlfriend and seven others. Lord! Two died, including the girlfriend. The kid was a Satanist, the paper said. That would fire up folks for the meeting that night, but it wasn't witches that were worrying him. And there was Wolfden's big story on page three across three columns:

Is the Twilight Zone Murderer Still on the Loose?

The Twilight Zone Murderer? What was that about? There were two photos: One of a Black teenager in cuffs, looking scared and being led down the County Courthouse steps by a big cop and a detective with a suit and thin tie. The other of an old Black man in prison garb leaning forward, talking to a young guy in a sport coat. The caption read, "Freeman Lane, age 19, after Damascus sentencing in 1960 (left) and (right) photographed in September of this year in conversation with an Innocence Project representative at Graham Correctional Center."

Buster decided to read it all carefully before he had to sit down with the boys out at the Dixie:

> Thirty-nine years ago today, October 2, 1959, CBS aired the first episode of Rod Sterling's *The Twilight Zone*, and on that very night just a mile north of Yonders, a gruesome triple murder took place.
>
> The case, the only multiple homicide in the history of the north-county community at the time, was solved by the Damascus Sheriff's Department in late November of that year when Freeman Lane, a 19-year-old African-American from Blunt, confessed to killing retired farmer Earl Wyatt, his wife Esther and daughter Rachel in their farmhouse during a robbery.
>
> Now, nearly four decades later, Lane, serving a 99-to-150-year sentence at Graham Correctional Center, has recanted the confession and claims that he was guilty instead of the murder of a Damascus businessman, Jack Crawford. Lane maintains that he was attempting to rob Crawford in a Damascus alleyway in the downtown area referred to in those days as "the red-light district," and that, when Crawford fought

> back, he killed him with a switchblade. He also claims he was offered by prosecutors the option to, in Lane's words, "swap murders" and thereby escape the death penalty. He now believes the switch was to avoid causing embarrassment to the Crawford family by having certain unsavory aspects of the victim's behavior revealed as part of the investigation of the murder Lane now admits committing.
>
> While the Marigold District Attorney's Office evaluates Lane's confession to the Crawford murder and decides whether to review the Wyatt murders verdict, Yonders residents will wonder if, after nearly forty years, the Twilight Zone Murderer may yet live among them.

Warry was right about one thing, Buster thought. Lane might be a murderer, but he never killed anybody in Yonders. Old man Wyatt, ornery as they come and armed to the teeth out there north of town, would never have opened his door to a Black stranger in the night.

He'd been sitting there reading for a few minutes, but he'd still be early if he went straight out to the Dixie, so he drove east out Hamilton to the fields and then cut down to Main and headed back west. The two-and-a-half-block business district was dying little by little, the stores sometimes changing names and colors two or three times before falling derelict along with the other boarded-up, ghost store fronts. So many places closed and all the parking meters taken up. And even though the Lorraine Theater, the sparkling jewel of Main Street, was still going, Mayor Tom said it was losing money hand over fist. The marquee advertised another one of those crap *Lethal Weapon* movies. Last movie Buster liked was *Lone Star,* but Ellen needed to get out so they went to the show every couple of weeks. Just walking down the aisle of the Lorraine took Buster back to his childhood days, but the grand old theater was starting to get a little ratty at the edges. Buster couldn't imagine Main Street without that grand marquee.

From the Lorraine to the C&EI tracks, there were only a dozen or so offices and stores still open, and there was Keelan Putnam sitting in the window seat of the Two Spot. Looked away quick, but he saw me alright, thought Buster. If he hadn't read the paper yet, he had something to look forward to.

Warry, if he'd ever been as sure about a suspect as Buster was about Keelan, would have found some cause to bring him in, charge him and hand him over to the county boys for questioning. Those old county detectives could get a confession out of a lunchbox. But what would Warry do in this day and age? Same as he was doing. Nothing or near nothing. But never forgetting.

Buster drove through the old downtown. Three insurance offices, Snider's Bar, Hook Electric and Real Estate, Midwest Auto Parts and boarded-up places that still had names most folks remembered. Both pool halls had been closed for years and so had The Little Lorraine where they used to show the kiddie movies. So much was empty and the emptiness gave him a lonesome feeling as he saw the warped reflection of the Interceptor rippling and surging across the long, tall windows of Dixon's Hardware and Hay's Ladies' Clothing. Hay's still had three dusty, naked, cream-colored ladies posing in the window. One was headless. Pitiful, Ellen said. They either ought to dress them and put the lady's head back on or get them out of there.

Some of the old stores belonged to the banks, but not to the defunct Yonders Community Bank, its name fading from the big ground-floor window of the Phillmore Building on Iroquois Street. The Phillmore still stood with her marble façade and five empty floors. Folks who shaded their eyes and peeked into the forsaken bank could make out the long counter with no tellers back of their little windows and no clerks at the desks behind the absent tellers. Above were four empty floors with narrow central hallways lined on both sides with offices. Names, all of them familiar to Buster, printed on the little frosted-glass, eye-high windows of the old doors:

Dr. Francis Masters
Dixon and Evans, Attorneys at Law
Lorraine Theater Management
Dr. Calvin Carver, Dentist

Buster remembered his mom taking him to the dentist, riding in the only elevator in town up to the fourth floor. The elevator operator said, "Going to the dentist, huh, Bub? Well, you're in luck. Doc Carver just got a new pair of pliers." In the office right across from the dentist's was the clattering ticker tape with prices of livestock, corn, soybeans, feeder cattle futures and also the latest stock market quotes. He remembered the two agents, the Tyler brothers, both big old boys with round, steel-rimmed glasses and red suspenders, sweating in swivel chairs in front of electric fans on that hot, summer day, making and answering phone calls to inform their farmer and investor clients.

The old, abandoned building was worth no more than its long shadow now, with the Action Group offering it rent-free to any company that could bring a viable business and a handful of jobs to town. He was glad Hook had not leased the Phillmore to the witches. All the town needed now was a circle of folks who called themselves witches dancing around on the roof of what used to be the second tallest building in the county.

Got a call a few months back from old Avery Jockings—lives just back of the Phillmore—saying he saw a flash and somebody looking out the window on the fifth floor. It wasn't the first time Jockings had called about seeing a flash up there at night, like somebody lighting a cigarette. Murdock had investigated once before and found nothing, but this time Buster climbed the five flights of stairs. He thought maybe high school kids were going up the fire ladder and jimmying the door, but the door was locked. Not a footprint on the dusty floors. All he found was an empty, crushed cigarette pack on the floor by the back window. Old Golds. Buster couldn't remember the last time he'd seen a pack of Old Golds.

The first time he saw the Phillmore building was when his dad took him to the bank. He must have been five or six years old. Look up, his dad said, and he did and he couldn't see the top. There used to be a red beacon on a triangular, ten-foot wooden tower standing at the front ledge of the roof, visible for blocks around in the winter when the trees were bare. The single police car had no radio, so when there was a call for the police, the night operator, who also acted as night police dispatcher, would throw a switch to turn on the beacon. When the night captain saw the red light, he called in from the nearest phone booth. The beacon was more effective on foggy winter nights. Buster remembered his grandmother saying, "I saw a devilish glow over the downtown last night when I couldn't sleep. Must have been some trouble."

That was back before Warry. Alba Rook was chief then, his picture alongside Warry's in the chronological row of black and white photos on the wall behind Buster's desk. Beside Rook was smiling Dean Jackson alongside Big Bobby Brown. There were three more: Elmer Hubbard with his bushy mustache, Tom Thornton with Roosevelt glasses, and Yonders' first police chief, Curnel Potter, barely discernable as he posed by a steam engine in a copy of a tintype. Buster decided his picture, when the time came, would be in black and white too, out of respect. His grandpa said that old Chief Bobby Brown, back in the twenties, used to wear a cowboy hat and ride a horse up and down Main Street. The shopkeepers had to clean up after it with shovel and bucket.

As he neared the tracks that marked the end of downtown, Buster looked in the long front window of the video store. The big blue letters read Yonders Video Rental & Tanning. A single clerk sat behind the counter watching a video on a small overhead screen. A McBride boy. They opened early so folks could return videos on the way to work. He had one to return but he forgot it. Used to be the Five-and-Dime store with big Christmas displays: bikes, cowboy outfits, Davy Crockett coonskin caps, doll houses and electric trains running around a Christmas tree.

Northbound freight whistling from the south, bells clanging at the Main Street crossing. He could make it if he goosed it, and he did, just as the gates twitched. The Interceptor's big police motor was quick. In the mirror, he saw the gates come down and do their little bounce. When he was a kid in high school working summer at Pride during pack, he always knew to allow for trains on the way to work. A long freight could screw up your morning if you were on the wrong side of it. He glanced again in the mirror. Another one of those mile-long, double-stack container trains. Didn't seem that long ago that there were still big, black steam engines. He missed the old steam trains with red cabooses, back before graffiti. Boxcars, gondolas and tank cars with their colors and names: Southern Pacific, Lackawanna, Rio Grande, Monon and the one his mom liked to say and sing, the Atchison, Topeka and the Santa Fe.

The dash clock said a quarter to eight. He was still running early, so he stopped. A police car always looks right wherever it's parked in its home town. He pulled into the vacant corner lot just across from the junior high school where the old Gas & Go! used to be, one of those gypsy no-brand filling stations that always hawked gas-war prices back in the gas-war days. Buster remembered once paying 19.9 cents a gallon at the Gas & Go!

He looked at his watch. He'd be right on time if he left in a couple of minutes. He cracked the window a bit to the chilly, dank air. Light drizzle. Something was coming. It wasn't even that cold out, but he ran the window back up and turned on the heater. Summer thinned out a man's blood. What was coming was winter. The older he got the more he loved the summertime. A brown and white mutt went high-tailing by on the sidewalk in front of the junior high school. No collar. An outlaw in leash-law days, but no dogcatcher to catch him. Good for him!

He was about to start his engine when a yellow Mustang—it looked like the one the druggie kid at Mike Bailey's place drove— went right through the stop sign at about twenty miles per hour, not thirty feet from where Buster sat parked in a black and white police car, for Christ's sake! He said out loud, "Did I just become in-goddamn-visible?" And he tore out, throwing gravel, lights flashing. All that Detroit power made him smile.

Buster gave the siren a hit and the yellow Mustang went to the curb. He was right. It was the druggie. Now what? The word from the sheriff's department was to lay off the drug kids unless they committed some major crime that couldn't be ignored. Since the 60's there had always been a few drug arrests in town—some years none, other years two or three—but the numbers were growing. Sheriff said it wasn't a case of it getting worse before it got better, because it wasn't ever going to get better.

He walked to the window of the Mustang. The kid, half smiling, wasn't looking him in the eye, but the empty eyes of a death head were peeking over his collar. Who in his right mind would tattoo a skull to his own damn neck? Malcolm Lutz would. According to his Illinois driver's license, that was his name and he was from Joliet, an upstate kid.

Buster carried the license back to the Interceptor and thought it all over. If he gave a ticket, he'd have to run his license and plates and then, sure as hell, he'd find the kid had an outstanding warrant for something and have to act on it. That could burn the raid. Last thing the sheriff wanted was for any of the three suspects to get arrested too soon and for the wrong thing, not after all the planning from Mexico to Houston to Chicago and with the Central Illinois Drug Enforcement Task Force from Mattoon chomping at the bit for the right moment to come rolling into town with their DEA Humvees, a dozen agents in full, go-to-hell battle gear, armed to fight Arabs, and with their drug-sniffing K9 named Gonzo. Sheriff McIntyre told Buster the dog's name, but none of the names of the men.

Buster walked back to the kid's window. It was still drizzling and the kid, all dry and warm in his yellow Mustang, was still not looking at him. He leaned down and handed the license through the half-opened window. The kid took the license, flicked it on the passenger seat and reached for the ignition but stopped when Buster said in a calm but stern voice, looking into the eyes of the death head, "I didn't say you could go."

The kid kept his hand on the key and didn't even look at the policeman standing in the chilly drizzle. Buster's tone was almost friendly, almost fatherly. "I'd advise you for your own good to look the man who's talking to you in the eye."

The kid looked up with a hint of a smile on his lips, and that almost made Buster yell Wipe that smile off your face! The words were on the tip of his tongue, old Chief Warry's words. And Warry would have had the door open and his big head stuck right in the kid's face. He'd have shouted so loud they'd have heard him downtown.

He remembered a speaker at the police chiefs conference over in Springfield a couple of years back saying that an officer should end every traffic stop on a cordial note, offering some friendly advice, appropriate to the conditions. Drive carefully. Watch for standing water. Watch for black ice. Or even, Have a nice day.

Buster almost said, And watch out for pot holes. But that just might be a little too appropriate, so instead he said, speaking softly but intensely in a cordial tone, "If you ever go barreling through a stop sign again right under my goddamn nose, I'll give you cause to regret the day your sorry ass was born."

Anybody driving by on this chilly morning would think he was just telling the boy to get his taillight fixed, inviting him to have a nice day.

Chapter 9

1998
Dead Man's Grave

"Morning, Chief," said Jezzie. "Nat and Rusty are waiting for you and the mayor. Mayor Tom's usually the late one."

Buster smiled. Hard to believe she and Keelan were brother and sister. They seemed as different as day and night. Looking around the Dixie, he saw a booth of Kramers and a booth of Benders. Old Bob Wilson, who used to own the sporting goods store till he closed it, was sitting at the counter with old Fred Dixon, the southsider who used to own the hardware store until he sold it to a man from Jericho who closed it, and there was a booth of women he could name if he stopped to think. Somewhere in there Buster heard Mary Weber's cackle. She was from his class and still had the same laugh. Didn't know the big boy in the Braves hat or the teacher-looking old lady sitting alone at the little side table. And there was the Hoosier who was installing equipment at the Illiana. Seemed OK, but you never know till you do. Knew everybody else. Hook and Rhodes were waiting for him in the corner booth. He slid in beside Rhodes, unsnapped his walkie-talkie from his belt, unclipped the speaker mic from his epaulet and placed both on the table. The three old friends grunted hello to each other.

"Look at that Jap crap Covington bought," said Hook. On the forecourt across the lot, Buddy was making change at the window of Melvin Covington's Honda Civic.

"That's brand-spanking new," said Hook. "Bought off that Honda lot down in Damascus where the old Starlight Club used to be at the bottom of Dead Man's Grade."

"I tell you what," said Rhodes, "I must have been thirty before I figured out all those old roadhouses was on Dead Man's Grade instead of Dead Man's Grave."

"That's what I called it too. I think we all called it that. Didn't know no better," said Hook. "All gone now, anyhow."

Gone now, the honkytonk, gravel-parking-lot, badass roadhouses south of Damascus where Rhodes, Hook and almost everybody else from back then, Buster too, more than a few times, had caroused and sometimes fought, usually with each other, seldom with strangers— they were shy of strangers—driving home half-drunk at eighty miles per hour, sneaking in the back door so as not to wake the folks. Those bars and clubs were all gone, swapped for strip malls and blocks of self-storage sheds. And now there was even a Japanese car dealer at the bottom of Dead Man's Grade.

Melvin Covington steered the little Civic, wipers wagging, onto the highway joining the straggle of light traffic, and Buddy Bowman hustled back through the drizzle to the office.

Jezzie came over with the coffee. "You boys scare us with these meetings. So far you got us a building full of witches complete with a fat man with a pigtail and a cape. We can't wait to hear what's next," she said, hand on hip, pouring coffee and blowing a stray strand of red hair out of her eye the way she always did, extending her lower lip and making a quick puff.

"One of your customers is wanting you, Jez," said Hook, nodding toward the far end of the diner where a man in a blue and yellow jacket was smiling Jezzie's way and holding up his mug. "That's the robot guy, ain't it?"

"There's high pockets now," said Jezzie, pointing with her chin to the mayor who was walking in from the lot. And she was gone.

"She changed that subject pretty fast," said Hook. "Who is that guy, anyhow? I been seeing him around off and on for a couple of weeks now."

"He's sent over from Kokomo Machinery to put in some box-stacking equipment at the Illiana that does a man's work for nothing. Them NAFTA Washington boys missed a few and he's here mopping up the last couple of jobs they forgot to send to Mexico or China. He's been back and forth, staying at Four Corners when he's in town. Somebody said they seen him and Jezzie at the show up in Jericho," said Rhodes.

"What's at the show up in Jericho that you can't see here?" said Hook.

"Jezzie and the Kokomo Hoosier, for one thing," said Rhodes.

"About time, I say," said Hook.

Those in the booths near the door greeted Mayor Wellington. The trucker and Jezzie's murdering lady looked up too. The mayor was six-foot-four when he was the First Team All-County center back in his day and he was still the tallest man in town. Wellington had settled an inch or so, but he made up for it with some shoes he ordered out of a catalogue, shoes that he thought nobody noticed. He scooted into the booth alongside Hook "You boys seen the paper?" Buster nodded, but Hook and Rhodes shook their heads.

"Well, you got some reading to catch up on," said Wellington. "Sounds like they're trying to unsolve the Wyatt murders."

Wellington laid the *Damascus Herald* on the table.

"Is that thing still on with the witchmaster tonight?" said Jezzie, back to take their order.

"Afraid so," said Buster. "He calls himself chancellor, but I like witchmaster better."

After they had all ordered, Wellington got down to business. "We all need to be at the First Church of Christ tonight to referee between the home team and the witches." Wellington lowered his voice and tone. "There's been a lot of talk and some of those in our evangelical community have taken umbrage. So we just need to be there to keep things on an even keel."

"Umbrage, huh?" said Buster, imitating Wellington's soft tone. "I went along with you on this, but I wasn't in my right mind at the time. Bringing witches into churches just might spark some progodious umbrage."

“Well,” said Wellington, smiling and almost whispering now, “in spite of you pushing it for the last fifty years, progodious is still not a word.” And they all laughed.

“It was that article Lisa wrote this summer that got some of the church people nervous. Words like witch and pagan kind of jump out at you in a newspaper, in ours anyway,” Hook said.”

“We might have been better off just tearing that old wreck down and putting in a little flower garden and a couple of benches,” said Wellington.

“It was the only real offer I got on that property, the only real offer the town got. What was I supposed to do?” said Hook.

Rhodes had been carefully reading the article in the paper while the others talked. He looked up and said, “The Twilight Zone Murderer?”

“I guess that’s how you sell papers. Anything likely to come of all this, Buster?” said Wellington.

Before Buster could answer, a sudden, heavy rain hit hard on roof, glass and earth.

Jezzie, walking past with a tray, said, “Looks like it finally cut loose.”

It was only a short cloudburst. By the time the four men had finished their breakfasts, the sun had begun to break through leaving a few blue patches amid the dark clouds. The mayor picked up the tab, but they all left tips and headed out to their vehicles. Buster sat in the Interceptor and watched the others drive away. His copy of the *Herald* was on the seat beside him. He hadn’t answered Wellington’s question, but he knew the answer. Nothing at all would come of an old convict changing his confession from three murders to one after nearly forty years. They dug folks up sometimes and found traces—no, they called them strands—of DNA on whatever hair or tooth or bone was left of the victims, but no Marigold County judge was ever going to order an exhumation to try and make a case against a man without having a shred of evidence or a single witness, especially if it meant embarrassing the bigshot Crawfords from Damascus. A cop's hunch wasn't enough for the law even in Warry's day, let alone now, but as Buster drove downtown the backway over the bricks of Hamilton Street, avoiding all those boarded-up stores on Main, he wondered what Keelan thought after he read the morning paper. And, more than that, Buster wondered why a man would come back to the one place where there might just be a cop who hadn't given up trying to put things right? Maybe even murderers get homesick.

PART TWO

SUMMER 1998

Chapter 10

1998
A LETTER FROM HOME

Keelan awoke to a familiar sound and for a moment he was back home, but he knew before he opened his eyes that he wasn't hearing a Nickel Plate freight and it sure as hell wasn't a streamliner on the C&EI either, because this wasn't Yonders and it wasn't 1959. The hooting out there was some Union Pacific container train leaving the yards back of the Eisenhower Highway in Reno and, whatever time it was, it was time to get the hell out of Nevada before Bobby Harkie's kid brother, Twitchy, got out and came after him. Twitchy Harkie! It was like having a comic-book character gunning for him.

The morning after he heard Twitchy was about to be released, any day now, from Southern Desert Correctional, he woke up in the bed that he and Betty had slept in for the last three years—since the lucky night when he won her at Harold's Club just a few weeks after he got early release—and he knew it was time to make tracks. He almost said that to Betty, but before he turned his head, he remembered that Betty was dead in her little jug and he was alone again.

His luck had already started to run out and now it was getting worse. Before his feet hit the floor, he knew there was only one place left on God's green earth where he could count on the righteous law to keep the likes of a Twitchy Harkie from gunning down a law-abiding senior citizen. He had never seen him, but if he looked as crazy as they said, he'd stand out like a goose in a hen house. Buster Lawton—Aunt Spite said Buster was still chief and going strong back home—would take one look at him and run him out of town. That's the way it used to be when Keelan was a kid, back in Warry's day, and Keelan couldn't imagine it changing much. When he thought of Yonders, it hadn't changed and neither had he.

It was during his third prison term that he found himself thinking for the first time in a long time about home. Prison had changed a hell of a lot since the sixties, and whatever they were singing about on the radio wasn't happening behind bars or in the yard. You might talk to the Mexicans and the Blacks on the street or in a bar, but in prison you kept to your own. Keelan never got a tattoo. Last thing he needed when he got out was a swastika or a double S or some other such Aryan Warriors shit. He was known as a redneck burglar who wasn't all that smart, and that was just fine with him. Good behavior meant taking courses in the recidivism reduction program. Keelan didn't find the courses all that useful except as boxes to check on his record as a model prisoner. He went to prison church on Sunday mornings, made license plates, watched Dallas, learned about American wars in high school classes. He got his General Educational Development credential and his high school equivalency certificate—class of '93 instead of '58. And, just a little at first and more later, he started remembering things back home.

He was in the second month of his third stretch when Aunt Purity showed up. Purity Ramirez, she was calling herself now instead of Tucker. He'd heard about her but never seen her. His mom always said she was a caution. He never heard her called Purity. She was Spite.

Aunt Spite, looking feisty and wearing tight jeans tucked inside high black boots, looked a lot younger than the sixty-some he figured she must be. She kept well, like apples. Married, she told him, for twenty years to an Oakland cop. They were sitting across from each other at a little table in the visitation room. It was the first time Keelan had a visitor and he was surprised to see most of the tables occupied, sometimes with whole families and little kids who couldn't sit still. It seemed like everybody had people. And, for a little while anyway, so did he.

"It's from your mom," Spite said. The envelope was blank. She could at least have put his name on it.

"Who died?"

"Your dad. He had a stroke."

Keelan, saw his dad bent under the hood of the Chevy, leaning into the gunfight on TV. He looked at the white envelope that Aunt Spite placed before him and asked if his mom told her to hand deliver it. "No. She didn't know how to find you, but my man looked you right up. I could have just sent it over, but I wanted to check up on the other crazy Tucker in the family. The rest are all still back where we left them. You going to open it?"

"You already told me what's in it," said Keelan. He started to put the envelope in the chest pocket of his blue uniform shirt but it wouldn't fit and he didn't want to fold it. He placed in on the table and kept his hand upon it. He might as well ask. "What about Mae and the baby girl?" Mae! First time he'd said her name in years.

"Surprised you even know she had a girl," said Spite. "Not even your mom knows what part of Kentucky they're in now. They never stayed in touch."

"Do you know her name?"

"I was told it was Keelan. I kinda like it better as a girl's name."

He saw Mae and made his mind look away. Spite reached across the table and gave his shoulder a push. It felt friendly. He didn't even know his kid had lived, didn't know it was a girl, didn't even know he was divorced until, on his first conviction, they ran his record all the way back to Illinois and found a divorce for desertion. They had him down as a deserter, a break-in thief and a filling-station robber, and they didn't know the half of it.

They talked for a bit about nothing much, about this, that and the other. Mostly about home where neither had been for so many years. Did she remember the smell of the factories during pack? Yes. Did he ever climb the water tower? No, but he went up the fire ladder and stood on the roof of the Phillmore looking out over everything. He would have liked to have lingered there gabbing just a while longer, but a guard said it was time. He thought about hugging Spite but only held out his hand. She squeezed it and smiled. It was the first time anybody had smiled at him, smiled that way, since he didn't know when. Since Yonders.

He waited till later when he was alone in the little bleachers by the basketball courts in the prison yard. It was just a half piece of paper, probably torn in two with a ruler—his mom didn't like to waste anything. "Your dad died and he's buried out at Floral Hill. He didn't suffer." The note was in ink but she signed it Mom in pencil. Maybe she only thought to sign it later when she was putting it in the envelope to send to Spite. He was glad his dad didn't suffer.

He could see Floral Hill, a green carpet of tombstones and trees rising away from the tracks where Double Aught crossed the end of Iroquois, right along the tracks and across from the old farmhouse. Sometimes when he was going to sleep, he'd find himself thinking about walking the tracks, but not out toward Floral Hill. He always liked walking out east of town. You could get out in the country quicker heading east, and he remembered as a kid going out that way with his BB gun and shooting at crows and tin cans. Once he even snuck out with his dad's hunting rifle and maybe he shot something, a fox or something. He couldn't quite remember, but he did remember walking the tracks home one time in particular, just at sunset, seeing the streetlights through the trees at the edge of town and the red light high atop the water tower. That evening at dusk he remembered a freight hard behind him out of the west, coming from town. No problem guessing it was a freight because the Nickel Plate quit hauling passengers when he was in first grade. He turned to face it, playing chicken with a Nickel Plate freight, the engineer hanging on the whistle. Keelan really didn't know if he was going to jump or not. It scared him, as the train screamed by where he lay face down in the cinders of the banking, scared him that he almost didn't jump. When he got home, supper was on the table and it was cowboy night on TV and he was glad he'd jumped, and, even with one thing and the other, he was still glad he jumped and it still scared him to know he almost didn't.

Whenever someone asked him where home was, he'd always say he was from Regret, Kentucky, the place his mom was always talking about. "Tell me about this Regret place," Betty said one night. He hadn't gotten two dozen words out of his mouth before she said, "You're lying through your teeth, Keelan Putnam. You ain't from no place called Regret, if there even is such a place." So, he told her about Yonders and she listened and said, "Well, my, my! You really do have a home, don't you? That's more than most people have." She said he ought to take her back with him for a visit. Folks need to be careful what they ask for unless they're not too particular how they travel.

Betty said she was from a little Missouri wide spot in the road that just blew away along with her folks and everyone she ever knew and that's all she'd say about it, but she kept asking him about Yonders, little things, and he didn't mind telling her as long as she just asked about the town and left him out of it. She liked him to tell about all the floats and the marching bands and the big steam tractor in the Harvester Pageant parade, and one day she said, "You're lucky. Not everybody gets to be from some place that's still standing." At the time he didn't think much about it, but now, with the word that Twitchy was planning to come looking for him, he knew Betty was right. He was lucky to be from a place that was still back there.

He was real lucky there for a while—for a three-year run that ended when Betty died of a heart attack while she was working behind one of the bars at Circus Circus. During those years he had a home. 2300 Prater Way, Sparks, Nevada. It had a solid sound to it, like it might have been a house with trees and lawn and big front porch instead of being a 28-foot trailer.

Those years under the same tin roof with Betty was the longest stretch he had ever voluntarily stayed in one place since he left Yonders. When he won Betty at Harold's Club he was working for City of Reno Maintenance, a job he got as part of what they called a re-entry program. He'd done three and a half years at Northern Correctional in Carson City back in the sixties for burglary, five years at Nevada State Prison in the same town for the same thing in the seventies and, most recently, he'd been back to State, convicted of robbery—and it should have been armed robbery. Betty was right. He was lucky. Dumb luck. His kind of luck.

It happened after his second stretch. He was just off parole and that meant he could finally quit the butt-busting road work job he'd had to take after getting out. While he was looking for something better, he decided robbing a desert gas station would tide him over. He took a drive out toward Pyramid Lake and found a little gas station and fireworks store at a lonesome crossroads a few miles down the road from a 24-hour Paiute casino. He asked the reservation kid pumping gas how long he stayed open. "As long as the casino's open, we're open," he said. The next night Keelan came back, wearing a bandana like a bandito in the movies. There was nobody around at 2 a.m., and he was in and out fast. He didn't point his gun at the kid—the same kid as the night before—but he showed it to him. The skinny kid wasn't about to get himself shot just to protect some paleface's money. Keelan emptied the cash drawer, grabbed a pocket full of candy bars and told the kid to lie down and stay down till he drove away. Next morning Keelan woke up to banging on his door. State cops, two cars full of them, surrounded his house like he was some big gangster. They found the pistol and the money still in his jacket pocket on the chair beside his bed. At the station during interrogation, they showed him the security videos and called him a dumbass for not covering his license plate. All this technical crap, thought Keelan, will truly be the death of us all.

It would be his third felony conviction and this time he was armed. The detective who questioned him seemed friendly, a little too friendly, offered him a cigarette and a light and then he said, "I want to congratulate you for being smart enough to have gone in there unarmed. A man with your record charged with armed robbery would be looking at serious time."

Keelan blinked, swallowed, nodded and listened. Something was up and he didn't have to wait long to find out what. Plead guilty to robbery, a Class B felony and, the detective said, he'd be looking at two to twelve, and he just might find himself eligible for early parole. If he was feeling cooperative, he might be in the breeze before he got much older. They needed a snitch who knew his way around inside enough to not give himself away. The detective leaned in close and talked low. "Sometimes shit goes wrong inside and that two year minimum turns into the full twelve, and twelve years is a long time for an old guy like you, but if you're smart enough to play ball, you'll have a happier and shorter stay as a guest of the state." How short? "Hard to say, but we'll find good use for you. Don't you doubt it."

Just as he was told, he got two to twelve. At first, he cooperated on some little stuff like tipping off the guards about who had drugs or a shiv and where they got them. They were testing him, but he was glad they got him a harmless cellmate. He was just five months into his first year when they told him he had another visitor, the second one he'd ever had. At first he thought it might be Aunt Spite again. Maybe his mom had died. They said it was some cousin he'd never heard of, but instead of escorting him to the visitation area, they took him up the back stairs to a room where the friendly detective was waiting. He had a name now. Detective Cartwright explained what Keelan could do for Nevada and what Nevada could do for him. They had just locked up a small-time, stick-up bandit, Bobby Harkie, convicted of a series of armed robberies, but they suspected him of an unsolved murder on an unpaved backroad in the desert northeast of the little town of Searchlight. They had nothing but a deputy's hunch. All they knew was that Harkie used to go jackrabbit shooting in the remote area where a man was found dead at the wheel of his truck with a bullet in his chest along a lonesome backroad. Harkie would be Keelan's new cellmate and his job would be to get enough on Harkie to bring a murder charge.

This new cellmate was not harmless. Bobby Harkie was batshit crazy, mean-looking and less than half Keelan's age, but Keelan knew how to play it, how to get him to brag on himself without ever asking a question. At first Harkie only talked about robberies, about how well-planned they were, about how smart he was. But one evening Keelan turned the conversation to Nevada State's most famous ex-prisoner, the flesh-eating serial-killer, Carrol Cole. Cole, executed by lethal injection at Nevada State back in '85, was a legend among the inmates. "I don't know if I'd have it in me to go killing like old Cannibal Cole," Keelan said, and Harkie snapped back, "Cole was a damn coward who killed women." It took a while, but finally Harkie bragged not only that he'd killed a man. He got his wind up and said he'd killed two men, one out back of a bar in Lodi, California, during an alley stick-up. The other was just for the pure orneriness of it. He said he was out practicing his aim one day, using an old Winchester 70 that used to be his dad's, shooting anything that moved in the hills north of Searchlight—rabbits, coyotes, buzzards—even said he drew a bead on a low-flying little single-engine airplane, but he was afraid he'd miss and they'd report him. Then he got the idea that he could probably shoot a man driving by in his truck down on the road and get away with it. Harkie said he got him with the first shot from maybe 50 yards. The truck just slowed and went off the road into the ditch. He got the hell out of there and found out the next day in the paper that the guy was dead.

As a kid growing up watching TV, Keelan believed that people murdered each other for good reasons, or at least for some kind of reasons. He certainly would never shoot somebody just for fun, although when he was a kid, the idea of taking a shot at somebody in a train window crossed his mind, like it would to any kid, but he grew out of it.

Keelan used the guard he worked through to get a message to the warden, and the next day three guards came for him. They searched his bunk, roughed him up and drug him upstairs. They pushed him around in front of Harkie to make it look good. The same friendly Detective Cartwright who arranged his plea with the prosecutor was waiting upstairs and did the questioning. The warden just sat back and watched.

He decided to keep the second murder to himself. One murder was all they asked for and, besides, he suspected that the Lodi alley murder was just made up. They said they needed more proof than a confession to a cellmate. So he went back to work, and it wasn't hard to get Harkie talking again. He talked himself into Murder 1. Not only did he give more details, he told Keelan that he left the rifle, his dad's Winchester, the murder weapon, in his little brother Twitchy's keeping. That was all they needed.

After a week of waiting, still sharing a cell with the man he was setting up for a life sentence or worse, he got taken back upstairs. "You're lucky. It all checked out," Cartwright said. They found the rifle among Twitchy's things at his folks' house. Young Twitchy himself was already in custody, awaiting trial for armed carjacking. They matched the bullet out of the dead man's chest to Harkie's rifle. Although he had no idea who he was killing and no motive, Keelan's testimony that Harkie had bragged that he "shot to kill" brought Murder 1 charges. Bobby Harkie was transferred to another cell block and Keelan was paroled after serving less than half his minimum. It wouldn't take long for the Harkie brothers to figure out why Harkie's cellmate, a three-time felon, was enjoying the fresh air so soon.

The Nevada papers called Bobby Harkie the Searchlight Sniper, trying to play it up, but it didn't catch on. The public wanted serial killers like Cannibal Carrol Cole or at least something a lot more gruesome than a psycho with an old cowboy rifle shooting some poor bastard driving along a desert road. Keelan never had to testify because Bobby Harkie pleaded guilty to avoid the death penalty. And Keelan was a free man again.

He didn't let himself think it while he was an inmate, but once he was out, paroled and walking free along the Reno-Sparks streets, he knew he'd sooner die than ever go back in that shade. Ten years of his life in prison was long enough, but he'd been lucky to be convicted before the three-strike rule. One more now and it would be life. Harkie was no gangster with the reach to send somebody halfway across the United States to settle a score, but Keelan knew he would be a dead man if he ever went back to State or if Twitchy ever caught up with him. But Twitchy, Keelan learned, was in the first year of a four to twelve sentence and that allowed for some breathing room.

After he and Betty got together, both working honest jobs, Betty at the casino and Keelan working for the city, he started thinking about moving somewhere quiet and far away. When Betty upped and died, she left him money she'd been holding out on him, not so much, but a lot more than Keelan ever had at one time, and when word got to him that Twitchy Harkie was due to be released for good behavior—that meant Twitchy must also have been helpful to the State—and that he was saying he was going to butcher the man who put his brother away for life, Keelan knew it was getting to be time to leave the desert. He was a free man, off parole and free to roam, and where would a free man whose roaming days were over want to go more than to the one place where he'd always know which way was north? It was time to go home.

He put Betty's money, his money now, in the big Bank of America on South Virginia Street. They looked at him as if they thought he was there to rob them instead of to open an account. Cameras everywhere once you knew to look for them. The money wouldn't be there long and neither would he. Nobody in Nevada wanted him to stay except Twitchy Harkie.

Keelan packed his suitcase and spent his last evening in Sparks watching a Dodgers game on TV in the trailer. He was the worst player on his Little League team—his dad had never played and nobody taught him—but one sunny day he hit a home run, inside the park but a home run all the same. He almost always struck out, but that day, swinging wild, he hit one hard down the right field line and ran like he'd never run before. All the kids on his team, the ones that usually made fun of him for striking out, were cheering and hollering for him. He slid into home even though he didn't have to. It was the last game of his last year in Little League and he didn't play Pony League—he'd started robbing by then—but he still liked watching baseball, remembering all the kids cheering for him and slapping him on the back. Once, watching a game on TV with Betty, she asked him what position he played. "Shortstop," he said. That was a lie. He always played right field and batted last, but it made him happy to tell her he was a shortstop.

He missed Betty. She was packed away for the trip. He didn't know what to do with her ashes. She wanted them thrown on the waters of Pyramid Lake so she could swim forever with the water babies that some old Washoe woman who cleaned at Circus Circus put in her head, but he never got around to making the drive up to the lake. It didn't seem right to throw them out or leave them behind, even if it was just a jug of old dirt, so he packed her urn in his suitcase. She always said she wanted to visit Yonders. He'd figure out something to do with her later.

When the game was over, he turned off the TV, set his alarm for 11 p.m. in case he dropped off to sleep, and sat in the dark listening to the radio until it was time to head out.

He locked the trailer, and put the key on the ledge above the door. He'd even paid up and given notice. The Greek that owned it would probably rent it to some cokehead and it'd go to hell. He was glad to be getting out. He picked up his old suitcase and walked past the little all-night bars and casinos on the way to the bus station. He didn't need a schedule because he had wandered down there a few times when Betty was working nights. He knew there was a midnight Chicago bus coming through from San Francisco. Once he drank a couple of beers at a little bar down the street from the station and watched the big, blue and silver bus ease past through the lit-up night. The destination board said Chicago, but that bus was Yonders bound.

Chapter 11

SENTIMENTAL JOURNEY

They couldn't sell Keelan a ticket to Yonders even after he pointed to where it should have been on the route map, but he knew there was a local that ran up the Dixie from Damascus to Chicago, so he bought a one-way to Damascus. It'd be another couple bucks up to Yonders.

He boarded the half-empty San Francisco to Chicago Greyhound and took the window seat of an empty row at mid-coach. It was always best for a smoother ride on long hauls to sit between the axles. He put his suitcase in the seat beside him, hoping to stretch out overnight.

"Is this seat taken," said the woman standing in the aisle. She started talking before they reached the outskirts of a place Keelan figured he'd never see again. So much for sleeping, but he didn't mind the company. It was almost interesting to hear about this woman's life: two husbands, six kids, a car crash when she was pregnant and driving herself to the hospital. Had the baby in the ambulance. Didn't say why she was driving alone and he didn't ask. She'd been visiting her mom and was going home just up the road to Winnemucca. She went quiet for a mile or so and then she started in on him. Where was he going? Home, he said. Whereabouts? Illinois, a little town nobody ever heard of. Was it a nice place? Yes, it was. How long since you been back? Getting onto forty years.

"I guess you're on a sentimental journey," she said, "Like the old Doris Day song."

"I guess," he said. By then she was all talked out and soon dropped off to sleep. He looked at her in the highway lights of a passing car. Probably a pretty thing once, like Doris Day.

When the woman got off in Winnemucca, he was hoping another one, younger and better looking, would get on. Nobody boarded and soon he fell asleep, but the sleep just wasn't quite right, a kind of half-dreaming. When he opened his eyes, everything seemed too real, and there was a mild-looking fellow with a little mustache sitting beside him in the diesel hum of the Greyhound night.

If you didn't know it was the Devil you'd never guess, but the Devil knew he knew him. He hadn't thought much about him since he was a kid. His mom never talked about God like other kids' moms, but she used to say, "You keep up your ways and the old Devil will grab up out of a leaf pile and drag you down to Hell by your skinny ankle." Sometimes she said he'd reach up out of a mud puddle or out of the ice. It was enough to make him watch his step, especially after dark. Hadn't given the Devil more than a moment's thought all these years, and now there he was riding through the night with him. When he sat through those prison sermons, the preacher was always praising God's mercy and bad-mouthing the Devil. It was the same way on the radio on those long drives in the night when no other stations would come in. Maybe the Devil had his reasons. Didn't they say nobody could be all bad?

The rest of the bus looked like it should—almost—and the badlands flowed by in the moonlight, but when he snuck a look beside him, the Devil was looking right back at him and his eyes were just too bright.

"How long's it been?" the Devil asked, friendly like, matter of fact, with an accent that sounded like home. Keelan almost answered but he stopped himself in time. He almost talked to the damn Devil! Crazy stuff in the night and after too many hours bouncing around on a bus.

The next time he awoke he was really awake and it was light out. The driver had turned on the inside lights and opened the door to the chilly dawn at the Salt Lake terminal. Folks were standing, talking, getting down luggage. "Forty minutes for breakfast," the driver said.

Keelan looked over and there was nobody in the empty seat, nothing to give away who'd been riding with him that night. Maybe it had nothing to do with him. Maybe it was just the first empty seat the Devil found when he managed to hop that bus running eighty miles an hour on the five-hour run from Winnemucca. But what was the Devil doing so far from Yonders? He'd seen that fellow before, walking down Main Street a long, long time ago. But that was crazy thinking.

Bacon, eggs and a coke instead of coffee. He needed to get the sleep he'd lost because of the woman and whatever else rode at his side till dawn.

"Lunch in Table Rock, eight hours to Cheyenne," the driver said.

And that got him thinking. Cheyenne was an Indian tribe like Apache, Sioux and Cherokee, and Keelan remembered playing cowboys and Indians along the tracks. One time he played like Jezzie was an Indian maiden and he tied her up to an alley tree and tried to strip her, but she made such a racket he had to let her go. You'd have thought he was killing her. Before he let her go, he told her not to tell, but she went running straight to their mom. You ever mistreat your sister that way again, his mom said, and I swear I'll skin you alive. That was what the Indians did too.

Jezzie wasn't much to look at till she started to bloom; then every boy in town was after her. She really thought she was hot stuff and she even put that damn tape over the keyhole to her bedroom door, something their mom was sure to see. She had no call to do that, since he was always quiet as a mouse and she had no way of knowing he'd ever squatted out there in the hall. She only thought he was peeking at her because she had a dirty mind. Seeing that tape and knowing she was in there probably primping in front of the mirror just got to him that day. He surprised her in her room when the folks were gone and she yelled at him to get out.

He was just playing around at first. The folks were at the park watching the horse show and there was nobody to hear her, but she yelled anyway and something went haywire in his brain and he wasn't thinking right and he was standing there seeing Jezzie's little tits under her torn shirt. Holding up a butcher knife to her own brother. He couldn't remember tearing her shirt, but he could see his hands doing it. Poor Jezzie. Her favorite cowgirl shirt. Where did she get a butcher knife?

He ran off and stayed out till after midnight just walking the C&EI tracks north, all the way up to Willows and back. When he got home late that night, his mom was waiting up and she gave him a talking to. After she finally let him go up to bed, he saw there was light at the bottom of Jezzie's door, but none through the keyhole. He wanted to say he was sorry, but when he tried the knob the door was locked. Locked with a damned key as if he couldn't pick any lock they threw at him. His own sister too. His mom must have given her the key to go with the butcher knife.

Rolling through the Wyoming morning, he dreamed he was treed and his shoes were on fire, and then Jezzie was running at him with the knife, her shirt torn open, running at him like Rachel across the living room, and she was Rachel with that curse in her eyes. Then he awoke.

With nobody riding beside him, nobody he could see anyway, he finally slept unbedevilled all the way to the Cheyenne supper stop. After supper, the bus, half-empty now, stayed lively. Folks tend to gab more when they are riding the green flatlands. The deserts and the mountains with their bleak little towns cause people to turn in on themselves, but every little town in Nebraska was bustling and happy in the sunshine—kids on bicycles, mothers pushing baby carriages, men telling each other what was what, walking the shady sidewalks of little towns with the town names riding high on the water towers, like back home.

There was a six-hour wait to transfer to the Indianapolis bus in Davenport, Iowa. Keelan was starting to get antsy. It was late morning when they crossed the Mississippi and rolled into Illinois: Bloomington, Le Roy, Farmer City, Mohomet, Champaign-Urbana, and about the time they crossed the Marigold County line at Ogdon, the fields and farm houses took on a familiar look. From the outskirts of Damascus to the bus station there wasn't much he didn't remember, but he wasn't home yet. He went to the ticket window and asked for a one-way to Yonders.

"We haven't gone through there for years," the grandmotherly Black woman said, studying him.

"It's on the way to Chicago," said Keelan. "The driver can just put me down at Four Corners."

"I know where it is, but we don't go up that way no more."

"Well, how do you get to Chicago without running up the Dixie?"

"Via Champaign and the I-57. Could you step aside, sir?"

Keelan stepped aside. A fucked-up way to run a bus company. Going up to Chicago through Champaign! He was twenty-five miles too far south and the taxi bastard wanted two dollars a mile. A dollar a mile up, he said, and a dollar a mile back because he had to drive back empty. Keelan grabbed his suitcase and started walking. He knew where north was, and once he found Marigold Street, he set out walking until he got to the fancy houses and the big stores and eating places and finally the car dealerships and the gas stations and the storage sheds and the big lots with tractors and combines for sale and finally, after walking nearly an hour, he reached the start of the fields and stuck out his thumb.

"I can take you as far as Milton," said the kid in the pick-up, listening to the most godawful music Keelan ever heard. Sounded like a woman trying to sing like a man and a man trying to sing like a woman. Keelan couldn't understand either one of them and he didn't want to. He was glad to get out at the stoplight in Milton just to get away from that caterwauling. Stuck out his thumb right away and the first car that stopped was a damn Milton cop, a kid cop not even wearing his hat.

"Sir, you can't stand in the road for the purpose of soliciting a ride from the operator of any vehicle other than public transportation," the kid said, sounding proud of himself for remembering all that.

"What if I am waiting for public transportation?" said Keelan.

"Then you'd be about ten or fifteen years late," the kid said, friendlier after hearing Keelan's talk. Keelan heard it too. It was all coming back to him—the smells, the feel of the air and sun and a way of talking and of listening too.

"Where you headed?"

"Up to Yonders."

"Well, your best bet is to hitch from the curb so as not to be in violation of the section that says you can't stand in the road."

Minutes later he caught a ride for the last five miles from a man in a farm truck who turned west at Four Corners, leaving Keelan standing with his suitcase at the southwest end of Yonders, and he was of two minds how to get home—whether to walk east on Indiana Road to Iroquois or north to Main. It was suppertime by his stomach, but his watch had stopped and he didn't know what day it was, as if that mattered. He'd never been at Four Corners without a car. He decided on north, and in a couple hundred yards he came to the Dixie Diner. It hadn't changed hardly at all and it made him feel for a moment that he hadn't changed either, that he had never been out west, never been to prison, never killed a soul, never got fired that day, never left town.

He thought about going in to get himself something to eat when he saw her standing at a window booth writing down an order. The same red hair and the same way of standing and almost as skinny. Wouldn't it be a surprise if he just walked in there and said, Hey, Jezzie, it's your big brother come home! She seemed to look out at him. It was her alright. Too far away to see her blue eyes. She'd just see an old man walking the highway with a suitcase, but he felt her eyes on his back when he turned to keep on walking.

It was a long walk home from the Dixie, about two miles, not as far as walking across Damascus, but the Yonders miles seemed longer. Folks downtown looked at him twice, carrying a suitcase. He wished he had one of those suitcases with wheels. He saw faces that made him think of last names and he could see some folks trying to put a name on him. He crossed over the tracks onto the north side, but the tracks were gone. That surprised him.

Once on the north side, there wasn't a street corner that didn't know him, not an alleyway he hadn't run. The old fire hydrant at the corner of Church Avenue turned him into a little kid and a red squirrel crossing the street stopped, hunched all up, its tail in the air, and said, "I know you. You're Etna Putnam's boy." But he didn't answer back to such foolishness. His mom always told him what rabbits and birds and squirrels were saying. Said they were saying Good morning, Keelan, Good morning, Jezzie. Talking critters, his mom said. There was a time he believed all the foolishness he was told.

And there was his house. If they'd painted it, they'd painted it the same color and some time back. He knocked and stood there, his face in the little square window, and she came to the door. He expected her to look older than she did. If he was fifty-eight, she had to be seventy-five or so. She didn't even look surprised.

"So, you've run out of places to be," his mom said, after she let him in. She never once spoke his name, but she turned and he followed her into the old living room.

He saw out the back door how much the trees had grown and saw that the alley fence was gone. When he was little, that fence was the wall of the fort when the Indians attacked, shooting burning arrows and whooping, and he shot every one he could, but they kept coming over the wall. There were so many of them wanting to tie him up and scalp him that once he went running into the kitchen and hugged his mom. When he told her who was after him, she went right out the back door with the butcher knife. "I run them off," she said. "They'll think twice before attacking this fort again." Now there was no wall to keep them out. Was that the same butcher knife?

"You got money for your keep?" she said after a moment of standing there, the two of them in the dusk. His mom never turned on the lights till it was full dark outside.

"You offering me a place to stay?" he said, but he knew better.

His dad was dead so there was nothing else they could have talked about.

"I'll drive you out to the Four Corners Motel," she said. "You know I can't have you here."

Then her eyes softened just a bit. "Have you et yet?"

"No, but you can drop me off at the Dixie and maybe Jezzie can roust up something."

That got the soft out of her eyes. They were standing in the same old living room. There was a new davenport, but his dad's big chair was still there. The TV was bigger, but in the same place. Used to be five of them watching it.

"You're never to set foot anywhere near your sister."

He wished he hadn't said anything about Jezzie. He almost wanted to tell her what the red squirrel said, but all that was over and done with, as if it ever was. She didn't offer him coffee, but she gave him a glass of water when he asked for it. Good Yonders water.

She drove him out to the Four Corners Motel in her old Caprice. His dad always was a Chevy man, but he sure never got that 283-inch Impala. She drove with no talking right past where Jezzie was probably still working and let him out in front of the office. Wasn't she going to say anything?

"I'm glad you're well," she said, and drove away leaving him in that close and familiar evening air—the smell of the good, black earth, she used to call it. He hadn't heard cicadas crying that loud or that way since he left for California in 1959. He walked into the little motel office toting his suitcase that held all he owned: some clean clothes, spare shoes, coat, his lucky 777 jacket, Betty's ashes and his Colt semi-automatic with a silencer already screwed on. He'd been gone too long to put a name to the unsmiling face of the woman behind the counter, but if he met her on the moon, he'd know she was from Yonders.

He hadn't done anything but sit and sleep and eat and talk and listen for the last day and a half, but he was dead tired, too tired to even want supper, although he did wonder if Jezzie would recognize him if he walked back up the road and went in and sat down in a booth. But he'd better mind his mom for now. He was asleep with his clothes on the minute his head hit the pillow, and when he woke in the middle of the night to take off his shoes and socks, he didn't know where the devil he was—not until he heard the whistling of a freight, coming at him all wrong. Hearing the engineer hold the whistle long for Hamilton and Main, Keelan located himself. He was out at the Four Corners on the edge of Yonders, but he wasn't home yet and he wondered, just before falling asleep again, if he ever would be.

Chapter 12

THE DEVIL'S IN THE PORCH SWING

I guess the Devil must be lonesome tonight, thought Harold. He was hearing it again, the soft squeaking of the chains, and he knew it was the Devil out there swinging in the porch swing.

This was the second visit. The first time, a month earlier on a blustery spring night, Harold awoke during a mighty thunderstorm and thought he heard something on the porch, just outside his bedroom window. He tried to ignore it, rain in the gutters, wind in the trees, but after a few minutes he got up and peeked around the edge of the blind just as a bolt of lightning, simultaneous with a godawful crack of thunder, ripped open the night, and he saw who it was. Harold didn't believe in the Devil, but he sure knew the Devil when he saw him. His mom always said the Lord had too much to do to be bothering around, but the old Devil never knew a stranger.

He didn't stay that time. The next flash of lightning, weaker as the storm moved on, showed the swing empty, as if there hadn't been anyone there a moment before. It couldn't have been the wind, because Harold knew the swing only squeaked when it held weight. What he didn't know was if the Devil would be back or if he was just passing by and came up on the porch to get out of the rain. In a downpour like that, thunder roaring and lightning flashing, maybe even a fellow who doesn't quite exist needs to find cover.

The next morning, after that first June visit, Harold decided not to try and make sense out of it. He was eighty-two and he'd seen enough to know you never know what's just around the corner. One day you're cutting meat at a butcher shop on Main Street and the next you are halfway around the world on the way to fight an empire, sleeping in the moonlight on the deck of a troopship with sharks and Jap submarines and God knows what else below. Next thing you know, you're an old man living alone in the house you were born in. He decided not to think about the Devil unless he showed himself again. There was enough to worry about.

But, sure enough, he did come back in mid-July. Harold had watched *Walker, Texas Ranger* before he turned in. He didn't care that much for the program, but his mom used to like it and he used to watch it with her. *Gunsmoke* was better but, like just about everything else, it was gone. Harold usually took a walk down to the corner of Iroquois and back, just shy of half a mile, before he went to bed, and sometimes he walked a lot farther, once all the way out to Indiana Road, but his knee had been acting up and he decided to give it a rest. The days were hot and close, but there was the start of a cool breeze and he went right to sleep.

When he heard the squeaking of the chains, he looked over at the luminous hands of the clock. A bit after 4 a.m. And he knew who it was out there. A man's notion of what can be changes over the years. His first week on Saipan he was just returning to his Quonset hut after chow when he heard a straggler coming in late from the day's mission. It was a big, silver B-29 dropping crossways out of the clear blue, its tail shredded, one engine trailing smoke and its landing gear only down on one side. It pancaked hard, tearing off half a wing on the low side and erupting in black smoke and red fire. Moments later, he saw men running from the wreckage.

One man was afire. Someone said he died, but someone else said he didn't. Harold was a cook and heard a lot of scuttlebutt.

Whenever Harold thought of the things he had seen in the world, that one took the cake, that burning man running from the burning bomber. That happened on a godforsaken island halfway around the world during the war, but this was closer to home. The Devil was in the porch swing. You couldn't get closer to home than that.

Just as he did back on that stormy night in June, Harold got out of bed and looked through the crack between the blinds. No lightning bolt this time, only the moon and starlight and the streetlight three houses away on the corner, and there he was—the Devil swinging away. Last time he vanished, if something crazy can vanish. Harold had to smile, remembering the silly old song they used to sing on the Glenn Miller radio show—The Little Man Who Wasn't

There. His sister Helen played it on the Victrola. His mom never liked it, and that egged Helen on to playing it all the more. Something about meeting a ghost or a spirit who wasn´t there on the stairs yesterday and again today. Harold hummed it but couldn´t remember the words— something like "I wish the man who wasn't there would go away."

I guess I better go out there if I'm going, thought Harold. The Devil in the porch swing swung casually, the toes of his thin, shiny black shoes holding place and the heels rising and falling soundlessly. Harold opened the screen door and stepped forward, one slippered foot on the porch, the other still back on the threshold.

The Devil, or whatever that was sitting is his swing, seemed to wait for Harold to speak and, when he didn't, it did. "If this old swing could talk, what stories it would tell. But now just you sit alone here, after all these years," the thing said in a most friendly voice.

"It's not me sitting there now." Harold came fully out into the moonlight, both feet on the porch, closing the screen behind him, careful not to let the spring bang the door shut. The moon was at the Devil's back, but Harold could make out his features now, his black hair parted right down the middle and flat to the sides the old-fashioned way, a trim moustache…a fine-featured man, dapper and spiffy, maybe a tad smaller than Harold and thinner too in his white shirt, dark pants, pointy shoes. Eyes bright in the dark, as if they had their own light.

"Can I offer you a seat in your own swing on this lovely night?"

Harold looked down the block of dark houses and especially toward the screened-in porch of the Goodman house, just a moonlit lawn away. Ed Goodman would be out there sitting on the coaster with his loaded guns, watching the night through the video cameras in the trees.

Once, years back, Harold discussed Ed with old Doc Kline, dead now out on Floral Hill. "He sits out there all night and watches," Harold told him.

"Well," said Doc, "if you got to have some poor old shell-shocked Marine sitting up dusk to dawn on the porch and armed to the teeth, better it be a good man like Ed, a man with war medals."

The visitor, sitting nearest the banister, slowed the swing, and Harold sat down at the opposite end nearest the front window. Together, as front-porch folks know to do, they resumed swinging slowly again without getting the swing wobbly. Harold had built the swing in shop class his senior year and put it up at a ninety-degree angle to the street so that it faced due west. The porch roof and the tree tops blocked most of the summer sky. In the winter, when the limbs were bare, the sunsets were beautiful, but it was too cold to sit out long. Even with all the leaves in summer, someone sitting to the far right could see the trains passing on the C&EI five blocks west, beyond the end of Swisher Avenue. That was where Harold's mom had always sat and where he sat after she died. It was where this other fellow sat on this night.

They swung quietly and Harold, after a time, looking straight ahead and, sitting at the end of the swing he hadn't occupied since the last time his mom sat with him on the porch, wondered calmly if he was losing his mind. But, nope, he dismissed that thought. Lisa Canova, Gabriel Heatter and Paul Harvey…his mind was working fine as long as he could remember those old radio names. Working fine with maybe one exception, Harold thought.

"Ask you a question?" said the voice beside him.

Harold looked over. Still there. "Shoot," said Harold.

"How did you come to crash into the graveyard gate that night?"

That was an easier question than he was expecting. "I'd driven up from Louisville to visit Mom and it was my first drive with my new car. I left Louisville early and got all the way to town when I started hearing a rattle in the dash. New cars shouldn't rattle, so after supper I decided to drive out to Floral Hill to see if I could find out where it was coming from. It was after dark and there were no cars. Seemed like something was rattling around just behind and above the glove compartment, and I was leaned way over fiddling around, trying to feel where it was and drifted out into to the middle of the road. The last thing I remember is a black car with no lights coming right at me out of nowhere and then switching on its lights. That's the last thing I recall before waking up in the hospital."

"Can you remember what kind of car it was?"

Yes, thought Harold. Yes, that's the right question, the one Chief Warry asked him over and over. He wished he had the answer.

"I don't remember a darn thing after that car jumped out at me. Next thing was waking up in the hospital down in Damascus on my back in a white room looking at my brother's face and not sure if I knew him or not."

"What kind of car was it? You should remember that. It just hasn't come to you yet," said the Devil, looking down the street.

Harold had not turned away since the Devil asked his question. "I believe," he said, studying the smooth, plausible profile of his visitor, "you are one of those hallucinations that I used to get for a time after my accident. But, funny you say that about things coming to me, I'm just getting a notion that I saw you in a flash of lightning standing at the foot of my bunk one stormy night back in the war, but you didn't look as real then as you do now."

"Maybe I just went back after you crashed and slipped into your memory so you'd recognize me when the time came for us to get to know one another, Harold."

Harold thought that was crazy talk, but he didn't say so. He didn't want to offend him.

The Devil turned and Harold saw his eyes did have their own light. "Since I'm a hallucination and you're out here talking to yourself, you'd have to be the one to figure out who's talking crazy."

Harold looked away and saw a little flick of light on Ed Goodman's front porch. Ed, lighting up a Lucky, sitting there with his guns, like every night, thought Harold. Watching for whatever he watched for.

"Did you ever smoke, Harold?"

"Never took it up."

"Better for you. I must have started and quit a thousand times. I used to smoke Old Golds. Remember the old ad? 'Smoke Old Golds. Not a cough in a carload.' An evening like this almost makes me want to start up again."

"Can the Devil get cancer?" said Harold.

"So that's what you think, that you're talking to the Devil?"

"Well, who else could you be? If I thought you were just real, I'd call Buster to come after you. Sitting on my porch in the middle of the night."

They were quiet for a bit, swinging, listening to a lonesome mockingbird. The squeak from the chains was deeper with the weight of the two of them. Finally, Harold spoke, "I can't remember if we believed in the Devil in the First Church of Christ."

"You said that kind of loud. I fear you might get Ed over there nervous with your talk. Feel like taking a turn on deck this warm night?"

Harold looked over to Ed's dark screen porch, all alone over there after his folks died. So, this fellow here knows everybody in town, he thought. Makes sense if anything does. Harold started to say no, but he realized his knee felt a lot better. He never liked to miss his walk, his constitutional. "I'll get dressed. Can't very well go traipsing around outdoors in my bathrobe and slippers."

When Harold came back out, he saw the Devil was still there and he was almost glad he was. They went down the steps into the moonlight, turned west and set off side by side. The lightning bugs were still around. Harold was limping just a bit from that old car wreck, but after the first few steps the Devil stopped, turned to him and said, "I expect you can recall something about that crash, Harold. I'd venture it'll come to you if you study on it."

They stood in the moonlight under a break in the shadows of the tall trees halfway between Harold's house and the Goodman house.

"Old Chief Warry must have asked me about that car a hundred times. I never had an accident before and I never had one since. It was all on the same night that young fellow from Damascus came up here and killed the Wyatts. A colored boy, it turned out."

"That's hard to believe."

"That's not the only thing that's hard to believe," said Harold.

They both laughed a little at that, and the Devil reached over to give Harold a light pat on the back, and he almost felt it. It was the first time Harold had laughed for a while, but he figured, by the looks of him, the Devil liked a laugh now and then. Nobody had patted Harold on the back for a long, long time. His brother Jack wasn't much inclined to go touching people. Nobody in the family was. It wasn't the Yonders way either. You only shake hands with a man when you first meet him or when he's going off to war or coming back from a war or when he's going off somewhere for good. His mom, walking by out to the kitchen or coming back, used to put her hand on his shoulder as she passed by, but she was dead.

The Devil shook his head, "A colored boy from Damascus drives twenty-five miles north to a town where any black face would stand out like a sore thumb and then drives out to a farmhouse on a dirt road in the cornfields and kills everybody. Does that sound right to you, Harold?"

"I think they established it was a robbery. We all knew old man Wyatt kept a lot of money around. He was always buying and selling guns out the door of his farmhouse and not all of them sold by their rightful owners, according to what we heard."

The Devil was already talking before Harold finished. "I refuse to believe there is any way that boy could have known any of that. How would that boy from Blunt even know there was a man name of Earl Wyatt, let alone know about how he kept a cigar box full of money in his desk? No. I don't believe a word of it. This needs straightening out." The Devil seemed dead serious as they took up their walk.

Harold was thinking, how does he know all that and how does he know what I knew and what I didn't? And then it came to him, right out of the long-ago night.

"I can see that car racing around the corner right at me. It was the kind with the two-piece windshield and a divider in the middle. A Ford, a '49 Ford!" Harold told the Devil.

"Or a '50?" said the Devil. "Or maybe a '51?"

The Devil knows his cars too, thought Harold. Trying to trip me up. "Maybe a '50. Not a '51. It was, sure as shooting, a '49 or '50," said Harold. "You know it by the grill."

He looked over, but there was nobody there, if there ever had been, and that old lone mockingbird was making a hell of a racket up in the trees.

Chapter 13

The Watchman

Ed Goodman, sitting on his screened-in porch smoking a Lucky Strike, his loaded Colt 1911 beside his leg on the coaster and his Remington 870 12-gauge shotgun at the ready on the coffee table at his knees, watched Harold Dresher come down the front steps and walk past in the moonlight. He was fifteen years younger than Harold and had grown up seeing his neighbor, over the years, putting up ladders to paint the house, driving his first car and then, after Scooter Keen went down to his death in the belly of the Arizona at Pearl Harbor, watched him in his white Navy uniform going off to the war in Chuck Kelsey's taxicab, waving back to his mom on the porch.

When Harold came back from the Pacific after doing his part to win the war in time to be home for Christmas of '45, Chuck Kelsey, still driving the same cab, honked all the way from Third Street. It was a Sunday noon and everybody came out to see another Yonders boy come home. Harold was wearing a black peacoat and a white sailor hat, his duffle bag slung over his shoulder. His mom came running out to the curb in her apron in spite of the cold, and folks were waving and standing proud on their porches and in their front yards all up and down the block. Ed was a freshman in high school, watching from the driveway with his mom and dad.

Ed feared he had missed out on war, missed out on the train rides, the ocean crossings and all the excitement, but he didn't have to wait long for his war to come along. He graduated in 1949 and joined the Marines down in Damascus right after cornpack. He would have joined the Army but that summer, only a month after graduation, he and a couple of friends drove down to Damascus to see a gangster movie, but there was a short documentary on the Marines at Guadalcanal before the feature started. After that, only the Marine Corps would do. Ed was itching to fight a war, and it seemed the North Koreans needed fighting. Paris Island was no tougher than he expected and he was a good marksman, one of the best. His dad had taught him to shoot and he was good enough to be assigned right out of boot camp as a counter sniper and chosen to train with a modified M1 rifle fitted with a telescopic sight. It was supposed to be accurate at over 600 yards, but it needed a good dose of Kentucky windage.

He saw brutal combat at Chosin shortly after deployment and thought he would surely freeze to death or be shot and then frozen, but he survived the nightmare retreat with nothing worse than frostbite only to be captured by the Chinese when his platoon was overrun a month later. It was over two years before he was repatriated in Operation Big Switch, but instead of sending him straight home, the doctors kept him for a couple of weeks. They were conducting a study on torture and asked him if he had been tortured or brainwashed. He said he hadn't been washed much at all to speak of. The man questioning him just wrote that down like it was a serious answer, but there was a young combat veteran doctor there, an Iowa farm boy, who laughed right out loud. Ed said he couldn't remember how he got the cigarette burns on his neck and palms, but he remembered. He never talked about the worst of it to the doctors or to anyone.

Ed just wanted to get home. He thought if he could just get off the train downtown and walk down Main and over the tracks and home, it would all be over and done with. He decided just to say it was hell but he got through it. Say that, he told himself, and they'll let you be. And once he was home, the Korean would never come for him again. But if he did, Ed would be ready for him.

Some of the other boys who had survived the winter death marches and had been prisoners with him later at the POW camp along the Yalu River told of the way he risked his neck sneaking around the camp at night, sometimes way below zero, to steal food from the kitchens to share with them, keeping out of the moonlight to avoid throwing a shadow, squirming out through a couple of floor boards, replacing the nails when he returned. They gave him two medals: the Prisoner of War Medal and the Navy Marine Corps Medal. He got the Corps Medal because of what the boys in the POW camp told about his food raids. But he was caught one night and that was the beginning of the worst. After that, there was one who came for him at night, not always, but sometimes. It was always the same man, the same big Korean. Ed learned to tell the difference between the Koreans and the Chinese. It was a Korean who always came for him, slumped and walking slowly, never in a hurry, taking his sweet time with his tools, enjoying his work.

Lloyd Myles from the newspaper wanted to interview Ed about his time as a POW and Ed said okay, that he'd call when he was ready to talk about it. He never called, so Myles sent a young reporter, Lisa Riggs, a northside girl still in high school, hoping to at least get a picture of Ed with his medals. Ed's mom finally talked him into posing, but he didn't want to talk. He got his medals out of his old duffle bag and had his picture taken with them in the backyard by the lilac bush. Lisa asked him what the POW Medal was for and he said, "For getting caught." She asked about the Corps Medal and Ed said, "For stealing grub."

After Lisa left that day, Ed took the trash out to the alley, came in smoking a Lucky and went down in the basement to clean his guns. His mom saw both medal cases open and empty on the dining room table. She yelled down the stairs to ask where the medals were. He yelled back that they were where they belonged. When he came up for supper, he didn't say a word about the medals and his mom didn't either, because she'd already recovered them from where they hung around the neck of Nighthawk, the big Indian brave, seven-foot-tall, formed out of two welded-together sheets of 8-gauge stainless steel that Ed cut, welded and painted for a senior high school project called Garden Art. His dad got him the steel from work, and he did all the cutting and welding in his dad's backyard workshop because the school didn't have the facilities. He even welded on a steel feather. Before he went off to Korea, he set Nighthawk in concrete out in back by the walk that came down from the alley. "He's to watch over you and Dad till I get back," he told his mom.

Lisa made some calls after that visit and a couple of weeks later, on Memorial Day, his picture, hair combed, almost smiling but with a looking-away look in his eyes, was on the front page. Lisa's article entitled "Our Hero" told that he had received the Navy Marine Corps Medal for "extraordinary bravery."

Now, fifty years later, Nighthawk still stood by the alley, and the medals were safe in his mom's little wooden box on her night table. After his mom died, Ed looked at them once but he never took them out. He kept his folk's bedroom as it had been, windows open in summer, an extra blanket at the foot for cold winter nights and the medals in the keepsake box on his mom's little night table by her stopped clock and her photo of all three of them at the park on the Fourth of July when Ed was in first grade.

When he first came back from Korea, he got on at Food Equipment where his dad worked as a welder, and he rode to work and back with his dad in his dad's Pontiac. Ed still drove then and sometimes he drove alone in the evening along the old, familiar roads, but he never strayed far. He went to the VFW a couple of times with his dad, but being there reminded him. One Friday night he went down to

Damascus with old friends from high school to see a movie, but when he was coming out of the restroom at a gas station on the way home, he came face to face with a big Korean in the narrow passage back to the toilets, and he was back there again. He saw the Korean's face change and saw him back up a couple of steps and then turn and hurry away. Ed's first impulse had been to attack. He took a step toward the man, but he caught himself. It scared him that he had thought of killing that man at a Damascus gas station.

After that, he quit going out of town and quit having much to do with people except when he had to at work. And then he started making mistakes. They had to put him in the grinding room after he ruined a couple of patterns in the press. His mind wandered. There were sounds deep in the boiler-making section of the factory that took him back to the battlefield and others that took him to the POW camp. When he cut himself grinding, even his dad agreed he shouldn't be there. After he was let go, his dad took him back to the VA in Damascus and they put him on temporary disability.

He just needed to rest his mind, he said, and then he'd be fine and dandy. In order to get out of the house, he walked downtown and shot a little pool by himself at Brownie's, but he didn't like being out, didn't like having people behind him and beside him and didn't like people coming around corners at him. He just wanted them to let him be. He puttered around in his dad's machine shop out back and watched the Cubs and the Bears and the Illini on TV. He nearly quit talking altogether except to say good morning and good night to his folks. When his dad died, he didn't want to go to the funeral, but his mom made him go. Then when she died, he made himself go to hers, but after that he stayed home except to drive downtown to the grocery store or to the bank to deposit his VA check—it was permanent disability now.

One evening shortly after Harold's mom died, Harold came over from next door to talk. Ed came down from the porch and talked to him, but he kept his back to the house. Harold said he should come over some time to watch a ballgame on TV or join him on his walks. Ed said he might, later. But he never did. Still, it was good having Harold close by.

There they were, the Seabee and the Marine in their old, memory-filled, two-story houses set between the street and alley of their boyhood days. They'd been boys at different times and had gone off to different wars. They both kept to themselves, but they nodded to each other. They were different about the lights. Ed kept his place dark and hardly ever turned on a light. His summer porch screens were black and, when he put up the winter storm windows, he kept the Venetian blinds half-closed. Harold had a powerful back porch light that lit up his walk all the way out to the alley, but what good did that do if no one was watching? Still, Ed watched over Harold's place too.

The VA booklets they sent him kept changing the name of what was the matter with him. Shell shock was the old name till they started calling it combat neurosis and then something else, but it wasn't just the combat and the explosions. It was the sound of the key in the lock when he came for you.

A few months after his mom died and he was left alone, Ed took some precautions. Using his dad's painting ladders, he put two video cameras in the box elder tree over the front sidewalk and another camera above the back door looking out the walk to the alley. The cameras fed a console of three monitors. He kept a powerful Fulton military flashlight at his side on the coaster along with his Colt and his Remington 12-gauge, and when he went down in the basement to sleep at dawn, he kept his guns in easy reach. He had hunting rifles too, his and his dad's, but he never hunted after Korea. He drove out to the gravel pit a couple times a year to fire them all and keep them ready.

When Buster heard about Ed putting cameras in the trees, he came by to see how he was doing. Ed knew Buster for a good man. The chief, square-jawed, blue-eyed, barely grinning, asked him, "What's all this for, Ed, these guns on the porch and all them cameras in the trees?"

"If I hear something out there at night, I need to know there's nobody coming up the back walk and I like to see who's walking down the sidewalk out front too. I even got backup if the lights go out." Ed pointed to the two car batteries connected by cables to a power inverter. "I know better'n to shoot nobody, unless there was cause."

"Well," Buster said, "if you ever do see anything suspicious that you think might require you taking some action, I want you to call me up straight away, day or night. We wouldn't want you to be shooting the meter reader or the Brownie Scout cookie girl."

"As long as neither one of them's not coming up my back walk in the middle of the night with a gun." Ed said, smiling. His hair was white and long and wild, his eyes blue and darting.

"Wouldn't that be a sight for sore eyes? An armed, night-prowling Brownie Scout cookie girl," said Buster, and they both laughed.

They were quiet for a moment. "It's my nerves," said Ed.

"Nobody could ever begrudge you that," said Buster. He asked Ed for some tape and stuck his card to the bottom of the central monitor. "You call me if you see something unusual that you think I ought to know about. This number rings straight through to my desk day or night, Christmas or 4th of July, and if I'm not in, Ronnie or Sally will get me on the radio. Anything strikes you unusual you call, you hear?"

The first unusual thing Ed saw came that late-July night when Harold came down from his porch and stood on the walk halfway between the two houses talking to himself. He'd been talking away on the porch earlier sitting all by himself at the wrong end of the swing, but there was no reason to call Buster about that. A man can sit at either end of his own swing, and if a man can't talk to himself, who can he talk to?

It was a bright night, the leaves as still as in a photograph. Harold came down from his porch and started west toward Ed's, but then stopped in the moonlight. Ed heard him talking but could only make out a few words. "You know it by the grill," Harold said, and then started walking again. Ed wondered what Harold was talking about, but more than that, he wished he knew who the devil Harold thought he was talking to.

After Harold walked by, Ed only heard a mockingbird carrying on for all it was worth. Must have lost his mate. Ed's mom said it was the lonesome ones that sang all night, poor things. One monitor showed Harold faintly in the moonlight walking in the middle of the humped brick walk now. The other front monitor showed the empty sidewalk to the east and the third one showed the path leading up to his backdoor. Even when it was pitch dark, he could see a dog or a cat, so he knew he could see a man.

All quiet and it wouldn't be long before the light of dawn. Then he could go down in the basement and get some sleep before the heat set in. Not that he believed the Korean was out there, but in the dark what you believe is one thing and what you think is another. They wrote in the paper that the old war wasn't really over. There was just a truce along the 38th Parallel, but he knew, truce or no truce, a man had to be careful because when he came for you it was always out of the night.

Chapter 14

TWO-LANE SOUTHBOUND

Whizdom Lahae, driving due south in the blue Honda Civic, heading down old Illinois Route 1, watched houses, farms and fields flow by. The road sign said: "Historic Dixie Highway." His mom, in jeans and T-shirt and wearing her silver, five-pointed witch-star necklace and brass-beaded earrings, had dozed off once they broke clear of the city. He kept the volume low as he poked the seek key on the radio.

Although Whizdom had planned the drive carefully, he wasn't surprised in the first minutes of the trip when his mom, map on her lap, changed the route. He wanted to take Interstate 57, but his mom said no. "We'll save time," he said.

"No," she said, "that road takes us past the walls of the old insane asylum at Manteno where they ran ice picks into people's brains. We can't go this way." She said this with her eyes closed. He didn't argue. He´d learned not to ask, but he never knew when some barrier in his mom´s mind or memory would send them on a detour, a real detour this time. Ice picks, she said. Someday he´d ask, but not today.

He pulled into a gas station for a quick look at the map. They'd take the 94 to the 394 at Wampum Lake and then south all the way on Route 1, even though it took them through the heart of Chicago Heights for a quarter-hour crawl until they broke out into the country south of Steger, all to avoid passing too close to some abandoned insane asylum that he'd never heard of. His mom went back to sleep—she'd been up packing all night—but he was sure if he had driven anywhere near Manteno, she would have felt it and sat up wide awake.

One by one the familiar Chicago music and talk stations crackled, tangled and faded, finally giving over to country songs and Sunday morning sermons in the twangy voices of the central Illiana farmlands.

An hour gone and an hour and a half to go, he lingered on one station just long enough to catch a line of a man and a woman singing in duet, "You're the reason our kids are ugly." He'd never heard that one on Rock 103.5.

He stopped his search on an oldie station he thought his mom would like, even in her sleep. It was "White Rabbit" on the radio and white silos jutting high over the tall, late-July corn and a railroad line running alongside Route 1, the straight and narrow highway once known to southerners in the days before Interstates as The Dixie, the road Yankees drove to Florida. Whizdom looked it up on the Internet. He wasn't sure where he was going, but driving the patchy two-lane between the fields, the only thing he really knew was that he was good, really good, good like his dad. Twenty-three years before, a Chicago sports reporter wrote of his father in words that Whizdom memorized. "Clifford Lahae combines lightning quickness with deadly accurate shooting. His joy at playing the game brings the crowd to their feet even on the road. If he continues to develop, Clifford Lahae is going places."

He did. First, he went to prison and then to his Maker, as Granddad Lahae put it, cut down by a stray Saturday-night bullet in an Inglewood drive-by.

That old clipping, safe in Whizdom's suitcase, was accompanied by two very similarly captioned photographs published many years apart in the *Chicago Sun Times*. One caption read: "Clifford Lahae led all scorers, but in a losing cause as Gage fell to the mighty Morgan Park Mustangs." The other: "Sophomore sensation Whizdom Lahae came off the bench for the Huskies to score 14 points but it wasn't enough to topple Downers Grove."

Whizdom put both the clippings side by side in a single frame. Behind glass, both young men were in the act of shooting. Whizdom was at the peak of his jumpshot, the ball just free of his extended fingers. His father had completed the release and the ball was out of the picture, his right wrist gracefully arched, fingers spread and pointing down. Both photos showed soft hands that sent the ball spinning on its way.

The only memory Whizdom had of his father was of being held high overhead, his father's big hands clamped tight just above his knees. He held a tiny ball, and the bottom of the chain net was just above his eyes. He felt his father crouch and spring and felt the power of the jump. He was rising in the air to the rim and above the rim and he dropped the little ball into the hoop. Men's voices cheered him. There were traffic noises in the distance, and close by the sounds of dribbling, the scuffing of gym shoes on concrete and the laughing and shouting of men and boys playing the game in the noonday heat of a sweltering Chicago Sunday.

Clifford "The Kid" Lahae was from the South Side. Rose, Whizdom's mom, wasn't, and that's all she let be known about herself—just that she wasn't from Chicago. He asked her once, when he was nine, who her mom and dad were, and he never forgot her answer. "My father was a shadow and my mother is a ghost." He wanted to ask more but she stopped him. "The past is tightly woven and cannot be undone, but we weave our futures freely."

As a little boy, Whizdom didn't know that it was unusual for his mom to talk that way and to be a witch. He didn't see any similarity between his mom and the silly TV witches, but he learned early that she was not like his friends' moms. When he was six, Yvonne, the little girl next door, wanted to know if his mom was a really-witch who did magic or just a play-like witch. He asked, and that was the day she fizzled a cloud out of the sky.

"Want to see some magic?" she said. She led him into the backyard and pointed to the summer sky. "See that little cloud way up there?"

He looked into the sky and saw a small puff of lonely cloud. His mom turned her eyes to the sky and squinted hard and the world seemed to darken around them. The cloud, white and bright against the blue, slowly began to shrivel and fade and in only a couple of minutes it had vanished from the sky and everything was as it had been, bright and warm, but the little cloud was gone.

"What did you see?" she asked. He said he saw the cloud just faded slowly away, and his mom asked, "Do you believe I can stand here in the backyard and fizzle a cloud thousands of feet up in the sky?"

"No," he said, "but you did it."

"No, I didn't," she said. "Little clouds shrink and disappear on their own all the time and it is a trick to tell people you can take them down by staring at them."

The only real magic, she told him, was in seeing things others don't see and knowing things others don't know and sometimes even knowing what you don't want to know.

Now, as a seventeen-year-old driving away from his home, his friends and his place in the starting line-up, his mom confused him. A year earlier, she refused a transfer to the upscale Aurora branch of the bank to avoid having to move and pull Whizdom out of Oak Park just when he was starting to shine on the JV team. Yet now, at the worst time, they were moving downstate to a place called Yonders. What kind of future was this she was weaving?

He looked over at his sleeping mom. Her past was closed but she told him all she knew about his father. She took him several times to visit Granddad Lahae who lived alone in Back of the Yards, the neighborhood where his father grew up. On those visits, before the old man died in 1993, Whizdom learned about his father and, accompanied by his grandfather, he walked the streets of an area the papers called Gangland. Unlike Oak Park, almost everyone he saw was Black except his mom, but she walked with him and his grandfather as easily as she walked the tree-lined streets of Oak Park and, Whizdom knew, as easily as she would walk whatever streets awaited in Yonders.

Whizdom's father, the ex-high school basketball star and paroled drug offender, was twenty when he met Rose, the young witch from nowhere who worked in a bank and had no past. Rose and Clifford fell in love, married, had a baby boy and lived happily for just over two years until Clifford was shot dead at the wheel of a UPS truck by random gang gunfire on a street corner. His mom was sitting up reading and felt the shot, she said, across forty city blocks and knew Clifford was dead long before the policeman came to the door. It was just another hot-summer-night, south-side, stray-bullet killing that got an inch in the crime pages.

Rose said Whizdom's father was a spirit in the wind, watching over, but to the boy he was a newspaper clipping and a thin envelope full of pictures. His mom was only in a couple of them, a tall white girl, almost six feet, so his father must have been 6'3". She was dressed all in black with her gypsy earrings and bracelets.

By the time he was in high school, the only magic that interested him was Magic Johnson, although his hero was Michael Jordan. He watched every Bulls game on TV and listened, when he could, to their out-of-town games on the radio. At an afternoon practice, he and another freshman were put into a scrimmage against the varsity. Whizdom was used to being the best player on the floor in JV games, but in this practice session something magic happened. He had been scoring and playing strong defense. He was already 5'11" and fast, but there was a moment when he broke between two defenders and launched a floater in the lane just over the fingertips of Oak Park's All-Conference, 6'7" center. When he saw that ball in the net, he felt he could do just about anything, maybe even really fizzle a cloud. But the magic was not making the shot; it was a sudden, faint voice in his head: "Whizdom Lahae is going places. Yes, sir! This kid has got something special." He recognized the voice of Wayne Larrivee, the voice of the Chicago Bulls on WGN, a voice he had heard for hundreds of hours listening to Bulls games, sometimes in bed and half asleep when the Bulls played late on the west coast.

Larrivee's voice was still with him his sophomore year, still in the background, but louder after that final game in the regionals against Downers Grove. As he showered, he heard Larrivee say, "The sky is the limit for Whizdom Lahae."

The coach told him, "Keep sharp, stay out of trouble and grow. I'm counting on you for next year." He knew if he kept his grades up he might attract the attention of college scouts. On the bus after the final game of the season, Larrivee said it. "Doesn't look like anything can stop the kid next year." The kid. Whizdom liked that. That's what they called his father.

It was at the end of basketball season, two months before the end of his sophomore year, when his mom came home excited and said she had big news. The coven had grown to sixteen, well beyond the ideal of thirteen, and it was past time to hive. Whizdom knew what hive meant, but he wasn't prepared for what he heard next. The Chancellor had funding to lease a building in a little downstate town that would become the new central home for the Whisperers. As the Internet grew, Yonders would become a campus, a center for online classes and their new building a warehouse and distribution center for Whisperers merchandise.

"It means I can stop wearing this disguise," his mom said, holding out the beige lapel on the pants suit she had worn to her job at the bank that day. She made it sound like she was changing jobs, but the Whisperers had always been something else. Afterhours. Like church or a club. Now she was going, rent paid and with a salary from the Whisperers. Witch's wages.

At first it would only be his mom, the Chancellor and his wife, and Lilith Zon with her two little girls, six Whisperers to start a new coven. Whizdom wasn't the seventh, his mom said.

He would not be a Whisperer. The Chancellor asked why and she answered. "Because he is a shooting guard."

Yvonne, somewhere in between childhood friend and high-school girlfriend, was mad. She said, "You know what they're gonna call you down there? I do. They'll call you a nigger son of a witch if they don't call you worse when you run your half-black hide out on the court to play for the Podunk Piranhas or the Hicktown Hoot Owls or the Yonders Yodelers, or…"

But he stopped her. "Come on," he said, "this is 1998 and this is Illinois."

"Up here it is, but they're taking you back to 1950, to

some town where they probably drive around with Confederate flags painted on the roofs of their cars. My dad worked at Caterpillar down in Peoria, and I'll tell you what he said. He said, 'Kentucky starts in Kankakee.'"

The library computer told him the Yonders Harvesters played in the Two-gun Lawton! It Conference, but there was no Marigold Valley or any kind of valley on the map of those flat farmlands. The town had four factories and an annual Miss Harvester Pageant. A note at the bottom of the page said that two of the factories had closed. Yonders High, a little Single A school, won ten and lost ten the year before, fourth in conference. The school mascot was Shucks, a humanized and grinning ear of corn, and they had some returning starters. He found pictures. Yonders had one big farmer-looking kid listed at 6'3", but it seemed only one team in the Single A Marigold Valley Conference, the Blunt Wildcats, had any Black players. Well, the Harvesters had one. They just didn't know it yet. He studied the picture of the Yonders sophomore class, his junior class. He showed Yvonne and she called them barn dancers.

When he laughed, she said, "You got no idea what's down there." But she was wrong. Like every Chicago area basketball player, Whizdom dreamed of someday going downstate, but that meant playing in the State Finals at Peoria, not going downstate to live. He knew the top teams: Moline, Peoria Manual, Quincy, Collinsville, Decatur, Springfield, Carbondale and Damascus, just down the road from Yonders. The Damascus Bulldogs had Wendall Truman, All-State Second Team. Everybody had heard of him, but Damascus and the other top downstate teams were all Double A schools. Yonders was just Single A.

Since breaking out of Chicagoland and into the open countryside of broad fields and occasional little towns, the only face he´d seen that wasn´t white was his own in the mirror. As they pulled away just after dawn that morning from the only home he had ever known in his seventeen years, he had taken a look back at the trim, white, single-story, shingle-sided house. Beside the front door, he saw the rectangle, brighter against the sun-faded wall, where the red and white hand-painted plaque in his mom's spidery script had hung.

Rose Lahae, Pagan Psychic
By Appointment Only

The plaque rode south now in the little, single-axle U-Haul trailer along with what Whizdom called his mom's witch kit of books, candles, charms, robes, gowns and trinkets.

Those who came for sessions in Oak Park were usually women, but Whizdom remembered two white men in suits who came on a cold winter evening. Their gray four-door had the cheap little dog-bowl hubcaps usually seen on government cars.

Some months after that visit, a reporter came to the door and asked his mom, while Whizdom listened nearby, to comment on the help she had given the Northbrook Police in locating the body of a slain teenage girl. She said she couldn't talk about private consultations and sent the man away. Whizdom, fourteen then, asked what the reporter was talking about, and his mom said, "The poor girl was staring up at the light from under the ice of the Skokie Lagoons."

The road sign on the southern outskirts of the little town of Jericho read:

Yonders 25
Damascus 50

He kept to exactly 55 mph for fear of white TV cops charging out from behind billboards. Whizdom turned off the radio and drove the last straight and flat twenty-five miles in silence looking up the road for the first signs of town. Just a few miles out of Willows he saw the Yonders water tower standing white above the corn. The town slowly rose out of the horizon; first a single tall building, a pair of silos, factory stacks and then the trees and houses. His mom still slept and didn't see what Whizdom saw when he drove up from the dip under the railroad viaduct. There on a large billboard, Shucks, the giant, humanized and half-shucked ear of corn, barefoot, carrying a football and a pair of spikes and dribbling a basketball with its fist, leered down crazy-eyed under the words, in giant blue letters:

WELCOME TO HARVESTER COUNTRY!

Chapter 15

Dog days

Lisa Riggs, reporter since high school and now the writer of the town paper's most-read weekly column, "News and Views on Main Street," was waiting at her desk when Lloyd Myles got back from lunch.

"We got to talk," said Lisa. "That's the second column of mine you've killed this summer." Myles started to speak but, seeing her face, gestured toward his office with his thumb. The only other person there was Herman Parker, working through the noon hour at his desk just outside the door to the publisher's office, banging away at the keyboard, hunt and peck, hitting the keys as hard as he used to pound the old Underwood typewriter, now on display beside his computer screen.

Myles stood behind his desk facing Lisa. "How mad are you?" he said.

"About halfway between wet hen and hornet," she said. She didn't smile.

"Could you shut that door?"

The door, with "Editor-Publisher" painted on the frosted glass, muffled the sound of Parker's heavy keystrokes. Myles waited until Lisa was seated before sitting across from her at his cluttered desk. With the window at his back, Myles was silhouetted against the three-block American Pride Food Container Corp. factory, known as "The Tin Can." A dozen cars and pickups were parked diagonally near the employees' entrance. The rest of the curbing was bare for the length of the old redbrick factory. Only three years earlier, Pride had rattled and banged day and night during corn pack to make the cans for the year's new crop. It used to be so loud that it drowned out the car radios of people driving by. Now they only made lids, ends they called them, and the clattering racket was gone along with hundreds of jobs. One of the two canneries had closed and the surviving one, the Illiana, was still canning, but nothing like before. The town used to ship three million cases, two dozen #303 cans to the case, seventy-two million cans of Yonders sweetcorn, all grown locally and hauled, in the old days, to the factory cookers in wooden-sided corn wagons hitched to tractors driven by farmers whose names most folks knew, or sometimes by the farmers' fourteen or fifteen-year-old sons or daughters, too young to work in the factories but proud, in their straw hats and baseball caps, to be doing their part in pack. Now, the town was down to a half million cases of local asparagus, red kidney beans and peas, but none of it sweet corn—no corn canned in the Sweet Corn Canning Capital of the World. All of this was in the first of Lisa's stories, "The Quiet on West Main," that

Myles had filed in his limbo drawer that summer. Myles said that title was depressing.

The other drawered story was "The Whispering Witches are Coming to Town," a title Myles considered disturbing.

"Look, Myles," said Lisa, "I guess you've got a point about the factories piece. The factories aren't coming back and everybody knows it, so I guess there's no point crying over spilt milk, but most of our readers don't know about the witches yet. They're about to find out though. Rhodes' truck was parked out front of the Township Building all day yesterday getting it ready, and they're there today too. They've got a power company man walking around on the roof. At least he was when I drove by. He might have fallen through to the basement by now. How long you think it will take for it to get out that we got witches? And don't you think people might expect to read about something like that in their town paper?"

"I just don't like you calling the Township Building a witch church. Those words don't go well together," said Myles.

"Whatever these Whisperers believe in has been designated a religion by the Virginia Supreme Court and the IRS. Is it the evangelicals you're worried about or the Catholics?"

"Here's the thing," said Myles. "Most folks will just think this is all some new kind of foolishness. Catholics don't scare easy. They probably even have a saint just for running off witches like they have one for finding lost car keys. It's some of the good old folks, the Bible-reading people, who aren't going to like any of this. I don't want the cat out of the bag until we figure out the right way to present it. The one who worries me is Preacher Simms. He calls a lot of the shots with the Godlier among us."

"And what makes you think Preacher Simms and every preacher, priest and reverend in town hasn't heard that Hook has rented the Township Building to a coven of upstate witches?"

"They don't even move in until the last week of August."

"I forgot. You don't have any school-age kids or grandkids and you spend all your time cooped up in here listening to Parker beat that poor computer to death."

"What are you talking about?"

"Witches is what I'm talking about," said Lisa. "They're already here, walking around downtown, one of them night-walking the graveyard and another one jumping in the park. None have been seen flying as of yet. Anyway, they'll all be moved into town in a week or so."

Myles was stopped. The typing from the outer office stopped too. After a moment, he spoke. "Moving in where?"

"You know that empty place just across the alley from your house? No, I'm kidding, but you ought to have seen your face," said Lisa. "Nat Hook not only turned the Township Building over to them, he's renting the lady with the two young daughters the old Tucker place up on Fugate Hill. The tall lady and her boy are moving into a little house on First Street that Hook bought off the bank and fixed up. The one with the pigtail that calls himself Chancellor is going to have an apartment in the school or the church or whatever you want to call the old Township Building. For now, they're all staying down at a motel on this end of Damascus while Hook gets the utilities and the plumbing working, but they've already been to town, looking it over."

"How come they're staying down in Damascus instead of at Four Corners?" said Myles.

"Yeah, I wonder."

"It does need a little work, I guess." Lisa shook her head and smiled, and Myles went on, "How many have we got, do you think?"

"Seven of them been counted so far. There's the Chancellor, three grown witch ladies, two little girls and there's an African American boy too, son of the tall woman in black with all the jewelry. She's the one nobody's likely to forget seeing."

"What's so special about her?"

"I haven't got a look at her from up close yet, but my mom saw her when she was visiting graves last week. It was late when she got there, just before dark. Mom was tidying and tending to weeds around Dad's grave when she saw a tall figure walking by just a few graves away. It kind of scared her at first, a woman dressed all in black and wearing necklaces, bracelets and rings like a gypsy queen. Mom said the woman stopped and was standing for a while in front of the Wyatt plot."

"There's no law against any of that," said Myles, leaning across his desk and speaking softly. Behind him a big crow appeared and lit on the window sill. Lisa looked at the crow and Myles followed her eyes to it. It cocked its head to look inside, then began to preen.

"Maybe we should go out and talk in the car," said Lisa.

Myles waved his hand toward the window and the crow lifted off and flapped its way above the highest trees to the water tower.

"What do you think she was doing out there?" said Myles.

"I'm going to guess you mean the witch in the graveyard," said Lisa. "You tell me what she was doing and, while you're at it, tell me what our readers are going to think this Sunday or the next when some of our preachers start preaching about Devil worshipers cavorting among our dead."

"Walking in the graveyard doesn't constitute cavorting."

"I didn't know we had an ordinance that defined what constitutes cavorting," said Lisa.

"You're having way too much fun with this," said Myles. "That's what's wrong with your witch story. There are always enough people out there to make fun of anything that happens in every small town that doesn't ramp up to an Interstate, so we should be the first to avoid Mayberrying ourselves."

"That's a good one," said Lisa. "I might use that."

"How do you know so much about all this?" said Myles,

"My niece, she'll be a sophomore, told me the other day that Winona Burns, the one they call P K, Preacher's Kid— she's the daughter of Reverend Burns from the Universalist Church— told her that the folks taking over the Township Building are pagan witches and that the Black kid shooting baskets in the park for the last few days is the son of the tall witch lady. He's probably out there today too, running and jumping in the ninety-degree heat."

"How tall is he? Is he eligible?"

"If he was an inch taller than Mayor Tom claims he is, could I run the column? And yes, he'll be a junior transfer. Fully eligible for the season."

"His mother, the woman in the graveyard, is she all right? I mean, is there something wrong with her?" said Myles.

"If I said I was a witch, would you say there was something wrong with me? But, as you say, there is no law against dressing up like a witch and night-walking in the graveyard, and no law against being a witch, whatever that might mean, especially if that boy of hers can hit the broad side of a barn with his jumpshot, which would be an improvement over last year. What I'm saying is that unless we write something that makes sense about this, some sermon about Devil worshipers eating children is going to be the only story out there."

Lloyd Myles was already dialing. Seconds later Mayor Tom Wellington at his farmhouse on Indiana Road, closer to the Indiana border than to the water tower, heard Myles say, "Tom, one of your damn witches is strutting around the graveyard and scaring folks. You told me we had till late August. I figure you are about a ten-minute drive from here, so I know when to expect you."

"Did you hang up on the mayor?" said Lisa. The typing had stopped again.

"After I talk to Tom, you can run him down and write whatever you think best," said Myles. "Just try and play down the religion part of it. Call it a spiritual organization. The main thing is not to rile up people who don't need to be worrying about witches or the Devil any more than they probably do already."

"I'll give Tom a call this afternoon, after you two have your story straight, and I'll do you one last rewrite, but if you don't run it, I'm sending it down to the *Damascus Herald*," said Lisa. "They always get a kick out of the things we get up to."

Myles accompanied her out of the office, past Parker and to the entrance. As she left, he said, "And see if you can find out how big this kid is and how good."

"Ask Preacher's Kid. She's scouting him, not me," she said over her shoulder, stepping from the air-conditioned offices into the breezeless dog-days heat.

Chapter 16

The Quiet

There was no one on the tennis courts at Scooter Keen Municipal Park, no one on the baseball diamond either, and there were no kids in the swings and no dogs on the grass, but in the still and moist midday heat, the new boy was on the basketball court. It looked to the kids in the red Ford F-150 pickup cruising the park ring road that there was a solitary player shooting baskets—fadeaways, turnaround jumpers, rainbow three-pointers and soft, running floaters—but there were really two old rivals matched up on a new court. One was Whizdom Lahae and the other, also Black, was, as usual, invisible.

Whizdom, the lanky, 6'2" kid, never stopped moving, going left, going right, faking a ghost defender out of his jock with a crossover dribble and then putting up a sweet, soft, slow-spinning jumper from the top of the key that hit the back of the rim just right with the top of the ball and went straight down the hole.

The three boys on the bench seat in the cab of the pickup were Yonders High varsity starters from last season's basketball team: Junior center Zeke Grandey drove, senior forward Butch Dawson rode shotgun and senior guard Cory Wilson sat in the middle. Watching from the truck bed were Grandey's kid brother and a girl with stick-out ears and sunglasses. Nobody said a word and the truck carried on, creeping past the courts.

It was the girl, PK—only her folks called her Winona—who organized the reconnoiter. She lived out West Hamilton and could see the basketball court from her bedroom window. She took notice the first day because she had never seen anyone shooting out there in the hot sun and because the boy who was shooting looked like he might be Black. He was. She confirmed this by taking a ride around the loop road. She drove by again the next day to try and get a better look at him.

She had her own car now for her junior year, a 1994 Oldsmobile Cutlass Supreme, and she often stopped at the Dairy Queen for an ice cream cone after lunch. Four boys were eating ice cream at the picnic table under the awning when she drove up. "You guys heard about a new Black kid our age moving to town?" she asked.

They hadn't. She said, "Well, for the last three days he's been shooting baskets at the park. I think he's from a new bunch of people moving down here from Chicago. I heard my dad talking about one of them being Black and high-school age."

"Let's go cruise by and see what we see," said Grandey. "You coming along, PK?"

Grandey entered the park's one-way ring road off Hamilton and drove the anticlockwise loop, but he and the other four couldn't see the basketball courts until they passed the maintenance barn, and then they could only see Whizdom. They couldn't see that there was a game of shadow H-O-R-S-E. going on between Whizdom Lahae and Michael Jordan.

Whizdom saw the red pickup easing along past the courts just as he had seen the Cutlass laze past earlier that day and on each of the two previous days. And there she was, the same girl, the tousle-headed brunette with Top Gun sunglasses who drove the Cutlass, riding in the truck bed with some other kid. Jordan had just made a long three out of the corner and Wayne Larrivee was putting the pressure on Whizdom. "Now we'll see what this kid from Oak Park has left in the tank. It's not just the shot, it's the moves," said Larrivee.

Whizdom, very aware of that slow cruising truck, made the moves and drilled it. "Good from the instant it left his hand," said Larrivee.

MJ watched the truck go out of sight, shrugged his shoulders and walked well back of the key. Larrivee was on it. "MJ is moving back. Gonna test this boy's range from deep." Jordon hit the twenty-five-footer, but Whizdom followed with a miss bouncing high off the heel of the rim. He now had H.O.R.S. on him, one letter more than MJ. "Trouble for Whizdom. Michael could put him away with one more of those. We've seen the kid come back before, but right now MJ is in the catbird seat."

Jordan took his time deciding on a shot and then hit a twenty-footer just as the truck reappeared. Damned if that truck wasn't back around already, thought Whizdom. Must have broken the 10-mph speed limit, but it slowed back to a creep as the five kids watched Whizdom answer Jordan's shot with an identical turnaround jumper, although it rattled the rim before falling through.

Both players walked to the water fountain in the grassy shade beside the court. Whizdom was thinking about that red pickup truck and the kids in it. They wouldn't come around again, he decided. That would be too much. He took a deep breath and looked around him. The heat in Yonders was different. There was a scent of earth and fertilized farmland in the air and there was a silence just behind the town noises—somebody honking a horn somewhere, a single-engine aircraft droning over, a freight whistling through town, the humming tires of a big rig on the Dixie. Back of it all there was the quiet out there. When the honking quit, the plane passed over, the train whistle faded and the truck was gone down the road, the deep quiet remained. He drank at the fountain. The water was cold even at midday and he was hearing the silence and standing still, stopped and almost relaxed for the first time since he and his mom drove away from their little house in Oak Park, and then he saw the pickup coming around again, one time too many, he thought. This was why he drove his mom's car fifty miles a day, shooting around at the park in Yonders instead of practicing at a Damascus playground.

MJ was watching too, but it was Larrivee who spoke. "The kid is wondering if that's the welcome wagon or the Cross and Dragon truck."

There was a rebel flag, the sticker of one, pasted in the back window of the truck cab, not big, maybe two-inch square, but big enough. Yvonne might still be right after all. He read that there were more Klan members in Indiana than in Mississippi and he was only seven miles of fields from the Indiana border. When he learned about the civil rights movement in school, it all seemed like something that happened way down south a long time ago, but downtown Yonders looked to Whizdom like that rerun TV show with the Black detective and the tough old white guy as police chief, except that downtown Yonders was all white people, as white as an old Christmas movie.

"Don't let it spook you. This is just a Larry Bird town. Say hello to the folks," said the greatest basketball player in the world.

Whizdom took a step forward, the orange ball against his hip. When the truck was barely twenty yards away and parallel to the court with all five looking at him, he nodded.

First Grandey, then Cory and Dawson returned the same, somehow solemn, nod. Grandey's brother and P.K. waved cautiously from the truck bed.

"They look like Cubs fans," said Michael Jordan.

PK leaned out of the truck bed and said to the three in the cab, "Last name's Lahae. Funny first name, like Winston maybe. He's part of that bunch taking over the Township Building. Some folks are saying they're Satanists, but my dad says they're just pagans."

"Pagan son of a bitch can shoot," said Wilson.

MJ vanished, quitting while he was ahead. They'd finish

the game some other time. Whizdom wanted to get out of the sun, but he couldn't go until he hit at least nine out of ten jumpers from seventeen feet. Sometimes it could take a while, but he never left till he hit at least nine, and this time he hit all ten right away. Larrivee was quiet but he was never quite gone. When Whizdom hit the tenth jumper in a row, Larrivee said, "The kid is ready for the Harvesters, but are they ready for the kid?"

Whizdom wondered what those kids in the truck were thinking, wondered what kind of people lived in a Larry Bird town.

He needed a couple of gallons of gas for the run down to Damascus and the Marathon was on his way. Light traffic on the Dixie Highway, no cars on the empty forecourt of the Marathon station. Hot and quiet.

Ding! Ding! went the bell when Whizdom's car rolled over the little black hose across the forecourt of Bowman's Marathon. He went inside to pay. Same place he'd bought gas the last time he was in town and the same little man watching him from behind the counter. This time the little guy spoke. "I'm guessing you are the new boy I been hearing about," Buddy Bowman said. "Coach Dornfeld says you played up in Chicago. Who'd you play for, DuSable, Dunbar?"

"Oak Park."

"I knew it was one of them up there. What's your position here, do you think?"

"That'll be up to Coach."

"You met Coach Dornfeld yet?"

"No, I've just heard about him."

"And you can be sure he's heard about you too. He'll be running shootarounds after about the first two or three weeks of school, and, it's none of my business, but here's what I think. Shooting guard. That's your spot and that'll keep Wilson out front dribbling where he belongs and spare us from his intercontinental bricks."

Talks some trash, thought Whizdom, trying to figure him out. He looked up at the black-and-white framed photo on the wall behind the cash register. An upside-down, barefooted cheerleader cartwheeling down the court and some little player standing there in his Yonders jersey and smiling like he'd just done whatever was causing the crowd to all be standing. Everybody else on his team was jumping, all of them in the air. The other team looking miserable. The little guy must have done something big.

Little Buddy was straight-faced, but his eyes were smiling when Whizdom looked down from the old photo. "Every dog has his day." he said, handing Whizdom his change.

He pumped the two gallons of regular and as he drove away the bell went Ding! Ding!

▪▪▪

A month later and a week into the new school year, as Whizdom was settling in, big Zeke Grandey came up behind him at his locker.

"How come you ain't out for football, if you don't mind my asking?" he said.

Whizdom recognized the voice and turned to face him—the guy with the flag in his truck window. "I'm no good at it. I never played."

"You ought to give it a try, or do you guys just play one sport?"

You guys? Whizdom didn't answer.

"I'm guessing you're coming out for basketball. So, we'll see you when coach starts shootarounds, won't we?" It didn't sound like a question.

One day a week later after P.E., Coach Dornfeld called out to Whizdom as he walked by the coach's little office. "Hey, Whizdom, come on in here a minute. I'll write you a pass if you're late." Whizdom had been observing Dornfeld, waiting for the coach to ask the question. The coach was one of those square-headed, square-shouldered guys with a ring of keys at the belt—quick to laugh among themselves but slow to smile to strangers, especially strange strangers.

Just a chat. No need for a pass. What was said was simple enough. Whizdom was planning on coming out for basketball. After Whizdom left, closing the door behind him, Coach Dornfeld took one of his many keys and opened his basketball drawer, under the football drawer and over the baseball drawer. He took out a clipboard of play charts and made some notes and rocked back in his swivel chair, set his chin and nodded in agreement with himself.

When Sunday afternoon shootarounds started at the end of the first month of school, Whizdom never missed a one. At the second session, Coach Dornfeld, who did no coaching at shootarounds, only watching, brought a visitor to courtside. Whizdom recognized the visitor as the chief of police. He'd seen him drive by a few times.

There were only six kids at the gym that day and all but Whizdom were starters on the football team. They were just shooting, playing a little H-O-R-S-E. but no three-on-three because big Zeke Grandey and Cory Wilson were both limping a little after the road win on Friday night over the Mariah Marauders. Cory shouted out "nice one" when Whizdom hit a long jumper out of the corner.

"Hey, Whizdom," Dornfeld yelled. "Come on over here a minute. I want you to meet Chief Lawton."

Whizdom was thinking, this is the scene in the movie where the colored detective meets the old police chief. He took a last shot from three-point distance and banked it high off the backboard, missing the rim completely. "Brick!" yelled Grandey.

Whizdom walked to the edge of the court where the two men stood. This would be a hand shake, he thought. He wiped his hand across the front of his practice jersey. Property of Oak Park High School, it read.

He hadn't quite looked at Buster yet, but he did when the policeman, gun on his right hip, old-time, scrunched-down police hat a little off to the right with some attitude, extended his hand. This would be his second Yonders handshake. The first one with Coach Dornfeld went wrong because Whizdom didn't put enough shake into it and hung on too long. This time he matched Buster's squeeze and was ready for the shake, just one little shake, short and quick, and then let go. Whizdom had it figured.

Yonders men don't hold hands any longer than absolutely necessary.

"Hearing a lot of good things about you from Coach here. How you finding our town?" this tough-looking little cop said. Friendly eyes. Maybe.

"Good, good," said Whizdom. "I'm finding it good." And he thought his answer was dumb as soon as he heard it, but he wasn't going to say he was finding it like the first fifteen minutes of a movie he hadn't figured out yet.

The cop turned to Dornfeld. "Haven't we got us a Harvester shirt for this boy?"

Boy probably didn't mean anything. They said that a lot, but did boy mean something different, like in the movies and TV, if the boy was him?

"Well, we have to be so damn tippytoe-careful with the State Athletic Association rules about distributing new gear out of season, but I can probably scare one up," said Dornfeld.

The cop smiled, "Pleasure to meet you," he said, "and looking forward to watching you play. I'll let you get back to it."

Trotting back onto the court, he imagined himself wearing a practice jersey like Grandey's. Property of the Yonders Harvesters, and with that half-shucked ear of corn that was painted on the gym wall. They had it on the door of the police car too.

He looked around him. It was still a strange court. Shucks grinned down at him from the wall, the cop from *The Heat of the Night* was standing at courtside next to the coach from

Hoosiers and the big red-headed kid with a rebel flag in the back window of his truck—a kid named Zeke with a crew cut who looked like Biff in *Back to the Future*—was shooting sweeping, old-school hook shots.

In his movie, he'd take the Harvesters to the state title, play for a Big Ten university and study philosophy or literature and then play in the NBA and then run for governor or senator or something…and win!

He grabbed a rebound. Dribbled out and turned quickly behind the arc and fired up a hard, low-trajectory jumper, too low and way too hard. The shot lacked loft, hit the front lip of the rim, bounced off the backboard and to the inside of the front rim, pinballed and fell though the net. "Friendly rim," said Larrivee. "Home-court bounce. It's a good sign."

When he got home he called Yvonne in Oak Park.

"Howdy," he said when she answered.

She laughed. "Whiz, you survived!" And they talked and laughed for a half hour and the more he heard her voice the more he realized how far away he was.

Part Three

Fall 1998

Chapter 17

HANDYMAN

The old crow flapped and glided in ascending circles, riding the drafts up to the Yonders water tower. From there, two hundred and fifty feet above the town, sheltered beneath the catwalk and out of the drizzle, she saw all there was to see: the police car pulling out of the derelict Gas & Go! station to chase down the Joliet drug dealer's yellow Mustang, Nat Hook and Rusty Rhodes parking side by side at the Dixie Diner and, halfway up from Milton to the south a long freight heading for town, but the old crow cared only about Keelan Putnam, crossing Main to enter the Two Spot. The old crow never forgot a face and, even through the light morning rain and from the highest perch in town, she saw the enemy, a stoner of crows.

From the day Keelan set foot back in town, he had the feeling he was being watched. He'd been back since June, but the dogs on his own block still snarled at him. Even the damned birds squawked at him from the trees when he came walking home in the evening. And whenever that goddamned Buster came slinking up behind him in his prowler, Keelan could feel eyes on his neck. Who else did that Buster have watching him? Even that tall woman Dandy said was a witch was trying to get in his eyes, gawking at him as if there was something wrong with him, and her dressed up like Halloween at the nuthouse. Sometimes Keelan felt he was being watched even in the deep of the night when he sat out back on his porch stoop, minding his own business.

It was harassment. Dogs, birds, cops and witches. Especially Buster Lawton. There he was, a free man with money in the bank and a perfectly good truck parked in his drive, bought right there in Yonders, and the law wouldn't let him drive it. First week back, two days after buying a yellow '90 Silverado pickup—that was the only color they had— from the lot on Four Corners, and there was Murdock, Buster's flunky, parked in the shadows back of Turk's, just waiting for him to come out with a couple of drinks in him. Never even put the key in the ignition. Had him blowing into some tube that said what anybody who'd been drinking with him for the last two hours could have told you. As if the rest of those boys weren't going to drive home too. The law said a man could be arrested for being drunk and having a car in the lot and a key in his pocket. Automatic six-month suspension. That's how far they go to make a man miserable. Two months to go. Walking him right into the teeth of winter, the same way they ran him out of town. It was Warry then, and Buster was the flunky, cruising his block, slowing down in front of his house, asking about him in the stores, snooping. Did he pay his debts? Did he buy anything expensive? Checking at the bank too, for all he knew. Warry was closing in back then, watching him whenever he went downtown. Keelan knew, even back then, that once they took you down to Damascus, you were done for. Who wouldn't have run for it, wife or no wife?

No way ever to know if they would have figured out it was him because some Black kid from down in Blunt suddenly got railroaded into confessing to three murders he sure as hell didn't commit. If there was one thing in this life that Keelan was sure of, it was who killed the Wyatts.

If he'd kept in touch with his mom, he might have come back home a lot earlier because the West wasn't half what it was cracked up to be. He got an old boy at the prison library, a trustee, to find out for him what ever happened about the Wyatt murders, but by the time he found out he had nothing to fear back home, he was awaiting trial in Washoe County Jail.

Looking back on it all from his table in the front window of the Two Spot, he had to admit he'd had his share of luck. He was a free man with Betty's money in the bank, enough to last him for a while, especially if he kept cutting lawns, sweeping leaves, cleaning eaves and generally doing piddle work for old folks on the south side, but the time would come when he'd have to figure something out. He was too old now to go robbing guns and getting chased up trees. Besides, even if he did steal some guns, he'd have to find somebody local to sell them to because his last buyer was out of business. No, Keelan was retired for now, a senior citizen with money in the bank, and once he got his license back, he'd drive down to Damascus to see if any of the old red-light bars were still open. He hadn't gone out to Floral Hill since he got back, but he knew his dad had bought a family plot out there with a place for him to rest—or to rot, more likely. But if there did happen to be something else beyond, like they say, he'd just have to take his chances.

"No man is beyond redemption," is what the God Behind Bars preacher told the sorry group of inmates who sat through his sermons during his last hitch at Nevada Correctional. It reminded him of the times Aunt Unity used to drag the whole lot of them—Uncle Amos, the cousins, his mom and dad and little Jezzie and him—off to the Baptist Church to hear old Preacher Hurley give everybody hell. Always carrying on about the Devil as if the Devil owed him money. The God Behind Bars preacher told it about the same, telling all the poor bastards they were sinners and had done evil because Satan possessed them, as if the old Devil didn't have nothing better to do than to put a man up to such petty-ass shit as stealing a car, slipping into a man's house to steal watches, jewelry and guns or robbing a gas station. If the Devil had any interest in him, he'd already got his money's worth long before he jumped on that Greyhound just to vex and torment him, if that even happened, which it most surely didn't since he wasn't nuts. Keelan smiled at his thoughts. If the time came when he had to plead insanity, he'd just tell the judge about talking squirrels, riding the night bus with Satan and talking to a woman in a jug. That'd sure as hell get him a one-way ticket to the funny farm.

The drizzle was just a sprinkle now and he had a backyard job waiting for him over on Hamilton Street for old Doc Kline's widow. Something about a birdhouse or a birdbath. Hard to hear on the telephone. Said she saw his name up on the bulletin board at the library. Handyman. Old folks on the south side were always needing something done, sending him up a ladder to clean leaves out of the rain gutters or setting him onto yardwork or changing ceiling bulbs on rickety stepstools. And when he was done with whatever tinkering they needed him to do, there was no place worthwhile to spend the pocket money he was paid. The town was quiet as a graveyard after Reno and quiet compared to how he remembered it, but that had its blessings, its bright side. If he heard a knock on his door he could be pretty sure it was the Jehovah's Witnesses trying to save his soul, or some little girl selling cookies, instead of Twitchy Harkie come to cut his throat.

Sitting at his window seat table onto Main Street, still waiting for his breakfast, watching occasional spots of rain on the glass, he felt himself getting mad again. He needed that truck so as not to be limited to the Two Spot or The Depot for his morning coffee and toast. The coffee at The Depot tasted burnt. The Two Spot had better coffee but the slowest service in town. Once he got his license back he could drive out to McDonald's for their Senior Breakfast or maybe even to the Dixie Diner where little sister Jezzie worked, except if he did, she'd go running to Mom.

Jezzie looked right through him when they passed the other day on Main, him walking and her driving an old green Ford. Whatever happened to bygones? They were just kids, and he'd heard of a lot worse. It didn't mean as much as folks made out. All that was forever ago anyway. He couldn't really remember much about it unless he studied on it. Sometimes he did, but it gave him pictures of things he didn't believe happened.

Finally somebody managed to figure out how to pour coffee in a cup and get bread hot enough to call it toast and how to rub butter on it. The waitress, Dandy's daughter and not a whole hell of a lot better looking than he was, was headed his way and might get there before Christmas.

"You done with that paper, Myers?" said Keelan to Frank Myers at the close end of the counter. Myers had the same chin as his big sister who was a year ahead of the two of them in school.

"Huh? Yeah," Myers said. And he looked almost friendly when he recognized who was talking to him.

"Well, give it to that young lady who's speeding past so I can see what they thought of next."

With his paper, coffee and toast, Keelan settled back in his window seat and enjoyed a few seconds of peace before he saw the police car and the man driving it. Wouldn't you know it! Nodding at me. Look all you want. You don't know when to quit. Good morning, you sawed-off bastard!

Keelan nodded back grinning and looked down at his copy of the *Damascus Herald*. He looked first at the date. October 2. Again. It comes around once a year like his birthday and Christmas. Those would do for days to remember. And one more—the Fourth of July, the day he won Betty. The front page was full of what the president had been getting up to. Made you ashamed of your own damn country. There was the usual stuff about politics and wars and there was something about a kid down in Mississippi killing his mom and his girlfriend and then playing hell at high school with a rifle, which just goes to show you what we're up against these days, he thought, but he skipped that for later and opened to page three. He was about to take his first sip of coffee but the cup stopped short and there it was. It was all about him. It seems like a man can't win for losing.

Keelan read it a couple of times while his coffee and toast got cold. So that's why Buster was nodding at him. They always know about everything before it goes in the paper. The paper is where fools find out what's going on after it's already too late. The Twilight Zone Murderer. You had to hand it to them for that.

Keelan knew one thing for sure; he wasn't ever running again. They had no more on him now than they did then and nobody was the wiser. The only person who knew what he did that day—the very same day and a Friday too back in '59—was his mom and she had no proof and wouldn't turn him in anyway and spoil that Putnam name.

Now what was Dandy carrying on about? Everybody laughing at the far end of the counter by the grill where Dandy was burning food. Keelan caught a phrase: "Whizdom Lahae and his Yonders Globetrotters."

Dandy was generally full of shit, but since he never shut up, he was Keelan's best source of local news. Lately, he'd been talking about witches coming to town and Keelan saw with his own eyes that tall, gypsy-looking woman walking around downtown all dressed in black. But now Dandy was saying that some old ladies out at the north edge of town were starting up the old talk about seeing dead Rachel in her yellow dress running the alleys again. There was crazy talk like that right after it happened, grown people believing that dead idiot girl was out there by night. Old northside folks always talked about seeing ghosts and the Devil and such, as if people didn't have enough to worry about. Keelan knew for a fact that he was the last person to see Rachel Wyatt run and that was before she was dead.

The Two Spot was starting to empty and he was about to go when the rain hit hard. He could never tell what the weather was going to do in Nevada, but he knew, watching the rain pound the sidewalk just outside the window, that this was just a passing storm. It left him with nothing to do but wait it out, eat his cold toast, drink his lukewarm coffee and read the article in the paper again. The Twilight Zone Murderer could be anywhere, it said. Not without his damn truck, he couldn't.

"See you later, Dandy. See you later, Keelan," said Myers at the door, nodding as he hurried out to his car. It was raining harder. Neighborly of him, calling him by his name like that.

By the time the rain had stopped, Keelan was calm again. He had nothing to worry about. There wasn't a damn thing to connect him to the Wyatts no matter what Buster had figured. One thing he had learned from those jailhouse lawyers was that only three things can put a man in the two-thousand-volt hot seat or put a poison needle in his arm or get him strapped down to a bench in the gas chamber: witnesses, evidence and confessions. That old boy down in Graham could change his story as many times as he wanted and Buster and Murdock and the rest of them could burn as much gas as they wanted cruising around his block, but unless Wyatt and his old lady dug their way up to the daylight and swore out a warrant, there was nothing to hold him on. Even if Rachel herself jumped out in front of the police car and accused him, nobody would take a dead idiot's word against that of a retired senior citizen. He smiled thinking of that court room scene, imagining his mealy-mouthed public defender piping up with "Your honor, we object to dead people making accusations" and getting overruled.

He must have been smiling because Dandy asked him, "What's so funny?" The place was almost empty and Dandy was wiping down the counter.

"The funnies," said Keelan.

"That's not the funnies page you're reading," said Dandy. Keelan looked down at the paper, open to the Twilight Zone Murderer headline.

"I was reading about the president," said Keelan. "Those boys do have their fun in Washington."

Dandy laughed, but there was nothing about the president on page three. He was slipping up. Time to get out of there. The walk over to the widow Kline's would ease his troubled mind.

The ten blocks took almost half an hour. Mrs. Kline was happy to see him. Birdbath fell over in the windstorm the week before and the fountain was full of leaves and she needed the grass troweled along both edges of the walk from the back door out to the alley.

She came out once to say what a fine job he was doing, but when he was done and wanted to get downtown for lunch, he couldn't find her. Knocked and then stuck his head in the kitchen door. Nobody. He needed paying. There was a big, clean stove and a Frigidaire, three times the size of his, and little yellow curtains in the window and a view of the garden. Jesus Christ hung on a cross and then hung on the wall. Pictures of old times too. His mom never had any pictures in the kitchen, not enough wall. This kitchen was as big as his mom's living room. There was a black and white picture of the Kline house with a big, long Imperial in the drive and everybody standing together out front: Doc and Mrs. Kline, kids that must be grown up and dogs that must be dead, have to be if that Imperial was new.

"Hello?" he said, speaking up, not yelling, and there was another door half open and he walked in there on a rug so thick it could trip you and there was a big old table and chairs and a sideboard with a big mirror and more pictures and knickknacks and doohickeys and little cups and saucers, and he saw himself in the mirror, out of place in that fancy room. That's what a murderer looks like in a nice old lady's dining room.

But she couldn't see it in him. She came carefully down the stairs smiling, pretty as you please, little old bun-headed lady no bigger than a child, and said, "Oh, Mr. Putnam!" Smiling. Not scared of him at all. "I thought I heard a knock but I wasn't sure. Forgive me. Have you finished with the birdbath?"

"Yes, mam, it's back up for you."

"For the birds, you mean," and she laughed. "That would be fifteen dollars, I believe, and a little extra for your shoe leather." Then she looked up at the ceiling and said, "Do you hear that? Oh, my goodness, I do believe I've left the water running." And she tottered off up the stairs leaving him in a dining room with doilies, a long table with a white table cloth and six chairs all tucked in tight.

He watched after her as she pulled herself up the carpeted stairway by the oak banister and when she was out of sight, he started going through the drawers of the sideboard. It would be so easy to kill her if he was of a mind to. Break her chicken neck with one hand. Not a day went by since Keelan came home that he didn't see a chance to kill somebody without even using a gun and with nobody knowing, and sometimes he wondered just how far he could get with his automatic and a pocket full of mags right down on the corner of Main and Iroquois. Crazy thinking. When he used to get to thinking like that, Betty'd bring him around, even get him laughing. What did she go and die for? She'd have probably liked Yonders, made friends of the neighbors. He must be getting funny in his old age, talking to four certified pounds of ashes and, what was worse, listening too. That's all a woman is, a man too—just enough dirt to fill a pot. He had to sign for her. Four pounds and four ounces. But he was glad he hadn't thrown her to the water babies. She was like company and it wasn't so much he could hear her talking as he knew what she would have said. She always said what needed saying.

Nothing in the drawer but knives and forks and spoons.

"I'll flood the whole house someday," said widow Kline, coming down the stairs and clinging to the banister. He closed the drawer and stepped back. She went over to the sideboard and took her pocketbook out of the drawer beside the one he had just closed and paid him, but he couldn't see if there was a stash in there. He looked over her shoulder into his own murdering face in the big sideboard mirror. Some folks just don't know how close they are to getting killed. If he killed widow Kline, she wouldn't run the backstreets and the tracks like they said Rachel was doing. She'd just sit out by her birdbath.

He took his fifteen dollars and two more bucks, the old lady's idea of the cost in shoe leather of traipsing all the way from North First Street.

She walked him through her fancy living room and out the front door and waved goodbye to him from the porch like he was somebody. In spite of himself he waved back at the little old lady and wondered if she did have money or valuables in that other drawer, maybe her burying money the way folks used to. But it didn't seem right to kill an old lady and steal her burying money too. That struck him funny and, as he chuckled, a lady sweeping leaves off her walk saw him passing by and damned if she didn't wave too. And he waved back. The southside sure was nice. Nice for some.

He thought of the newspaper article again. Folks wondering if the Twilight Zone Murderer might still be among them. He was walking up Iroquois past the little flower shop and he looked in the window and saw the reflection of The Twilight Zone Murderer walking by, and he winked. They both did.

He was feeling pretty good, fresh money in his pocket and the sun breaking out, and then he saw it plain as day. Wouldn't you know it! Harold Dresher's damned green Chevy parked in the visitor's slot right there in front of the police station on the corner of Iroquois and Franklin. As far as he knew, there was only one green Chevrolet Lumina in town unless he'd missed one, or maybe the car parked in the visitor's slot in front of the police station was from out of town. No, he was just about sure he was looking at Harold Dresher's car.

Keelan walked on past the police station. There wasn't a nick or a dent on that car. He didn't have pencil or paper, so he said the license plate number to himself a couple of times. He'd write it down when he got home and check it out, but he already knew what he knew, unless it was just a coincidence. There were a lot of reasons Harold Dresher could be in there talking to Buster about something other than the night of the murders. Sure, Keelan thought, they were probably just talking about why water don't run uphill.

The walk along Iroquois always took him past his mom's house. He looked over at the closed living room drapes of the house he grew up in and out at the garage where his dad showed him how to set points and gap plugs. That was the yard he played in with Jezzie when they were little. But that wasn't his home. He had to keep walking three blocks farther to his shack by the tracks. He had just turned the key in the lock when a crow scolded down from a rung of the telephone pole. He stooped to reach for a throwing rock from his handy pile, but the old crow knew what was coming next and flew off squawking and thumping the air with her black wings.

Chapter 18

Sunset

The two old cops were sitting in the porch swing at sunset out at the west end of Damascus, Buster's shiny black and white Interceptor parked in the gravel drive beside retired Marigold County Chief Sheriff's Investigator Ira Cockrell's black Lincoln Town Car.

The sun had just begun to flatten on the horizon, glowing golden orange beyond the fields of soybeans and corn. Both men watched the sunset. Neither spoke at first. It was a relief for Buster to sit out on the porch after spending all afternoon with the sheriff going over the latest plans for Operation Marigold North. Buster did ask a few questions about Freeman Lane's confession, but all he learned from McIntyre was what he already knew. Cockrell, being an ex-detective and a Damascus boy, would know more about who to ask. McIntyre was from way down in Cairo.

"I didn't stay up to watch the extra innings last night," said Cockrell. "How did all that come out?"

Buster didn't even look at him and Cockrell smiled. "Well, they'll get them back tomorrow at Wrigley," he said, and they were quiet again, each smiling a little. Buster wondered what it would be like when he retired. Maybe he'd do some coaching. It was nice just to sit for a minute with no talking.

Cockrell finally said, "What the hell is that you got painted on your door?"

"You know damn well what it is, same as it's always been."

On the white door of the new Interceptor was a badge in the shape of the state and on the badge a half-shucked ear of golden sweetcorn at about a seventy-five-degree angle. Above: Yonders. Below: Police.

"Didn't any kids ever paint a pair of balls to the bottom of that? I'd be careful where I parked that around here. I'd say that constituted maintaining an attractive nuisance." Cockrell looked over at Buster, but Buster's eyes were on the sunset.

"You done?" said Buster, not quite smiling.

"So," said Cockrell, "what do you think of the price of beans now, after what our boy wrote in today's paper? I'd have told you sooner, but I only just found out yesterday about an hour before I called you."

"Took me back forty years," said Buster

"One shy of forty. Hell, that was '59. I'd been on the force six years, but it was the first big murder case I ever worked."

"What's a little one?"

"One without rich white folks wandering onto the reservation."

"That'd be Jackson Street," said Buster.

"Now, don't tell me you got lost down there once yourself?"

"Nah, I pretty much stayed on the straight and narrow. Besides, we got married right after I got back from Korea," said Buster. "But what really happened with that Jack Crawford murder anyhow?"

"Crawford was a big shot around here in the day. When he got himself killed, they had us all on it at first. It was quietly known back then that Crawford was given to prowling the red-light district."

"I remember Warry saying something about that," said Buster, "and I seem to recall the Black kid, Lane, was the only suspect in the Crawford murder. So how did a Black kid who nobody ever remembered seeing in Yonders end up confessing to killing the Wyatts?"

"That was a hell of a month. First your farmers got themselves killed, and a couple of weeks later they found Crawford with his throat slit in the alley. We hadn't never had so many murders in the county in such a short space of time. Four in a month is still a lot, but we beat that in July of '96."

"You're not answering my question, Ira."

"You're right. I'm not. Can't very well answer a question about an investigation that I got taken off of, can I?"

"What kind of bird is that up there? Looks kind of like a bobolink," said Buster pointing to an overhanging branch of the oak in the front lawn. "Can you make out any white on him? I see some red or orange too."

"I can't see it too good without my glasses," said Cockrell, "but that's no bobolink. It's long past time for the bobolinks to be headed south."

"Shit, he flew off. Must have heard us talking about him," said Buster. He looked at his watch. Still plenty of time to get back for the witch meeting.

"Your old chief you had back then hadn't informed the sheriff's department of any suspects at all and then we brought this kid in for questioning about the Crawford murder, and he just ups and confesses to killing your farmers," said Cockrell.

"Did that happen often? People just up and confessing out of a clear blue sky?"

"We were all surprised, I'll admit," said Cockrell. "I was off the case by then. The Sheriff and the DA were playing their cards close to the chest because of who Crawford was. We all thought it was strange, but when somebody just confesses like that and knows all the details, you've got to listen."

"Chief Warry had a line on a couple of Yonders boys," said Buster. "He was working it slow, watching, but then your detectives decided—and this is how Chief Warry explained it to me—decided to assign your murderer to our murders for internal and local reasons that had to do with the reputation of your victim's well-respected Damascus family."

"That'd be one way of putting it."

"Is there another way?" said Buster.

"If you consult the trial records, you'll find that Lane confessed and his confession, dictated to a clerk, contained details of the crime known only to the murderer."

"...and the interrogators," said Buster.

"...and the interrogators, who would never divulge that information, because that would be tantamount to corrupting an investigation."

"Tantamount as hell."

"And the accused waived jury trial and was sentenced to life in prison, and that truly did surprise me, 'cause old "Sparky" Rutledge was on the bench and that usually meant the hot seat. Anyhow, after nearly forty years living at taxpayer's expense, Lane seems to have suddenly remembered cutting Crawford's throat over on Jackson Street," said Cockrell. "You smoke, Buster?"

"No thanks."

"I wasn't offering, I was trying to bum one. Thought you might have taken it up in your old age. The woman goes through my pockets and throws them out, but this is police business and I can't discuss police business without a smoke. You just keep swinging for a minute."

Cockrell stood, glanced in the front window and softly and quickly went down the steps and out to his car. He came back smoking.

"You have to pussyfoot around like that just to get a smoke?" said Buster.

Cockrell inhaled deeply, held and then slowly exhaled. The horizon, beneath the scarlet rippled sky, was a line of gold. "She's in the kitchen making a pie for the grandkids, but if I hear her coming this way I'm handing this to you. They say these coffin nails will kill you, but they seem to be taking their sweet time in my case. You guess how old I'll be next month?"

"Well, if you'd put in six years by '59, I'd make you late sixties. How come you retired so early?"

"Because I was a Damascus lawman. Hell, Buster, you should see the crazy sons of bitches we have to deal with, some of them so fucked up on meth and who knows what that there's no place to send them. Hospitals just drop them off in the alley somewhere and the prisons got no place for them to be. The insane asylums have all gone out of business. We arrest the same ones over and over and they'd as soon shoot you as look at you. Yes sir, if I'd been a Yonders cop, I'd still be giving speeding tickets, arresting drunks and chasing window-peepers."

"We get our share of burglary and the like, and lately we got some out-of-town boys in the wholesale marijuana distribution business too, as you well know, or I imagine you do," said Buster.

"I still hear things now and then. I'd even guess you and the Sheriff might have been going over that this very afternoon, but it only takes one little thing, illegal search or entrapment, to burn it. Ask a suspect the time of day and you got the ACLU on your ass for failing to let him call a lawyer. How many guilty men do you reckon got off because of that Miranda bullshit?"

Buster didn't answer. Twilight was becoming night. The corner streetlight came on and then twinkled and began to flicker off and on.

"That light's been doing that when it first comes on since spring. Annoying as shit. I've phoned it in a bunch of times." said Cockrell. "You know, I, honest to God, don't think we ever sent up a truly innocent man in all my years in the department." He glanced sideways at Buster.

"Sometimes a guilty man might not be guilty of what he is convicted of," said Buster. "That convict, Lane—he'd be pushing sixty now—must have had a pretty compelling goddamn reason to stand up to three homicides just to avoid embarrassing one of your prominent Damascus families."

"That the way you figure it? That he was compelled?"

Buster took his hat off and looked inside it as if there were a message written there. "Well," he said, "I've never talked about this before, but I guess there's no harm now. The chief had an eye on two boys up home. One of them ended up trying out the Nevada prison system a few times before he got old and came home just this summer to sit on the back porch by the tracks and do a little yard work for old folks. The other one went missing over in Vietnam. He was the one, the MIA boy, that Warry liked for it the most and right from the very first. He was an out-of-state boy from Missouri, in trouble down there and sent to live with his grandmother. They threw his ass right out of high school and he was still carrying on, getting in fights, until one of our girls straightened him out. Funny thing was, the girl was the other suspect's sister."

"That's the problem with your small towns. You haven't got enough people to play all the parts," said Cockrell. "Would I be likely to have ever come across either of these boys you're talking about?"

"The one lost over in the war was Clive Barber," said Buster. "You may have had a run in with him out at Dead

Man's Grade yourself at one time or another before he changed his ways, if that's what he did instead of killing the Wyatts."

"Barber? Can't say as I ever heard of him, but my memory's not what it used to be. I had an old boy at Walmart the other day come up to me and ask me if I knew him, said I run him down in an alley and tackled him for window breaking when he was a kid. Now, you'd think I'd remember a thing like that. Said I chased him two blocks before I caught him."

"Did you arrest him, did he say?"

"Said I smacked him upside the head, gave him a kick in the ass and run him off. That does sound like me back then. I hated paperwork for small shit."

Buster smiled. "The other one the chief was watching was a northside boy, name of Putnam. He's the one that made it to prison out west," said Buster. "Came from a family of fightin' Kentuckians."

"Fightin' Kentuckians! I ain't heard nobody say that for years. We had some of them too. Good old boys, drinking and fighting each other. That was before we got the boys coming down here from Chicago, or wherever else they come from. That's when it quit being fun. Fightin' Kentuckians!" Cockrell smiled and lowered his voice. "God, I miss those days!"

They sat swinging, watching the last of the fading glory at the edge of the earth.

"You know," said Cockrell, "I remember driving up to Yonders a couple of times right after your murders. There was even a van of crime lab smart boys from Springfield trying to raise fingerprints off all the firearms. They thought they found fingerprints on the door handle, but it turned out the crime lab boys were finding each other's prints and sending them off to Springfield and identifying each other. We must have driven up there a dozen times scouring the place for clues."

"It must have come as a relief to Sheriff Foster to finally get his own big murder so he could look like he was doing something useful instead of wearing out the Dixie Highway, poking around in our investigation," said Buster.

"We always had enough to do. Nothing like now though. According to something I read, our county crime rate is one of the worst in the state, right up there with Cook County, if you can believe it. But back then when Jack Crawford managed to end up with his throat slit behind a row of trash cans, we hadn't had a homicide for several years," said Cockrell.

"And you never did solve it, or at least no one was ever charged. Maybe they'll let Lane pin it on himself so you can finally close that case. But I got to be going pretty quick. We got a meeting tonight between a group of new neighbors and the local community," said Buster, watching Cockrell.

Cockrell smiled. "Now where did I hear you had imported a half dozen or so witches down from Chicago? We had us some Satanists for a while, but they just kinda lost heart and faded away. I guess they took a look around and figured they didn't have much to add to our community."

The streetlight came on steady and cast a circle of light on the road.

Cockrell looked at his watch. "Shit, it's late. I got places to be myself. Hey, it's sure been good catching up, Buster. I'll take a look at what we had on Lane and give you a call, but now I got a meeting of the Athletic Board at the high school in about a half hour and I need to put on a clean shirt. We got us a hell of a football team this year, but our basketball team is the thing. That Wendell Truman grew another two inches over the summer."

"That reminds me," said Buster. "I nearly forgot the other reason I'm here. I got a basketball matter to take up with you. A favor to ask, really."

"I was wondering when you'd get around to that," said Cockrell. "Ask away." Suddenly he handed the cigarette to Buster.

The door opened. "You fellows want some coffee or anything?" said Mrs. Cockrell.

"Thank you kindly, Evelyn," said Buster, "but I never drink coffee after noon."

"Well," she said, "you'd be better off with coffee than those things." She went back in the house and reappeared with an ashtray and then withdrew again.

"You want this back?"

"No, I think she's just about figured it out. Better snuff it," said Cockrell. "So, what's this basketball matter, anyhow?"

"Ray Dornfeld, our coach—I think you know him—has been after me to talk to you, now that you're a big-shot basketball executive, about getting a little old non-conference game with your Bulldogs. Offering your Bulldogs a rematch."

"Sure, I know Ray from back before he went nuts and thought Yonders should play us. You know we're class Double A. We don't play little Single A schools much these days. We're merciful that way."

"I recall you did play us in 1960 and, if I remember right, it didn't go all that well for you. Dornfeld just wants to give the Dogs another chance, a rematch."

"Jesus, Buster! Our Dogs against your Harvesters? Didn't you read about our boys last year? We made Sweet Sixteen and we're even stronger this year."

"Well, Mayor Wellington—you know Tom—got talking to Coach after watching the boys shooting around on open gym night and just wanted to give you a chance to get even for that last game. Just a fun game for your Dogs. A chance to give your bench some floor time."

Cockrell was quiet for a moment. "I'm assuming that your coach knows he can't be running practice out of season."

"Don't be a pain in the ass, Ira. Coach doesn't do a damn thing. Just sits in the corner and watches this new transfer kid from Chicago canning long shots. I watched him the other day. Lost track of how many he canned in a row. I think it would mean a lot to the town to see the Bulldogs at Happ Hopkins again."

"You still playing in that old barn? I remember going to games there. Every time somebody came in the flags ruffled and you could feel the cold draft on your neck."

"We got double doors now."

Cockrell was looking at his watch and almost grinning. "Well, hell, why didn't you say so? And inside toilets too?

You know, we got a non-conference game penciled in with Kankakee at the start of the season, early November. An hour-and-a-half bus ride up to Kankakee compared to a half hour to Yonders. You leave that with me and I'll see what I can do you for."

"Coach Dornfeld would really appreciate it. And, if you can, rack your brain a little for me for anything unusual you can remember about that Crawford case."

"Something not unusual would be more like it," said Cockrell.

Buster backed out the drive and waved to Cockrell, standing on the porch. The streetlight was flickering again. Maybe something would come of all of this. Maybe he'd finally solve the Wyatt murders. Maybe Yonders would beat Damascus again in basketball. The first would be very unlikely, but the second would take a damn miracle.

A deputy in a big Marigold County Bronco waved over at him, smiling, sitting alongside the Interceptor at the last stoplight at the north end of town. Buster didn't care what they said. That ear of corn was staying right there on the door.

He knew every bump in the road, every farmhouse, every barn along the twenty-five-mile drive. The big Interceptor hugged the road and wanted to accelerate, but Buster held her down to a safe sixty, just over the limit, giving himself some time to think about it all.

Fightin' Kentuckians! Cockrell was right. It was kind of good to be thinking about them again instead of that kid with the death eyes peeking over his shirt collar.

Yonders water tower at twilight, topped with its red cherry, was on the horizon and, just like when he was a kid, the moon, running just as fast as he was and skimming the treetops, followed him home.

Chapter 19

Belly-Gunner Sermon

Buster had only a couple of minutes to spare when he got to the church. He hadn't given much thought to the meeting, but when he saw all the cars and trucks parked on both sides of Main he wondered if this mixer, as Ellen called it, was such a good idea after all. He'd gone along with it, but it was Mayor Wellington who had talked the Neighborhood Watchmen into turning their monthly meeting into whatever this was going to be. He had to park a block away, north of the abandoned Nickel Plate right of way.

From the crossing of the ghost railroad he saw the church, tall and dark except for the light cast by the row of sidewalk-level basement windows of the Community Room. He was about to walk into a meeting between Christians and witches just four blocks away from the stash house the Central Illinois Drug Task Force was planning to attack with an armored vehicle and agents in combat gear.

The deacons were starting to close the inner double doors to the Community Room when Buster came down the basement steps. He knew both men, a Drummond and a Carew. They greeted him silently and closed the doors behind him. The room felt restless.

When Buster told Ellen they were called the Whisperers and that he wasn't sure what they were all about, something to do with the Internet, she got right on the phone. Later, while he was watching TV, she told him the Whisperers were pagans. When he didn't look up, she said, "They're witches and they sell magic books, spells and hexes."

"I'll be damned," said Buster. Ellen laughed.

Now, six months later, a man seen around town in a cloak and calling himself Chancellor Austin and identifying himself as a witch was to be introduced at a special meeting of Neighborhood Watch. All the town really knew about the Whisperers was from a midsummer article in the *Chronicle* by Lisa Riggs titled "New Neighbors" and subtitled "Whisperers, Modern Paganism and Witchcraft." The first person to object to the arrival of the Whisperers was Naomi Moore, the Farmers Insurance agent and the head of the Chamber of Commerce. She said in a letter to the editor that recruiting witches was a perfect example of the kind of thing that discouraged new business.

The religious leaders were not in agreement on how to take the arrival of witches. The Methodists organized a prayer vigil to drive the Whisperers away. The Nazarenes did the same. The Baptist preacher dedicated back-to-back Sunday sermons to the Bible's admonitions against mediums and witches, and three of the four evangelical churches wrote a joint letter to Mayor Wellington demanding that the city reverse the decision of the Action Group to lease the Township Building "to heathens." The First Church of Christ and the Presbyterians, Buster's church or, more like it, Ellen's, were sitting back to wait and see, but Reverend Burns and his Universalist Unitarians, as most folks expected they would, welcomed witches and looked forward to their enrichening the community. Whatever Father Simon thought about it was kept within the walls of Saint Paul's, but Ellen, who was taking almost a sporting interest in the witches, called her very Catholic roommate from her college days. Her old friend told her that she was sending her a Saint Benedict medal to put over the bed as a scourge against demons. That, Buster told Ellen, was why you don't ask Catholics too many questions. They have remedies for everything, saints for toothaches, saints for impossible causes and doodads to scare off demons.

The one man of importance in the evangelical community who had not yet taken a stand on the Whisperers was Preacher Simms of the New Morning Church, the oldest of the town's religious leaders. Word had it he was asked at the church door after Sunday services, and in the presence of several members of the congregation, what he made of the witches. Those who heard him said he cited the Book of James: "Be swift to hear, slow to speak, slow to wrath."

That, when Buster heard about it, seemed like the right answer and the kind of answer that he expected from a solid man like Simms. Buster had never attended his church, but he'd talked a few times over the years with the old WWII vet and he considered him a good man. Buster knew that

Simms' judgement, when he gave it, would carry a lot of weight, but how would a churchman like Simms react to witches? He and the rest of the listeners would soon find out. Simms must have gotten there early. He was seated front and center, his wife at his side and flanked by a few members of the New Morning congregation.

Lisa Riggs was standing off to the side up front and snapping pictures of Reverend McClean and Chancellor Austin. Reverend McClean, the host, was waiting for the room to quiet. The Neighborhood Watch meeting usually had about the same twenty or thirty citizens, mostly men, sometimes with a couple of women if there had been any recent break-ins, but this time the Community Room was packed to around a hundred people, a third of them women. More people than chairs. A dozen men, having given their seats to women, stood at the back of the room. All studied, most furtively but some unblinkingly, the portly smiling witch, pigtailed and cloaked, as he stood in fringed moccasins beside Reverend McLean, waiting to be introduced. People shushed each other until it got so still Buster could hear the seconds ticking off the wall clock.

There was no microphone. McLean asked for "a warm Yonders welcome for Chancellor Austin, spiritual leader of a unique group of new residents." Maybe, if one person had clapped only once, the rest might have joined in, but Austin was greeted with silence. That didn't surprise Buster. If there was to be applause, it would be after this stranger had explained just what the hell he meant by telling everybody he was a witch and after he said what he was up to.

The purpose of this meeting, according to Mayor Wellington, was to convince the town that the Whisperers were just a group of new neighbors with different beliefs. After all, he told Buster, some people believed in angels and others believed in infant damnation and the Pentecostals believed in speaking in tongues. But all of that was relatively normal compared to what the audience was suddenly hearing from the first word out of Chancellor Austin's mouth.

"Abracadabra," he said. Someone from the back laughed out loud. "Yes," said Austin, "the old word has become almost a joke, like so many words and customs and beliefs. Like the word 'witch' itself. Until recent times a witch was often seen as an old crone boiling bones in a big pot, but modern depictions in literature, movies and TV tend toward Homer's notion. He wrote of the witch Circe as a radiant and beautiful goddess with a celestial singing voice. Unfortunately for you folks, the Fates have sent you me."

He looked about hopefully, but no one laughed and the clock ticked on. "Once Reverend McClean and I would have been colleagues, but today when this respected minister speaks of the prophesies and ancient truths, he is regarded as wise. If, however, it is a pagan who speaks of these things, he is not regarded as wise, but rather as an infidel or a witch. Yet, the origin of the word 'witch' is derived from the Anglo-Saxon 'witga,' meaning the wise one. In olden times, I could have been your preacher and the good reverend here your witch, and the changes in our messages would be as superficial as a change of clothes," and, gripping his cape and extending his arms to both sides, he assumed the form of a comic-book vampire. He looked hopefully over his audience, but no one laughed.

If he'd ever had a chance, he'd lost it now, thought Buster. Chancellor Austin had no idea what he looked and sounded like, fooling around up there like that before a mix of Yonders Christians and volunteer vigilantes and trying to tell folks he was a witch. He might as well have said that he was the boogie man.

The half dozen members of Neighborhood Watch Night Patrol, most sitting together in the back rows, a couple standing behind, were exchanging glances, rolling their eyes, shaking their heads. Good men, but sometimes they worried Buster when they cruised the night streets. Unless the tone of the meeting changed damn fast, they'd probably consider setting up a witch-watch patrol, and you really couldn't blame them, thought Buster. He figured Austin had already said more strange shit in two minutes than most people have to listen to in a normal meat-and-potatoes lifetime, but Austin looked pleased with how it was all going.

After telling everyone he was a pagan witch and Chancellor for the Temple of the Whisperers, he had the honor, he said, of presenting three fellow witches, women in black capes, hoods down, all black-haired. He named them, but they didn't stand. He introduced his wife as Raven. Beside her was Lilith Zon, the High Priestess, and beside her was Rose Lahae. So, that was the basketball boy's mom, the back of her head anyway.

Buster decided he should make himself more visible; the folks needed to see him, uniformed, badged, armed and with his radio on his belt. People needed to see the law now and then. He walked along the wall to the front of the room, coming to stand in the front corner beside Reverend McClean. It was getting a lot worse fast, Buster thought. Austin was talking about magic and reincarnation, for Christ's sake. And then he said it, the one thing that had never been said, probably never even thought, in the basement of the First Church of Christ. "We don't believe in God."

Buster almost felt McLean cringe, but Preacher Simms, sitting in the front row, showed no reaction, biding his time, holding his peace. But not everyone could. The shout of condemnation came from a short lady, even short sitting down. It was Norma Ketchell of the Waylon Avenue Ketchell bunch.

"Great God, forgive our ears!" she yelled. These words froze Austin. Norma, sitting by her man in the middle of the third row in a clump of Nazarenes, went on, lowering her voice slightly now that she had the floor. "You say you don't believe in God. Who do you believe in?" She had the holy look, the seething calm of an outraged, devout believer, surrounded by believers, all good righteous folks, but not to be trifled with, not to be incited, not to be brought to the basement of a place of worship to have to hear a cloaked and pig-tailed witch man in Indian moccasins say right out in front of everybody that he didn't believe in the Almighty.

Austin blinked and scanned the room, unable to pick her out at first from among the hostile faces. When he found her, he smiled a patient and almost benevolent smile, as if he were about to explain to five-year-olds that the light inside the refrigerator went off when the door was closed.

"I merely meant to say we don't believe in a single god," said Austin, "We are duotheistic and worship the Moon Goddess and the Horned God and…"

…but that was more than Mrs. Ketchell's ears could bear. Eyes afire, she cried out, "What's this here horned god's name? It wouldn't be Satan would it?"

Merciful heavens, thought Buster—his mom's words often came to him—where did Austin think he was that he could talk to these good people about a Horned God? The deacon ushers were standing taller now at the back of the room and Reverend McClean was looking sidelong at Buster, but Austin was still calm, as if he knew just what to say next.

Until he heard the next words, Buster thought saying he didn't believe in God was bad enough, but Austin said, "We do not believe in the existence of the Devil." That riled the room even more. Buster's mom always spoke almost fondly of the Devil as if he were a wayward uncle, a local rascal.

Buster saw Simms perk up and lean a little forward, smiling. Here we go, thought Buster. It's not every day that an old-time-religion preacher gets an opportunity like this. Simms was coming up with the bases loaded.

"Well, Reverend McClean," Simms said, standing. Couldn't be taller than five-five. A bandy rooster, Buster's mom would have called him. But he had the voice. "When you said you were introducing us to a group of new neighbors with beliefs different from ours, you said a mouthful." Buster had heard that voice more than once through the open windows of Simms' church on a warm Sunday morning, a voice that could carry all the way out to the road. Now he was hearing it point blank. There were some in town who mocked his preaching, but none doubted that he was a good man, a World War II veteran, belly-gunner on a B-17 over Germany. The word was he flew seventeen missions curled up with two 50-caliber machine guns under a roaring bomber watching black flak through the Plexiglass bubble and blasting away at enemy fighters. That's where they put the short and thin boys if they had the gumption. He never talked about it. They said hardly any of the bomber boys survived a full tour of duty over Germany. One thing Simms did say was that the only reason he was alive to preach the word was that Hitler had the good sense to kill himself when he did.

Buster was glad he had come in his police uniform. He had noticed a couple of men he'd never seen before, sitting together in the third row, both staring hard at the Chancellor. How this was going to go now depended on Simms.

"We just heard our new neighbor here disavow our Lord and speak of a goddess and a horned god, but he denies not only the Lord but also the Devil, and yet the Bible tells us we should not doubt other spirits of the air. The Devil has many names, but the first of his names is Angel of the Lord." Simms spoke in that twangy, friendly voice that went so well with his smile.

Now comes the good part, thought Buster. He was raised a Methodist before joining Ellen as a Presbyterian, but he once went with a friend and his folks to services at the Baptist Church when old Theo Hurley was still preaching. He was about thirteen then, and he remembered the cadence and the timing and the mixture of Old Testament phrasing with plain people talk.

Buster knew it was going to be a good one when Simms kicked off in Revelation. "In Revelation we learn of the beast with ten horns and seven heads that rises from the sea, and we are warned in First John 4:1: 'Beloved, believe not every spirit, but try the spirits whether they are of God.' So, the question here is not whether other spirits exist, for truly John tells us and Revelation shows us they do. The question is whether they are of God. To deny the Devil, the Angel of the Lord, is to deny the Lord Himself. The question is whether the Devil was expelled from paradise, or whether he was sent on a mission. Did he jump, or did he get pushed?"

Two or three seconds of silence passed, a long time when God and the Devil have been conjured up in the depths of a holy place and in the presence of confessed witches. The room was still and every head was turned to the old belly-gunner whose eyes were cast briefly upward toward the florescent lights and to Heaven beyond.

"Now, I won't claim to have seen the Devil, but I wouldn't be surprised if I have—if we all have. We may see him every day. Just another fella walking by on Main Street. You kinda know him but can't quite place him. He doesn't truly show his face in the Bible till Second Chronicles, although many believe that the serpent in the garden is really the Devil in one of his umpteen forms. But what is he really up to?"

He paused and looked toward Reverend McClean. "It'd be bad manners to carry on preaching in another man's church, so, with your permission, Preacher, I'll just get right to the point."

McLean nodded uncertainly and Preacher Simms stepped forward, turned and faced the room. "Jesus chose twelve apostles, but the Devil found weakness in Judas. That was, is, his mission. You can think of it like this. He's working undercover in the Celestial Secret Service. God chucks him down from Heaven and condemns and reviles him and that establishes his cover. God even sent the Devil to test Jesus. Yes, he did! The temptations are reported in Matthew, Mark and Luke, but I'm partial to Luke's version. Jesus came back from Jordan full of the Holy Ghost and was led by the Spirit into the wilderness and there he was put to forty days of test. And who tested Jesus? It was the Devil who put young Jesus, back from his Jordanian galivant, through a kind of divine boot camp. In Luke 4:9-13 the Devil took Jesus to the roof of the temple and said unto him, 'If thou be the son of God, cast thyself down from hence. For it is written, He shall give his angels charge over thee, to keep thee, and in their hands they shall bear thee up, lest at any time thou dash thy foot against a stone.' Now that's how smart the old Devil is, or how obedient, trying to get the Son of God to test God's word by jumping off the roof and making God have to try to catch him. Jesus didn't jump, but not because he feared God wouldn't catch him, but because he knew darn well he would. To jump would be to doubt. So, we see the Devil is sent forth by the Master to put all mankind, even God's only boy, to the test. But our new neighbor here says there is no Devil. What do you folks think? Does the Devil exist or not?"

"Yes!" came the answer from the room. Some shouted and the loudest shouters were Norma Ketchell and the two mean-looking out-of-towners. Hearing folks shout to affirm Satan in the basement of The First Church of Christ was a new one on Buster and, he thought, from the look on Reverend McClean's face, it wasn't what he was expecting that evening either. Simms surely had a way about him once you got him started.

"Now since both God and Jesus speak of the Devil, there are only three ways it can go: If a man says he doesn't believe in the Devil, which is the same as calling the Son and the Father a pair of liars, then that man is merely ignorant, which is to be innocent of the truth," and he held up one finger. "Or," he said, standing still as a stump but holding up two fingers, "he just might be the Devil himself in one of his many forms come to town as a secret agent on a mission from God, sent to test our convictions. Or," he said now holding up a third finger, "he might just be who he says he is, somebody who leads a group of folks, good folks as far as I can see, who have chosen the wrong path and are as wrong about God as they are about the Devil, but who strive after the truth and may yet find their way. One way or the other, no matter what anybody tells you, both God and the Devil, whether he be demon or angel of the Lord, are always amongst us." And Preacher Simms, his piece said, sat.

Chancellor Austin couldn't find his voice at first, leaving Simms's words unrefuted in the basement of the church.

When he finally spoke, it was too late and too weakly. "Our only wish is to become part of your community, respectful of your beliefs and in support of religious freedom."

"And who is there here who supports you?" shouted one of the two outsiders, his face reddened from holy fury.

His companion didn't shout. He spoke slowly in the grave tone of judgement, "Thou shalt not suffer a witch to live." And, after a second, he pronounced, "Exodus 22:18."

Simms rose again, ignoring the words from Exodus and turning his pleasant smile to the cloaked and startled witch. "Forgive us, Chancellor Austin. We sometimes get carried away when discussing things most dear to us." And to Reverend McLean he said, "I believe there is usually a question-and-answer period now, but I'd offer that the questions we all have would best be answered by the Lord Himself in the solitude of prayer. Reverend McClean, could you kindly lead us in a closing prayer so that our hearts may be untroubled even after such troubling talk?"

McLean didn't hesitate. He stepped forward. "Let all who can stand, stand and pray," he said, and then he spoke very quickly, head bowed, eyes closed. "We thank you, Lord, for this opportunity to come together in our quest for understanding even of those who do not share our beliefs in the hope that these tests will strengthen our faith. Amen."

At amen, the two deacons, ramrod straight, opened the doors to the street and the chill night air was on the backs of the listeners. The Community Room emptied, the attendees jostling to get out of there. The few who talked, talked almost in whispers and the Whisperers didn't seem to be talking at all. Simms, accompanied by his wife, was one of the last to leave. After shaking hands with Reverend McClean and thanking him for his patience, he nodded, said, "Chief" and shook Buster's hand, a quick, firm shake and smile.

Buster stayed back with Reverend McClean, watching from the doorway as the two outsiders, the man who had shouted and the one who quoted Exodus, both middle-aged and rough-looking, stood on the curb very close to the black Olds Ninety-eight that Chancellor Austin and the other three witches were entering. Buster and Reverend McClean watched the witches drive away.

The outsiders climbed into a green Ford pickup and stopped for a few seconds at the corner of Main, perhaps considering, thought Buster, chasing after the witches. He relaxed a little when they turned east.

"I've never seen either one of those two jaspers in town before," said McLean. Buster hadn't either.

The Indiana farm truck plates, bright red, were easy to read under the streetlight: 1472 H. Buster memorized it as Ernie Banks, William Perry, Harvesters. There were no numbers that Buster couldn't see on the jersey of a Cub or a Bear.

Nightbirds were singing over the quiet street.

"Did you ever hear the like?" said Buster.

"That was a slick job the way he filibustered that Chancellor Austin right out of the hornet's nest he'd talked himself into."

"Those two Hoosiers sure perked up when he started in on the Devil."

"The Devil's never been put to better use in the cause of peace," said McLean. "You have to hand it to him, to Simms I mean. He knows his scriptures, chapter and verse. If I wasn't busy on Sunday mornings myself, I'd drop in on a few of his sermons."

"I did like that part about the Devil being an undercover agent for God," said Buster.

"I wouldn't put it past him," said McLean.

"The Devil?"

"Either one of them."

Buster smiled. "Did you see Reverend Burns sitting over by the window?"

"I sure did." said McLean. "He looked like he was enjoying himself. You know, I asked that man one time if he believed in God and you know what he said? He said, 'Well, we could sure use one.' Makes you wonder what the Universalists talk about over there in that church of theirs."

"Ha!" said Buster.

He walked back over the tracks that weren't there and down the dark street to the new Interceptor, shining under the street light. Busy day. He stopped by the station to drop off the Interceptor, check with Sally at the night desk and pick up his truck. Sally told him that Ronnie had left him a note. "You might be able to read it," she said. "I swear the art of penmanship is dying."

Buster read: *Harold Dresher came by but you'd already left for Damascus. I told him you weren't coming in this weekend. He said he'd come back by Monday. -Ronnie*

Buster had no trouble with Ronnie's mix of printing and cursive, and as soon as he saw Harold Dresher's name, he had a hunch. It was way too late to go by Harold's place, but he wasn't waiting till Monday. It might be nothing, might be Harold reporting on kids throwing rocks on his roof or dog packs running the alley, but he had a hunch. First things first. He'd drop by Harold's Saturday morning and then he'd watch Illinois-Northwestern in the afternoon and the Cubs in their last-chance game against the Braves that evening, and if Ellen said anything about going to church on Sunday, he'd say he'd had enough church for a month of Sundays.

Chapter 20

Walking the Tracks

Keelan thought the Twilight Zone Murderer looked pretty good in the headlines. Newspapers loved murderers, especially if they had killer names like Cannibal Cole. Now they were calling him the Twilight Zone Murderer, except they didn't know it was him. He was no Bobby Harkie, taking potshots at folks in their cars. Buster knew, but not even Buster could prove a damn thing. That wouldn't save him from harassment though. Nothing better to do than poke around in something that happened thirty-nine years ago to the day instead of doing his damn job and looking into whatever those druggies were up to on Swisher Avenue. Dandy said they were drug dealers, and from the looks of the place—grass uncut, loose siding, blinds pulled at noon—he was probably right.

To Keelan's way of thinking, there ought to be some kind of statute of limitations on murders committed by youngsters. Now they were saying the old boy who got himself convicted for killing the Wyatts was trying to renege on his crazy confession.

He had listened to the jailhouse lawyers talk in the bleachers out in the white man's section of the yard, bragging about how smart they were. So smart they were in prison with him. In each of his convictions he only had contact with public defenders, never with real lawyers, but you can't go to public defenders until they already have you dead to rights. He couldn't see walking into a lawyer's office and asking him… asking him what? You couldn't trust nobody. They were all in it together, police and lawyers and judges. Thick as thieves.

Keelan wished he had somebody smart to talk to because seeing Harold Dresher's green Chevy parked out front of the police station the same day the Twilight Zone Murderer story came out was a bad sign. That is, if it really was Dresher's car. He only managed to remember the first three numbers, but that'd be enough if he could get another look at it. He decided he'd take a stroll past the old man's place in the morning to take a look at the plate to make sure of what he was already sure of.

He was just going in circles, sitting on the davenport where he'd been sitting since he came home from the widow Kline's. The Twilight Zone Murderer could yet be among us, they said. Maybe he just ought to just fire up that truck and get the hell out, but where to? He was too old to go through all that again. When he first headed out for the West, he was young enough to do whatever he had to, and he wasn't so bad looking either. The ladies will help or at least comfort a man that they can stand to look at. Now he was past it and his face would stop a clock unless he worked around to smiling and that was hard to do. He needed a barroom mirror for that, a mirror and a glass of whisky. There's times when a man has to talk to somebody that ought to give a damn, but there was only one person he could talk to besides Betty.

"Well," he said aloud, looking at Betty's jug, "am I going over there, or should I just go out and howl at the moon?"

Betty was too dead to answer so he had to answer for her. "Go see your mom," she said in his voice. Glad I didn't chuck her in the lake, he thought. Otherwise, I'd be a crazy man talking to myself instead of a crazy man talking to a pot of dirt.

Now he knew what he was going to do, at least the first thing. He put on a clean shirt and the 777 Harold's Club jacket that he got as a prize for being the seven hundred and seventy-seventh person to come in the front door of the casino on the 4th of July, 1993. He was just two months out of prison and on parole back then. It had an American flag and the date on the pocket and, below, the words "Your Lucky Day!" Hardly ever wore it. He wasn't superstitious but he didn't want to use up his luck. They also gave him seven hundred and seventy-seven dollars in chips. He had a good time that night, got his picture in the Reno paper and, best of all, he met Betty. She thought he was a big spender and he was too, until he lost the seven hundred and seventy-seven and another hundred or so of his own, but that started him running around with her. She was nuts and a few years older than he was, but a good-looking woman for her age. She was the prize he won at Harold's Club that night, the jackpot.

He never really expected her to still be there when he woke up. He asked her straight out what she saw in him now that he'd blown all his lucky money. She said she was done with pretty men and done with smart ones too. A few weeks later, after he told her he'd been divorced for desertion while he was in prison, she organized a wedding in Virginia City and invited all her friends from work. As weddings go, she said, it was her best one so far. She had been married three times before.

When he went to collect her ashes, they were waiting for him with the bill. The whole thing, permit and fire and urn and all, cost him over four hundred dollars and an extra twenty for the special blue ceramic jug—a scattering urn they called it— and ten extra for one with a yellow butterfly over her name. Betty Putnam 1936—1998. It was her money anyway and she'd have liked the butterfly.

His mom must have seen him coming up Iroquois in the fading twilight because when he got to the house he saw the door was open and she was standing just back far enough to be out of the light.

"Mom?" he said, and she turned her back and walked into the kitchen. He followed.

"You want a cup of coffee?" she said.

"I'll have one if you will."

She turned to the stove and he sat down at the kitchen table. The backyard still looked wrong without the alley fence, nothing to keep the redskins out.

She put the cups on the table and pushed the sugar bowl toward him. He lumped in three spoonfuls. "I see that ain't changed," she said. "Doc Kline made me give it up before he died and I just never started up again."

She was talking to him. Not smiling but not frowning either. First civil words to come out of her mouth to him since that day. They sat across from one another at the same old kitchen table.

"You see the paper?" he said.

She nodded.

"So, what should I be worried about?"

"In this life or the next, if there is such a thing?"

"It's the here and now that I care about. What if they had some way of proving I was out there that night?" He said it plain and she didn't blink.

"Save your worrying till you got something to worry about."

"Walking home this noon, I'm pretty sure I saw old Dresher's car parked out front of the police station. Unless Murdock gave him a ticket for driving too slow, I can only think of one reason that old man would be visiting Buster on the same day as the piece in the paper. I don't know what to do."

She was looking into her coffee cup, waggling her spoon. "You don't need me to tell you what to do." She knew what she'd said as soon as she said it, but it was already said and all there was to say.

He thought maybe she'd say something more, but she was just looking at him, waiting for something it seemed, and before he knew it, he was the one doing the talking. Talking and talking and his mom listening and looking into his eyes till there was nothing left in him to say. The light in the windows had faded. He must have talked a half-hour straight. He started to look down, but his mom put her hand to his cheek. He remembered that touch. My poor dishwater hands, she used to say, but the fingertips were always soft. For a while longer they sat listening to the ticking of the kitchen clock. "You better be going, Keelan," she said. It was the first time she had said his name since that night.

Hearing his name coming from her made him want to do as he was told—to get going before something changed. Talking can change things and he'd always talked too much and said the wrong things. He didn't say a word and he was already on his feet and headed for the door, doing as he was told. He walked out past his dad leaning forward in his big chair watching *Gunsmoke*. If he looked, he could have seen them all, seen himself too, all watching TV and his dad cracking jokes now and then. He might even have seen Jezzie smile at him if he could've have looked back far enough. Back to before.

He wondered if his mom was still sitting at the kitchen table as he stepped down off the stoop. Maybe she had gotten up and walked to the door to watch him go, but he didn't look back to see. It had gotten dark. On evenings like this he used to help his dad fiddle with the Chevy in the garage until his mom called them in for supper, and then, if there was something good on, they'd all watch it together, especially on cowboy night.

Before he'd taken two steps, the porch light came on behind him and Keelan felt like he was a little kid going out to play after dark. Nightbirds were squawking in the trees like he always remembered. His mom used to tell him and Jezzie what they were saying.

▪▪▪

Etna stood watching him walk out of the light in his nice red and white jacket. He never had nice things as a boy. Some folks get born into nice things, nice houses, clothes, cars, but she never coveted what others had, not even as a little girl. Why was it that she could be happy with what she had, and Spite couldn't never act right no matter what? And why did her pa have to kill Ukiah Corrothers and the others they said he killed? And why did Keelan do what he did? She and Vernon would have done their part for Keelan and Mae and their little baby. Why did the Tucker men always have to go and spoil every damn thing? Old Mr. Owl says Who? but only people say Why? Aunt Unity said that.

She stood at the front window watching him walking in that red and white jacket, a little scooched down like he always walked, like he didn't want notice taken of him. He stopped at the curb to look both ways just like he was taught for crossing Iroquois. And now he was living over by the tracks on First Street, three blocks from home and lost forever.

"You don't need me to tell you what to do," she said. She didn't know if she'd said the right thing or the wrong thing, but she'd told him the truth. It was all up to him. She hoped he might pick up and run, get in that yellow truck of his and drive to where old Harold Dresher's memories couldn't touch him, but she saw in his eyes that he wouldn't run. He had no place left to go.

Was killing always evil? From all she could remember of her pa, he was not an evil man. He was fighting and being fought, and he went to the electric chair not for being evil, but for getting caught. Ukiah Corrothers, from what Aunt Unity told her, would have killed her pa first if he'd thought of it in time.

Her boy was ornery, mean and foolish, but watching him walking away on Iroquois, there was no way she'd ever call him evil in spite of all he'd done. And whatever was going to happen to him in Yonders must be better than what he was running from. One part of her wished he'd never come back, but the other part wanted to go after him and bring him home.

▪▪▪

It was just four months back at the start of summer when she was weeding in the garden and heard the phone ring in the kitchen. "Mom," Jezzie said, "I just seen Keelan." Etna didn't ask if she was sure. "He was walking by out on the Dixie carrying a suitcase. He looked right at me. He was way out there by the road but I seen his eyes as if he was standing right in front of me."

"How long ago?" said Etna.

"Just now, Mom."

"Well, you go on about your business. I'll tend to him when he gets here."

Etna knew it'd take him the better part of half an hour unless somebody gave him a ride, but nobody would know him. That gave her time to think.

Poor Jezzie figured she knew the worst of him, thought Etna, but she didn't have the slightest notion of the whole of it. Jezzie only knew what happened ages ago when Keelan came home and found her alone. Etna asked her what happened, but she was never sure what to believe. It was Jezzie's to say what happened and hers to believe her daughter whether she did or not. And best to leave it however Jezzie said.

"I run him off with this," Jezzie said that night. The knife had no blood on the blade. She was thirteen and he was fifteen. Jezzie, eyes red and clenching her teeth, buttons torn off her cowgirl shirt, said, "I hate him! I would have killed him."

Etna hugged her and hushed her and said "You think I wasn't raised in the same house with two big strapping boy cousins? That's why I gave it to you. Not for red Indians jumping over the back fence and climbing in your window. Now dry your eyes and get to bed. It won't never happen again. That or nothing like it."

Etna told Vernon it was nothing, just kids mad at each other, and he went off to bed, but she stayed up in the dark living room waiting for Keelan. He came sneaking up the grass beside the drive so as not to crunch the gravel, headed for the back door. He stepped into the dark kitchen and closed the door behind him just as the light came on. He turned to see his mom standing in the corner by the sink.

"If you ever misbehave like that again with your sister, son or no son, I'll put you out and you'll never set foot in this house again."

He started to speak and she said, "And don't you say nary a word. Get up to bed or out the door, one or the other!" He looked down and went up the stairs.

Jezzie didn't come down for breakfast and she stayed home from school that morning, but when they had the house to just the two of them, Vernon off to work and Keelan at school, Etna took her up some breakfast and told her about the time she faced the same. She had no parents to turn to, but she had sister Spite, barely twelve. Spite was big for her age, old for her age too, and she took a chair to stand on and got Uncle Amos' shotgun down from the top of the hall closet and went right into Homer's room with it. Pointed that double barrel right at where it needed pointing and said, whispered, because Amos and Unity were down in the kitchen, "I got a barrel for each one of your puny red balls, Homer Tucker." And then told him just how deep in pig shit his ugly head should be stuck.

Homer must have known Spite could just as easily have pulled the triggers as not, one after the other, and he must have said something to Floyd too because the Tucker boys changed their ways like all men do when they imagine a double-barreled shotgun a half a foot away from their crotch and pointing south.

Jezzie laughed a little when Etna told her all that, laughed just enough for Etna to know that her girl was alright. Jezzie spent the rest of the morning organizing her room, helping in the kitchen and she decided to go to school in the afternoon. Etna wrote her an excuse and watched her walk off to school, almost as if nothing had happened. Almost.

After the day Homer Tucker laid hands on her and Spite stood up for her, Etna took things into her own hands. She took her birthday money and bought a big kitchen knife at the White Elephant store and strapped it up under her bed where she thought her aunt Unity would never find it. But she did. Etna knew she did because it was strapped back wrong. Spite slept in the other bed in the girls' room and when Etna showed her the knife, Spite took it, held it up to the light and swiped it though the air like a pirate in a movie and gave it back and said, "That'd do, but I'll stick with my hatchet."

So long ago. Etna smiled and shook her head. Time had a funny way, she thought, of making things bearable and almost funny if you live long enough, but there'd never be enough living time to turn up the funny side of her boy murdering a whole family, especially a good woman and that poor, simple girl. And now there was no way out of it and nothing she could do to stop whatever was coming without bringing more harm to her boy.

▪▪▪

The streetlights had come on and night had set in when Keelan turned up First Street. Every house on the block except his had lights in the windows and most had the porchlights on, waiting for whoever was coming home from work or shopping or playing.

Not a soul to be seen, but as he started up the walk to his door, he saw a figure pass under the corner streetlight a half block away and he knew him. It was the dream man from the bus out Cheyenne way. Call him by his name, Keelan. It was the Devil, if there could ever be such a thing.

And that is why a man has to be careful where his mind goes when he's living alone. That was no more the Devil than the man in the goddamn moon. All that foolishness was just a rolling Greyhound dream anyhow. Keelan knew a man could lock the door of his house but he couldn't lock anybody or anything, Rachel or the Devil, out of his damn dreams. After a supper of hamburger and boiled potatoes, two beers and the bottom inch and a half of a bottle of Old Crow, Keelan went right off to sleep and, sure enough, the Devil was waiting for him in the corn. He couldn't see him at first, but he knew he was out there.

Keelan was walking along the Nickel Plate tracks out east of town. It was summer but he couldn't tell if he was a grown man or a little boy until the Devil, looking spiffy with that little mustache and wearing shiny, black, going-to-town shoes, came out of the field and up the banking to join him. Then he knew he was a grown man because he was looking the Devil in the eye. In fact, he was just a hair taller than the Devil.

"You're the man from the bus," he said.

"And so are you," the Devil said.

They walked the ties, but the ties were spaced wrong. The old hobos used to say the railroad spaced them that way just so they'd be a misery to walk.

"I know what you're thinking," said the Devil.

"It ought to be done with after all these years," said Keelan, adjusting his stride to the ties with a hippity-hop that made him feel he was about ten.

Now the Devil was prancing atop the rail, his arms extended to the sides like a tightrope walker. Keelan stepped up onto the opposite rail, spread his arms like wings, and matched the Devil's every step.

"Old Harold's got his memory back. He's remembering what the graveyard gate knocked out of him," said the Devil, going faster and now skipping along the rail like the schoolgirl across a meadow in a book Keelan's mom used to read before bedtime, sitting on the davenport between Jezzie and him.

"You can't rest until the reckoning," said the skipping Devil.

"I was resting just fine until you come along," said Keelan, dropping a bit behind.

The Devil stopped and turned and said, as he began to vanish, "What was its name?"

Black crows in a blue, blue sky, soft wind over the fields on a hot summer day that wasn't then or now or anytime and Keelan was all alone, standing out east of Yonders under a remembered sky so blue that it made him a little boy playing hooky again, and he was carrying his dad's rifle. His dad didn't know he had it. Would've whipped him if he had.

He heard a tingling and a clicking in the tracks and knelt down to put his ear to the hot rail. She was coming hard out of the east. He stood and looked out toward Indiana and saw the black speck jiggly in the heat waves at the horizon where the rails joined and, just a little later, he heard her crying out for the gravel pit road crossing…long, long, short, long.

When he was a little boy he once stood between the rails as long as he dared, until the black locomotive, billowing black smoke and snorting steam, was looming down so close that he could see the engineer leaning out the cab hanging on the whistle cord, and he leapt away, just in time, feeling the wind and the heat, hearing the wail, the giant drive wheels and flying rods only feet away. But this time his dream held him tight to where he stood, his feet locked to a tie, that black, towering engine rocking on the line, the cowcatcher coming for him a mile a minute, and the whistle broke into a scream.

Out back of Keelan's house a fast, southbound freight thundered past in the night, rattling the windows, whistling for the Main Street crossing—long, long, short, long—and he sat up in bed, tears in his eyes for the first time since he shot that poor, little tan dog, shot him for no earthly reason. Its name was Shadow.

Chapter 21

Black-eyed Susans

Saturday dawned sunny. There was nothing open that early except the graveyard and it was way too early to go knocking on Harold Dresher's door. He was probably up, but you don't go bothering folks before eight or eight-thirty unless it's to arrest them. After coffee and toast, Buster drove the truck out to Floral Hill, as good a place as any to start a day. The sign on the gate said "Closed Sundown to Sunrise," but they quit closing the gate at night because people, kids mostly, kept overshooting the turn onto Double Aught and running into it every few years. It cost more to fix the gate than repair or replace the tombstones they broke or knocked over.

When Harold Dresher had his crash the night of the Wyatt murders, he was running about forty. Any faster, Chief Warry said, and he'd have ripped the gate out of its moorings. Most of the time the collision just warped the gate so that it had to be taken down and repaired. When Harold clobbered it, he knocked himself into a twelve-hour coma.

Buster slowed to a creep as he drove by the Dresher plot. Harold Dresher was eighty-two according to the year of birth engraved on his stone. That meant he was forty-three the night of the murders.

Buster got out of the truck and stood on the moist grass in front of his folks' graves. Some people prayed at their parents' graves. Ellen did, but Buster, if there was nobody around, just talked as he would have done if his folks had only been out of town for a while.

"We're all doing pretty good these days. The kids too. Thomas is still working over in Indianapolis. He and Lucy are just fine and their boys are both going to Indiana University. Mary and her family are still living off in New Mexico. Ellen is still teaching. I can't get her to quit, and I'm still chief for a bit yet." He was quiet then. It can't hurt to talk, he thought, even if you're talking to memories in the wind.

As he often did, he walked west from the Lawton plot up the little slope that gave Floral Hill its name. The big stone said WYATT and to the left and below Earl F. To the right Esther Lee, and to Esther's right a smaller stone of lighter color with a reclining lamb carved above the words Rachel Wyatt. It must have been relatives from out of town or friends who arranged all that. All three with their year of birth and the same year of death, 1959. Buster knew the day. Yesterday. October 2. There were no flowers. The Wyatts had no relatives left living close enough to visit. The three Wyatt graves looked down on the tracks running into town and along the cornfield that covered the two acres where the Wyatt farmhouse, barn, out buildings and lawns had once been. There was not a trace left. The cornfield took it all back after the house burned. Folks said it was arson but more likely it was some hobo's cigarette. There were still a few hobos riding the boxcars back in the early sixties when the old place sat derelict. Nobody wanted to buy or rent the murder house. It sat empty four or five years before the fire. Some folks said it was haunted and that poor Rachel used to run the ragged weeds along the railroad bank waving at the trains. Hector Kelly, stopped at the crossing one night, swore he saw her in the moonlight, but there were reasons to doubt anything Hector swore so soon after closing time. After the farmhouse burned, some said she took to running the tracks. For a while in the sixties, high school kids dressed up like Running Rachel at the Halloween parties and from time to time over the years after the murders, somebody, usually some old northsider, claimed to see Rachel running the tracks out by the graveyard. That all petered out during the seventies, but now Buster was hearing talk again of Running Rachel, just in time for Keelan's homecoming.

He walked back down the green slope passing gravestones. There was hardly a last name that he didn't know and there were graves that made Buster remember, almost hear, old voices. Some of the stones were so old there were none left to remember anything at all about the folks buried beneath them. That's when you're really dead, thought Buster. And there were the empty plots with stones set for people who weren't dead yet or even close to it. Some people had stones set in their family plots but went off and died far away and were buried there with their tombstones left standing at Floral Hill over empty ground. Served as reminders, Buster thought.

His dad had reserved space for him and Ellen, but Buster hadn't gotten around to putting up a stone and Ellen wouldn't even talk about it. She visited her folks' graves a few times a year but she told Buster she thought it was creepy to see your own grave unless you were in it and that graveyards were not parks, but Buster, when he was on his own, just found himself wandering out there every few weeks.

The black-eyed Susans were still in bloom, grown now beyond their beds and taken root around the stones that marked his parents' graves. They had ranged to spread their gold over the whole plot and beyond. His mom would love that. She grew up on a farm in Iowa near a little forest with a brook, and she told Buster how she ran free as the wind as a child. She loved wild flowers more than garden flowers and never kept a potted plant.

When she died, just three years before his dad, Buster set out a little bed of Susans, but the graveyard troll, as they called him, Harry Flint, a man who had problems with the bottle, tried to tell Buster that there were new rules about planting what he called nuisance flowers, and Buster told him two things: that he would take it upon himself to avoid spread and, second, that Illinois law said if a law officer had reason to believe that a driver might be over the limit on the basis of past infractions, the officer could stop that driver without any other cause and test him. And that was mostly true, at least in his town.

Harry never mentioned the flowers again, but they did get away just as he said they would. They could be found from the Scooter Keen Memorial all the way to the founder's crypt at the top of Floral Hill. Harry fought them as best he could, weeding them out, trying to dig out their roots, but he let them riot around the Lawton plot.

Whenever Buster saw the black-eyed Susans, he thought of his mom as a little girl running wild in her woods. He'd never been to Iowa and he wasn't sure where her farm was or how long her family farmed there or why they left. He wished he had asked more.

As he drove away, he looked back at the big LAWTON stone and at the patch of shady grass alongside waiting for him and Ellen.

He still had time to burn, so he headed back home and, on the way, went past Keelan's house. The streets were still wet and puddled from the rain the day before. Too bad about not being able to drive that truck, but Murdock was right to charge him. And if that's the worst he's charged with, he'll have no complaints.

Houses start looking like the people who live in them. Keelan's little house used to have kids playing in the yard and a dog sleeping on the walk; now it looked like it was looking back, hateful and resentful, dangerous even, sitting there with peeling paint in the shadows of a tall oak, older than any man or woman in town.

He drove back onto Iroquois, past Etna Putnam's house, lonely but proud, and turned east on Swisher. He wouldn't drive past the druggie's house, but from the corner where he turned off Swisher he saw O's black Ram 4x4 with Texas plates backed into the drive, facing the street, wheels cut toward the west, ready to make a run for it.

Buster never locked the house during the daytime. He couldn't imagine anybody trying to rob the home of the chief of police. Ellen always locked up but left the key under the mat. She wouldn't get home until after six, after the Illinois game. He brewed a fresh pot of coffee and fried some eggs and bacon. He could watch Mr. Potato Head on TV or a black-and-white movie with old dead actors talking in barky voices or a stupid quiz show with everybody smiling way too much even when they lost. It was either music or the president on the radio, so he turned it all off and read Friday's paper again. The Twilight Zone Murderer, huh? He remembered the program. Off the air for years now. He watched that show a few times with his dad. His dad kind of liked it, especially that one about the gremlin on the wing of the airplane. His mom hated it. Whenever that tinkling music came on, it was her time to do the dishes. If it was still on today they could probably make a program about Keelan living over there alone with Rachel's ghost running the tracks behind his house. That would be a good one.

At a quarter to nine Buster drove the two blocks to Harold's place, going the long way around to avoid driving past the drug house. A year before, Buster got a warrant and just the three of them—he, Murdock and Whitehead—drove out in two cars to arrest two out-of-town couples from up north renting out on West Waylon by the Dixie and cooking meth and selling down in Damascus and even to a couple of Yonders kids. Strictly a Yonders matter. Now they had the DEA, the County and the Drug Enforcement Task Force from over in Mattoon putting together—any day now, they'd been saying for weeks—what they called a strike force with agents in battle gear who would spring out of an armored Humvee throwing stun grenades and raising hell next door to Mr. and Mrs. Vigas, across the street from the Herman place. McIntyre said this was just the beginning of it. He said there was no limit to it that he could see. All we can do, McIntyre said, was peck at it to slow it down. If it was a war, like old Tricky Dick said, then we were losing it. Things would never be the same in Damascus, the sheriff said, and Yonders was next on the list.

Harold was old Yonders, one of the boys who fought in World War II. Ed next door, with his cameras in the trees, was Korean War. Clive Barber was Vietnam and Buster's own boy was Desert Storm. They'd have one for his grandsons too.

It took Harold a moment to recognize him. "Chief Lawton," said Harold. "I didn't know you at first without your uniform. Come right on in. The place is a mess, but I've got some coffee on."

The house was ship shape. The only thing out of place was the *Chicago Tribune* open to the editorial page on the coffee table in front of Harold's big chair. Harold's idea of a mess.

"I'm all coffeed out but I will sit a minute if you can spare the time," said Buster.

"I was up to see you yesterday but they told me you were at a meeting in Damascus."

"That's why I came by. To hear what was on your mind."

Once Buster was sitting, Harold settled into his big chair. "Welp," he said, "the reason I was up to see you was that article in the Damascus paper the other day about the old murders. You and Chief Warry, rest his soul, came by to see me down at the hospital after my accident back then and asked me what I remembered about that car I nearly ran into. I had only the foggiest recollections of that night and I was unable to help you."

"We suspected that the murderer was driving that car," said Buster.

"It's peculiar how a man will remember something. The other week I forgot the name of the Democrat that wore a coonskin cap and rode around in a dogsled. How could you forget that? He was the one who got after those gangsters on television, if you had a television back then."

Buster waited. He'd get there.

"Estes Kefauver. I never knew a man with either one of those names. I determined to remember it without asking anybody and one day I was making a pot of coffee and it came to me. Now, the way I remembered about that car was a little different." Harold hesitated, and then went on. "It came to me a couple of months back one night in July while I was out walking after dark like I do. I didn't figure it meant anything after all these years and with those terrible murders solved, but then I saw that piece in yesterday's paper and I thought maybe I better tell you. That car that jumped out at me that night was a 1949 or maybe a 1950 Ford. I'd swear to it on a stack of Bibles."

"A '49 or' 50, not a '51 or '52?"

"Your '49 and your '50 had the bullet-in-the-center grill, but the later model, you'll recall, had double bullets, one off to each side."

"Could it have been a '49 Mercury, do you think? A Merc of that ilk could look like a Ford in the night."

"I know what you mean. The Mercury did have the same split front window and a kind of toothy grill, but it wasn't anything like the Ford bullet," said Harold. "Besides the Mercury was fatter."

"And this car, this Ford, where was it coming from?"

"Coming off Double Aught with its lights off, from the very direction of the Wyatt place and, if the truth be told, it was more my fault than the other fellow's. My car was brand-new and it had a dang rattle. I was leaning way over onto the other side of the front seat fiddling around trying to find a rattle behind the glove compartment, and I'd drifted out to the middle of the road. I might not even have seen him if he hadn't put on his lights when he did."

"And what could you tell me about the man driving that Ford?"

"I just saw there was somebody at the wheel. A man, hunched down."

"Was he a white man?"

"You mean was he a colored man? No, I could see in my lights he was a white man. If he'd been a colored man that would have been the first thing I would have noticed. The car was black though, I do believe."

"Is there anything else you can tell me?"

"That's about it," said Harold.

There it was, just about all Buster needed to know and none of it worth a hill of beans in a courtroom, not after all these years and especially considering Harold was in a coma after the crash, but it settled any reasonable common sense doubt. Buster could picture that black Ford of Keelan Putnam's swinging onto Main Street off Iroquois one day a long time ago. He'd found out what he came to find out, but it wouldn't be polite to just get up and leave, so Buster stayed to visit a bit. "You gonna watch the Cubs this evening?"

"Yes, I believe I will watch them. I imagine it'll be our last chance to see them this year. You think we stand a chance?"

"Oh, hell yes!" said Buster. "I think we'll win three in a row and go on to win the World Series!"

"That's a good one," said Harold.

Harold was still smiling about that when Buster left, as if the Cubs would ever win anything, but he wondered what would come of what he'd told Buster. Probably nothing, after all these years, but you never know. And then he said aloud, "Just as well I neglected to mention who it was that jogged my memory." That made him smile.

▪▪▪

Keelan didn't like getting his feet wet but there was still standing water along the street after the rain on Friday. No problem if you were driving, but Keelan, thanks to Buster, was walking, and thanks to the rich folks who laid out the town there were no sidewalks north of Swisher Avenue except along Iroquois street. They ran sidewalks all the way out Iroquois to the north end of town just in case some rich man ever took a notion to walk out that way to look at the poor folks close up.

He didn't want to walk all the way to the 600 block of Swisher, but he had to make sure that the Chevy he saw parked at the police station the day before was Harold's. He had the license memorized except for the last three numbers, but if the first three numbers matched, that'd be good enough.

People sitting out in their porch swings just had to wave and say hi, hello, howdy, morning, good morning, nice morning, and he had to answer each one back because if he didn't they'd remember him. His doubt was whether to walk by on Harold's side of the street or on the other side. He decided on Harold's side so he could get a look at the door. He could pick any lock they threw at him. Screen doors were easy as pie. Storm doors were a little harder, but the storm doors wouldn't be up yet.

He was thinking about doors and locks, debating back-door break-in against front door break-in when he saw it. There was Buster Lawton's damn truck sitting out front of Harold's house on a Saturday morning. No need now to even check that license plate. Keelan was still a block and a bit away. He didn't want Buster seeing him where he had no business being but he couldn't just turn around on the spot. If he retraced his tracks, he'd have to be nodding and waving to every man and his wife who'd be saying Back already?

You forget something? They'd stick their noses in and testify that he was out stalking the murdered man's neighborhood, so he turned north on Fifth right past that house of drug dealers, according to Dandy, and he had to walk out in the road because there was no sidewalk.

Keelan didn't ask himself what those two could be talking about two days in a row because he knew after what he read in the paper. Now that the crazy old boy down in Graham Correctional had figured out who he killed and who he hadn't, old Dresher, who nearly killed him with his crazy driving that night, steering his big Chevy from the wrong side of the front seat, would be saying what make of car he nearly ran off the road and that, Keelan knew, would settle it even more for Buster. He remembered thanking his lucky stars that old Harold had his memory knocked out of him but, he read somewhere, people can get their memories back. That had to be why Harold and Buster were chummy all of a sudden.

So, was this what he came all the way back to Yonders for? Buying a truck, a yellow one that nobody else would buy, renting a house, contributing to the local economy, helping old ladies not get overrun by their gardens or having their gutters overflow or their birds having nowhere to take their baths? He should have stayed in Nevada, but if he had Twitchy Harkie would probably have already killed him by now. If it wasn't one thing it was another.

By the time he got home, walking in the street like a horse all the way from where he turned off Swisher, he was already starting to plan how to do it. Sure, he'd be the first one Buster would suspect, but this time he'd remember to wear gloves. Smartest thing he ever did was buy that Colt with the threaded barrel and silencer—"suppressor" the Reno gunshop clerk called it. Betty's money well spent.

He wished he could have had a better look at the house and he still could if he had his truck, but if he went walking past all those howdy-doodee front porches again, they'd identify him sure as hell and that's all Buster would need to have an excuse to start in on him. Once they figured out a way to haul you in for questioning, they had you. The important thing was not to attract attention.

He saw a TV program once about a man who made some deal with a genie or some such thing and got three wishes and the dumb fool frittered them all away and ended up dead with nothing to show for it. If he had a chance like that, Keelan thought, he'd be ready. He'd ask to be invisible any time he wanted, to live forever and to always be happy. That'd fix things. The dumbass in the movie wasted one of his wishes on being rich and another one on getting somebody to love him and something just as useless for the third one. If a man could make himself invisible, never died and was always happy, what difference would anything else make? If he had an extra wish, he thought, he'd use the fourth one for getting Betty back, and it surprised him that he thought that. He must be going soft in his old age.

Well, that was a useless bunch of shit to be thinking, but the next thing to invisible was staying out of sight. He could walk past Harold's at night, real late, and probably nobody would see him, but if they did that would be worse. That's the trouble with small towns. Even if you don't remember where you were, somebody else will.

One thing he didn't like was all those streetlights between his house and Harold's. Sure as shootin' there'd be somebody with nothing better to do than watch the night streets. He'd need to study this all out, but he was feeling better now that he knew what was what. "There's no turning back now," he said out loud, but he wasn't just talking to himself. He sort of wished he did have an extra fourth wish to get Betty back out of her little jug.

Chapter 22

UNAVENGED

Ellen left for school early as she always did on Mondays, but Buster took his time, had a third cup of coffee as he watched the sports news on WGN, listening to the analysis of the big games played over the weekend. LSU upset Georgia on Saturday. Buster watched that one on ESPN. It was a good game, but he didn't care who won. WGN didn't have a lot to say about the Cubs game on Saturday. They fell apart in the eighth. On Sunday the Bears finally won one the hard way, scoring three touchdowns in the fourth quarter at home to beat Detroit. But during all those games, even during the Bears' big fourth-quarter surge and the Cubs' eighth-inning collapse, Buster kept seeing, just behind the tackles and base hits, Keelan's black, bullet-grilled Ford barreling off the dirt of Double Aught and onto Iroquois, running Harold Dresher's brand-new Chevy off the road and into the graveyard gate. That picture was still at the back of his mind on Monday morning, like a spider in the dark corner of a web.

Buster parked his truck in the chief's slot and entered the station. He started to say good morning on the way past the front desk but Ronnie made two urgent gestures from behind the bullet-resistant glass, one hand up, steadily patting the air, palm toward Buster and the forefinger of the other hand placed to his lips. He turned and wheeled himself beyond view, reappearing in the hall doorway.

"I don't know if I did right," Ronnie said, talking low, "but I let the witch lady in your office. She wouldn't say what it was about. She's in there."

"What did you do that for?"

Ronnie was stopped, stumped. "I don't know. It just seemed like the right thing to do her being…" and he hesitated.

Her being a witch, thought Buster, but Ronnie finished, "…her being a lady, and there's no proper place to have her wait except the hard bench in the hall. She got here five minutes ago."

Buster thought about knocking on his own office door as doctors do after they have left a patient sitting up shirtless on an exam table for ten minutes, but he just rattled the knob a bit and stepped in. At his entrance, she stood and faced him.

"Mrs. Lahae. Sorry I kept you waiting."

She was dressed as she had been at the Neighborhood Watch meeting on Friday, a black dress and black shoes, but now he noticed a necklace with a silver, five-pointed star set in a circle with yellow crescent moons on both sides. The hooded, black cape hung from a hook by the door. He'd seen her sitting at the meeting, but he hadn't paid attention to her when everyone stood to leave. It felt backwards to walk into his own office and have a seated woman stand to greet him. She smiled, her eyes steady. He always looked for a criminal but he didn't see a criminal behind her eyes. What did he see?

"Have a seat, Mrs. Lahae. What can I do for you?"

Rose Lahae looked Buster in the eye. "Our ways must seem strange to you after some of the things Chancellor Austin said at the meeting. But I'm not here as a Whisperer. I seem to know something that concerns you. Some call it second sight. Sometimes I just seem to know things."

Buster almost said, Well, what do you know? but he said nothing and went behind his desk and gestured for Rose to sit. When both were seated, she went on. "In Oak Park, especially at the fringes, there was always some threat in the air, but I never expected it here. Yet, since we arrived here I've felt some danger..."

Buster raised his hand and Rose stopped talking to listen. "Those two men who made a commotion at the meeting are not from here, but we're keeping an eye out for them."

"No, not those two," she said, with a gesture as if flicking away a fly. "Listen, this may mean something to you now or later. After the meeting on Friday night, I found myself thinking about the unavenged murders in the paper. When I visited your cemetery this summer, I noticed the graves where those murdered people are buried. Something came to me as I stood by those graves. The daughter buried there was not like others, was she?"

"She was what they used to call feeble-minded. Now we say retarded, I guess."

"I was thinking of her at her graveside and suddenly I had a vision of a man looking up into the night with frozen eyes and there was someone bending over him. It was you."

Her voice was very soft, firm enough but soft, and the word she had used before was unavenged, not unsolved. He didn't see a criminal and he didn't see a crazy woman either. Chancellor Austin said she was a witch, but the more he looked at her, the less strange she seemed in spite of the get up and in spite of what he was hearing her say. She looked less different, almost familiar, like she could have been from town. But when she said "It was you," there was a look in her eyes that made him feel she was seeing beyond him.

He started to say I'll keep that in mind, but what would he keep in mind? Behind him a hundred years of police chiefs looked on.

After a moment, she said, "This is a good place for my son and I. The others haven't found their places yet. I hope they do. But, I'm taking up your time. You have things to do."

She stood and so did he. After she left Buster realized neither of them had said goodbye. He stood looking at the door she closed behind her. She was right about one thing. He did have things to do. He was expecting a call from the sheriff about the raid, but he decided not to wait. He needed to talk about something solid, so he called McIntyre.

"You must be getting psychic, Buster," said the sheriff. "I was just this minute getting ready to call to tell you Springfield confirmed a big shipment in the pipe, maybe five or six hundred pounds of Mexican pot hidden in the underbelly of a pickup. Could be next week or next month, but we're on it. They're setting up to sell to out-of-town dealers, opening trade routes out of small towns. That's their way lately."

"We'll be standing by," said Buster. "And by the way, did you find out anything about what's happening with that Lane thing?"

"I've looked it over with our prosecutors. Everything Lane says about the Crawford murder he could have read in the paper. Unless he offers some new information, I don't see much happening. As far as your end of it is concerned, I can't see anything at all ever happening unless you've got some breakthrough."

An eighty-two-year-old man suddenly remembers a black Ford in the night from thirty-nine years ago, exactly the kind of a car that Keelan drove back then. Buster knew how that would sound. "Nobody's confessing up here yet," he said.

"You can figure out why the Crawfords aren't pushing us to take Lane seriously. They still have a lot of clout down here and they still put stock in family reputations. They've already been onto the paper about it. The wife is still alive and her boy, Crawford's boy Ronald, is a big wheel down here in business and local politics. There's things they don't want dug up. They think all that stuff still matters."

"It does," said Buster. "Matters to them. So, what's your feeling about what Lane says about being coerced into confessing to our murders?"

"Wolfden thinks he's going to get him a Pulitzer Prize for his journalism, but I'm guessing the paper's gonna smack a lid on it. The prosecutor's office might take Lane at his word on killing Crawford. That would get an old, cold-case murder off the books, but they'll drag it out so long nobody will pay any attention. As for reopening the Wyatt case, there's no new evidence, just an old convict talking to a prison preacher and some lawyer from back east." Then, after hesitating, he said, "Unless you think you have the murderer. You do, don't you?"

"Nothing that would ever stand up in a court of law," said Buster.

"Anyhow," said McIntyre, "looks like the raid is gonna happen."

Buster wasn't thinking about the raid. He decided he'd drive out to the park and check on the ducks. They'd still be there a while longer. He looked back at the wall of chiefs as he left his office. He'd never noticed before that Chief Warry had just the slightest trace of a grin on his square jaw. They all looked like they were going to talk about him after he left. He wanted to say, What's the matter? You boys never seen a witch before?

"I'm driving out to the park to check on something," he said. Ronnie didn't ask him what. He knew whenever the chief needed to get out of the office and he didn't have anywhere to go, he'd go out and check on the ducks. It was kind of a joke between them. Started years back when the ducks were getting into loud squabbles and the park superintendent didn't know who to call to deal with it, so he called the police. Buster identified the troublemaker and after that there was peace on the pond. They sent the bully off to a duck farm in Damascus and he either got rehabilitated or maybe somebody ate him.

He parked the Interceptor just beyond the tree shade in the warm sunshine by the baseball field and walked down by the pond to sit on the lone wooden bench. A brass plaque on the backrest read "In memory of Roy Lee Harlan. This was his favorite resting place." Good old Roy.

Not much traffic on the Dixie. A motorcycle with loud pipes accelerated away from Four Corners and Buster recognized the noise as coming from young Rex Warner's black Triumph. One of these days he might have to give that boy a ticket, but probably not. Sounded good.

At least the ducks were all fine and the swan too, enjoying the last of the warm weather before they got trucked off to winter storage in Damascus. Kind of like going to Florida for the winter. Ellen said she'd like that someday, but Lester Wheeler said you couldn't get the Bears or the Illinois games down there, and then, after being retired just three years, they shipped him home just after New Year's. His widow was the only one at the funeral with a suntan other than Lester himself.

And Rose Lahae said she saw a man looking up with frozen eyes. His mom said one night she woke up and knew her big brother was dead over in Germany. She was a little girl on the farm in Iowa. She never told anybody, but she just plain knew it, she said, and when the telegram came and they told her, she didn't cry at first because she already had. That was World War I. He remembered when he was a boy and his dad was off fighting the Germans during World War II that his mom always looked up fast whenever she heard the mailman come up on the porch. She knew that military death notices were always delivered by Western Union, but the mailman's footsteps on the porch stairs always scared her till she made out the postal uniform.

There was a program on TV about a psychic detective and Buster knew that some police departments claimed that psychics and clairvoyants had put them on the trail. Just lucky guessing, he thought. If a blind hog roots long enough. All that sounded crazy to him. But there were some good lawmen up north who used city money to pay people who said they could see things or know things just by thinking about them or holding a piece of evidence. If he lived closer to Chicago it might seem less crazy but that wouldn't mean it was.

Buster left the ducks and drove back to the office to work on some assignment schedules. He was just getting started when the phone rang and he was glad to hear Ira Cockrell's voice.

"You're gonna like this. I found you the only man who might be able to tell you the real story about Freeman Lane's confession," said Ira.

"I'm listening."

"I just this minute got back from the sheriff's department where I had to report some vehicular vandalism. Our volleyball girls beat Decatur on Friday but we lost two taillights in the parking lot and somebody spray-painted

'Bitches' all up the sidewalk side of the bus, which is a risk your girls' teams run when the school mascot is a bulldog. Anyhow, just before I left, McIntyre came out of his office and said he'd had you on the phone earlier talking about the Lane case. Well, we got to shooting the shit and one thing and another and I asked who headed the Crawford murder investigation back then and he said it was Albert Tull. You remember him?"

"He still alive?"

"Still breathing, if that's what you mean but, from what McIntyre says, he thinks Clinton is a holiday and Christmas is president."

"He must have been working with somebody. Did you ask?" said Buster, leaning forward.

"I did and you'll shit when I tell you who it was not only arrested Lane but got a confession out of him too. It was your old sparring partner. You remember old Memory?"

"How could I forget him?" said Buster. Memory Branson, too big to be a man and too small to be a horse, was a living terror in south county back in the old days. Bar fighter, Purple Heart in North Africa, stock car racer, biker, construction worker, truck driver and loud-mouth fightin' Kentuckian who could back it up. Buster remembered that, for a very short spell way back then, Memory Branson, of all people, got hired as a policeman down in Blunt. That was when Buster was still in high school, but every man and boy in the county had heard of Memory.

"Are you telling me Memory got the kid to confess to killing the Wyatts?" said Buster.

"Hell no. He got him to confess to killing Jack Crawford. That was what he was arrested for. Nobody connected Lane with anything in Yonders, not till they convicted him of it anyway."

"What the hell did Memory have to do with a Damascus investigation?"

"The Lane kid was living down in Blunt and pimping up here on Jackson Street. The night Crawford got his throat cut, he, Crawford I mean, was seen walking out the back door of Sam's Place with a little whore Lane, or maybe Sam himself, was running. That was the last time anybody remembered seeing Crawford alive. So Foster told the Blunt chief—Hunter was his name—told Chief Hunter that he was getting a warrant and that he and Tull were going down the next day to make the arrest. Only problem was Hunter was sick as a dog and turned everything over to Memory."

"I bet this is good," said Buster.

"You got that right. Seems like Memory thought that was his chance to be a Dick Tracy. The Blunt cops were just supposed to stand by as back up the next day, but Memory, who never had a lick of sense, jumped the gun and made a warrantless arrest—thought he was doing the sheriff a service. Not only that, but he and another Blunt cop, another one who's dead, took it on themselves, at Memory's initiative, to interrogate Lane without even first charging him. They said they didn't want to disturb Chief Hunter but they must have disturbed Lane because they claimed they got a confession out of him before suppertime. It was pre-Miranda. You remember how it was. So, when Foster got to Blunt, he found the kid he was going to arrest already locked up in Blunt's only cell."

"Chief Hunter was still sick in bed?"

"Foster got him up and read him the riot act and Memory was fired on the spot since he made it pretty clear all of it was his idea, but I'd bet you anything there's no record kept of nothing."

"Where would a man find Memory these days?" said Buster.

"I believe you'll find a Memory Branson at the Old Soldier's Home up in Manteno."

"Is he still lucid?" said Buster.

"Was he ever?"

"Thanks for your trouble, Ira. I hope this didn't put you out too much."

"Just don't be telling everybody that I helped you on this. Jack Crawford's wife is still in her sixties and she's a big noise in the D.A.R. down here and proud of her patriot ancestry. Says her great grandpa was Abraham Lincoln's bodyguard."

"Not sure that I'd be proud of that one," said Buster.

"The story goes that Mildred Crawford's great grandpa was off duty the night they shot the president. Old Abe sent Mildred's grandpa off somewhere on some errand but he warned the president not to go to the play that night. If Lincoln had paid attention..."

"Jesus, Ira! To hear you Damascans tell it, everything that ever happened got somebody from Damascus right in the middle of it. So, let me get this straight. Memory Branson got a confession from Freeman Lane for the murder of Jack Crawford and then Sheriff Foster lost it or forgot to write it down and Freeman got confused and decided he killed some other folks and Abraham Lincoln got himself assassinated because he didn't heed Mildred Crawford's great granddad? Is that about it?"

"Yes, and there's one more thing. I got you your basketball game. It'll be our season opener, if it'll work for you. November 13."

"Here at the Happ?"

"Just like you asked for."

"That'll make Dornfeld happy. Thanks."

"I'd wait till after the game to do any thanking. Anyhow, when you go up there to see Memory, watch out for the ghosts," said Cockrell before his voice suddenly became urgent. "Gotta go! Old lady's in the drive!"

Buster smiled, imagining Ira Cockrell running to flush a tray of ashes and a lit cigarette down the toilet, fanning the air and thinking Evelyn couldn't smell the smoke.

Talking to Cockrell got everything back to normal again even though he said something about watching out for ghosts. So he was going up to the Old Soldiers' Home—the VA nursing home they called it now—on the grounds of the old mental hospital, the one everybody said was haunted. He had nothing urgent planned for Tuesday. Tomorrow would be as good a day as any to go up to Kankakee, which is what folks used to say when they meant Manteno. Folks would say, "You keep acting like that and they'll haul you off to Kankakee." The insane asylum had been closed and shuttered for years now, but folks said the ghosts of the poor lunatics still walked the cornfields beyond the walls of the old bedlam.

Chapter 23

The Old Bedlam

The nurse at the desk told him that Memory would be down in a few minutes and she gestured toward the chairs, davenports and coffee tables of the lounge area. Buster was in street clothes and drove up to Manteno in his truck. When he asked to see Memory Branson, he said he was a family friend. The nurse, a young blonde girl who looked like she ought to be in high school, said, "I'm glad you came. He needs cheering up."

Back when Buster knew Memory, knew of him anyway, most folks would have been able to think of quite a few things he needed, but cheering up wouldn't have been one of them. In fact, on a summer night back in 1962, Buster gave Memory what everybody at Turk's thought he needed, and even after that, even after getting what he most certainly needed, Memory was, once he managed to get into a sitting position amid the sawdust and cigarette butts on the linoleum floor, cheerful enough to say, "Buster Lawton, I didn't know you had it in you," and then suggested that, after he had a moment to get his eyes looking straight again, the two of them take a ride out in the country and have "a good old bite and gouge."

Sitting in a beige armchair and listening to family members laugh and talk with their veterans, some in ball caps that said World War II or Korean War and others that named the branch of service, Buster remembered the night he knocked Memory flat. He was in his first months as chief, taking over from Warry, and there were some who doubted that Buster, in spite of his days as an MP in Korea and his glory as an all-county guard and line-backer, was big enough and tough enough to wear old Warry's badge.

It was thirty-six years earlier that Buster, at Chief Warry's retirement ceremony, first felt the weight of the police chief's badge. It was still light enough not to tug down even on the summer uniform shirt, but it seemed to weigh a bit more, made of thicker stuff, or maybe it was just the word "Chief" added beneath the town shield that gave it that extra fraction of an ounce more than the badge he wore his first three years as an officer. The old badge was one of the chrome-plated copper and die-cast kind. Only the most veteran members of the police force still had the old ones: Buster at sixty-two, Murdock in his early fifties and Whitehead in his late forties. The outfit down in Carbondale that used to make the old badges went out of business sometime in the seventies and the new ones were made back east—still good quality, but stamped sheet metal instead of cast. The new badges still carried the same town shield and that angled, three-quarter shucked ear of golden sweetcorn that

Cockrell thought was so funny. It was kind of funny, Buster admitted, if you imagined being from somewhere else, but if you were from somewhere else nobody cared what you thought about it anyway.

And there he was, big Memory Branson crippling down the stairs, hanging on to the banister with both hands and with a steady, Black nurse in blue scrubs at his side, her hand under his elbow. He must weigh three-hundred pounds, thought Buster. Enough white, scraggly hair to stuff a pillow and the same smile that not even a knockdown punch at Turk's could wipe away. Memory had already spotted Buster and was beaming at him from across the lounge. Once he was on level ground he stopped and pulled himself up to his full height and, now towering over the blue-uniformed nurse, set out slowly but steadily for Buster. Buster stood and waited as the two approached. Damn, he was big and ugly, and Buster knew before he spoke that whatever he said would be in that same jokey tone he used when he suggested the two of them go out in the country for a good old bite and gouge.

"Flossie," said Memory, "this here sawed-off, square-headed old fireplug is called Buster Lawton and he's the best they can come up with for a police chief down in corntown."

The woman, maybe forty, maybe older—Buster never could tell about women—had fun in her eyes. "My name's not Flossie, Chief, it's Mrs. Florenza Beck. I am pleased to make your acquaintance. I knew it was just a matter of time till you found him and took him off to stand trial. Did you bring your cuffs or do you want me to get some rope?"

Memory spoke before Buster could reply. "Now, Flossie, why on earth would you think that of an upstanding man like me? You may be surprised to learn that I was once a lawman."

"Lord pity any folks had you for the law."

"Pleased to meet you, Mrs. Beck," said Buster.

"He gives you any trouble, young man, you just give a whistle and I'll be over directly to straighten him right out."

"Don't pay her no mind. We're planning to elope one of these days. You got room in your car, Buster? Maybe you could run us over to Indiana where I ain't got no wives at the moment."

Buster had forgotten Memory had once been up for bigamy but got off on some technicality.

"I'd sooner run off with a rattlesnake," said Florenza and she walked away. Even her back was smiling, Buster thought.

"Memory Branson. You're looking good," said Buster.

"To a buzzard, I'd be looking good. Are you a buzzard, Buster? You kind of look like one." They sat down, Buster in the chair and Memory taking up half the davenport.

"You know why I'm here."

"Cockrell called me. Said you wanted me to tell you how I broke the Crawford case."

"It didn't stay broken very long if it ever was. You figure it was Lane who killed him?" said Buster.

"That kid was guilty as sin and everybody knew it, but they couldn't have it in the papers that upstanding Jack Crawford was wandering the red-light district of the colored section down on Jackson Street."

"Did you beat it out of him?" said Buster.

"I never laid a hand on him, but if I hadn't pulled a gun on him he'd have run. Hell, Buster, me and the other cop, Vickers—Cockrell says he's dead like almost everybody else—found the damn knife and more money than that boy ought to have lawfully had in his pockets."

"Did he really confess?"

"Depends what you mean by confess. He was scared shitless and one of us, I forget which, said if he didn't tell us the truth he might get shot trying to escape whether he tried to escape or not. You know how it was back then. He owned up to it. He did it in the alley back of Sam's and we had the knife."

"So, there was no formal confession?" said Buster.

"We didn't take down no confession if that's what you mean. That was all what they were going to do in Damascus with the witnesses and the detectives, but he told me, told us both, exactly how he did it. Told us the name of the whore that led Crawford to where he was waiting in the alley, but he said Crawford tried to fight him. Maybe in the dark he didn't see the knife, or maybe he was too drunk to understand exactly what he was getting himself into, but Freeman Lane just cut his throat and held his mouth shut while he bled out. It didn't take Foster's boys no time to find the girl and she told them that she led Crawford out, taking him the alley way to her place, and that Freeman was waiting like they planned. She said she never saw no killing because she run off as soon as she saw the knife. The County Persecutor never wanted to know none of that." Memory was talking in his big, loud voice and causing nearby groups to look over. An old man sitting alone nearby whose cap said D-Day Survivor was watching Memory closely and smiling.

Persecutor! This is a man who talked just to hear his head roar, thought Buster, something his mom used to say. He was trying to imagine Memory telling his story from the witness box in a court of law.

Memory smiled at the D-Day survivor and went on talking more to him than to Buster, "So, if Foster had wanted to, he could have got an indictment and sent that kid straight to Sparky and been done with it, but that would have meant washing all Crawford's dirty laundry in public."

"And you got fired," said Buster, speaking softly.

"I wasn't cut out for the law no how. They said I'd keep quiet if I knew what was good for me."

"Would you say any of that in court?"

"Hell yes! But who'd believe me now? There's no records of nothing and you can bet that the knife, with all that DNA shit smeared all over it that we didn't know about back in the horse and buggy days, was long gone in no time."

Florenza was there again. "You fellows need anything? We got some lemonade. I'm not rushing you. Visiting hours don't end till eight. You got plenty of time, but I see Memory here all red in the face and thought he could use a cool drink. Are you okay, Mr. Branson?" Florenza asked.

"Mr. Branson was my sainted daddy's name," said Memory. "Would you believe, Flossie, that little Buster here knocked me flat once about a hundred years ago? Can you imagine that? You wouldn't know it to look at him. It took him but one punch and I wasn't even that drunk. They say he knocked me out but it was worse than that. He smacked me cross-eyed."

"Do tell," said Florenza.

"It was in the line of duty, ma'am," said Buster. "Memory here was terrorizing a whole bar."

"Yes," Florenza said, looking at Memory now, "I can feature that. I'm getting you both some cool lemonade and if you talk a little lower, you won't have half the folks in here listening to all your talk about knives and dead men in alleys."

"You know," Memory said when she left, headed for the lemonade, "I used to say nigger ever third word—we all did—but that woman there treats me like I was worth a damn. I said it in front of her once when I first got here and she just looked away like she didn't expect no better. I said I was sorry, that I didn't know no better and she said, yes you do or you wouldn't be sorry."

Memory looked around the lobby where some veterans were surrounded by family, some sat with a single visitor and others sat alone. "You ever wonder what the hell this is all about?"

"What what's all about?"

"This used to be a nuthouse and everybody told me when they sent me up here that it was haunted. You believe in that shit? I never believed in nothing or nobody. But since I got put up here, I been getting the feeling they're still out there, the ghosts of dead crazy people wandering around."

"It was better when you were yelling about knives," said Florenza, back with the two glasses of lemonade. "You don't need to be telling your old friend here about all that silliness." She looked at Buster, "Lately, when he gets started on that craziness, he can't talk about anything normal."

"I'll tell you both, I don't believe in spooks and haunts, but that don't make them go away. I look out my window some nights and I can almost make them out, the poor bastards they used to lock up in here and torment. They're out there wandering around between the old, falling-down buildings they used to keep them in." Memory lowered his voice and leaned toward Florenza. "One night I woke up and there was a pretty young lady with dead eyes like they used to leave the simple-minded with up here after they lobotomized them. I could see her sitting by my bed until I opened my eyes, and then she was gone. But here's what scared me. I seen she'd moved the glass I keep my teeth in on the chair by the bed so as to make room for her to sit down. I wasn't full scared till I registered that."

"See what I mean?" said Florenza, looking up and away from Buster.

"What I'm saying," said Memory, talking loud again "is that Buster here needs to step lively going out to his car to make sure nothing slips in there and rides home with him. But then, I imagine Yonders has already got its share of spirits and God knows what else if a man takes the time to see them."

After Florenza left to help a man with a coughing spell, the two sat quietly sipping lemonade, Memory extending his little finger delicately from the glass and, winking at Buster, said, "Drinking lemonade. Look at us."

"Most everybody is," said Buster quietly. "So, you think Lane got convicted for the right kind of crime but with the wrong victims?"

"I read all that in the paper about how Lane finally confessed to killing Crawford and took back what he said about killing your farmers. There was no way that boy could have figured out anybody to kill in Yonders. I think we both know what happened, and they sure as hell knew in Damascus. So, Chief, have you found your murderer?" said Memory.

"Could be, for all the good it'll do me."

"Does it make any difference after all this time?" said Memory.

"The statute of limitations never runs out on capital murder. All it takes is proof."

"Unless the murderer is dead or crazy or both" said Memory, "and can prove it."

"Proving a man dead," said Buster, talking as loud as Memory and smiling, "shouldn't be too much of a problem and you can take a dead man to trial—it's been done, but never in the county—but I suppose you're right. If a dead man facing capital murder in a posthumous trial could prove he was crazy he'd be not guilty due to insanity. Just being dead won't cut it."

"Aren't you two having fun! Now you've got the chief talking as crazy as you," said Florenza, again at their side. And they laughed: Buster, Memory, Florenza and the D-Day Survivor.

Buster said he had to be getting back home. Memory insisted on walking him to the door. That seemed to surprise Florenza, who looked toward the door at the far end of the main lobby. Buster followed her eyes. It was a long walk for a man in the shape Memory was in. The three of them moved slowly across the room, halting twice before they were halfway to the door. Memory, breathing deep, stood tall and stepped out the last twenty feet. Trying to boot-stomp in his slippers, thought Buster.

"He has a walker, but he won't let anyone see him using it," Florenza said to Buster behind Memory's broad back.

Buster turned to say goodbye at the door, but Memory said, "I think I'll get me some fresh night air with my old barroom buddy here, Mrs. Florenza Beck, and the conversation might be a little risky for your young ears, so, if I promise not to make a run for the hills, will you leave us gentlemen alone for a bit?"

Florenza, standing behind, looked at Buster, squinted and nodded toward Memory. Buster nodded back. Yes, he said, without saying it. I'll stay between Memory and the stone steps.

Out on the wide landing the wind was chilly. Memory inhaled and said, "Smell that night! Don't it make you want go somewhere?"

Memory, still standing tall, walked toward the stairs with Buster close at his side. He angled toward the wooden banister and took hold of it with both his big hands. He leaned out toward the dim parking lot, took a deep breath and exhaled.

"Let me give you a piece of advice," he said. "Don't never get old and if you do don't never end up in a place like this.

This night-air smell is torture to a dead man like me. If I could have anything in all creation, one last thing, it would be to be sixty again with a billfold full of twenties and some pretty woman tagging onto me for a night of dancing and drinking up and down the road, bar to bar, club to club, top to bottom of Dead Man's Grave! One more hog-wild Saturday night and I'd say, OK, I'm done. You can drag my ass off to hell now."

Buster waited. He knew Memory didn't want him to go. His dad was like that at the end, hanging on.

"Yeah," said Memory after a moment, "Freeman Lane never killed nobody in your town. Your murders was just handy, but I'm just telling you what you already know, ain't I? And you still care about it. It matters to you. You're lucky to have something like that to care about. You want to know what I care about? There's dead, crazy people wandering around here. It scares the bejesus out of me to think I could end up being one of them, but if such a fate was to befall me, you can be damn sure of one thing. I'm going back down home and scare the hell out of a few folks." And his laugh turned into a barking cough.

Buster reached out to steady the big man, but stopped short as Memory cleared his throat. "Flossie's standing right there behind me in the door, ain't she?"

"Like she was your mother," said Buster.

Buster nodded to Florenza and she came out and put her hand under Memory's elbow. "You ready to come on back inside now before you catch your death?"

"In a minute. Just want to see this man off," said Memory, and then he straightened, holding the banister rail with only one hand, standing tall and catching his breath. "I remember that sucker punch of yours. I was already starting my swing at you when you clipped me. It wouldn't have been much of a fight if I could've landed my haymaker."

"You telegraphed that by Western Union," said Buster. "A blind man could've seen it coming."

They laughed and shook hands and Buster turned to go but he was only two steps down the wide, stone stairway when Memory said, "You didn't come for advice, but I'll give you some if you'll hear it."

Buster stopped and looked up and back, waiting.

"You'll never get that Crawford case out of the dark as long as there's live Crawfords above ground who think folks still care about their Jack's carousing ways forty years ago. As far as your murderer is concerned, you got two choices. You can forget about it or become the avenging angel and make yourself a Charles Bronson movie, except he's a lot better looking than you are."

"I'll give that careful consideration," said Buster, starting down the stairs again.

"You drive careful now, Chief," said Florenza.

The chill wind had stiffened and begun to gust. Buster hurried to his truck, but before he climbed in, he looked back at the dimly lit entrance to the nursing home. It was only a quarter to eight but many of the rooms were dark and those that were lit had curtains drawn. Back under the feeble light of the entrance, the old giant, with Florenza at his side, waved farewell and Buster waved back. There used to be men like that spread here and there from East Kentucky all the way to Yonders and beyond, laughing, fighting, drinking, like the Tuckers up on Fugate Hill in the old days. Good men, his dad used to say, for raising barns and raising hell and mighty handy in foreign wars.

And now he knew. Tull and Foster and the DA, the persecutor, Memory called him, knowingly convicted a murderer for the wrong murders and let another murderer go free. What happened back then wasn't right and it wasn't settled, but old Harold's memory about a '49 or '50 Ford and the word of a dying old brawler didn't really amount to a hill of beans. Except to Buster.

He looked up at the racing clouds over the old asylum, stars appearing and vanishing and a waning moon jumping out and jumping back behind the rush of low clouds. A lot of the old buildings were shuttered and boarded up, some roofless with windows broken and doors gone.

The state hadn't yet gotten around to demolishing the last of the forty moss-covered, rotten-roofed brick cottages surrounding the mix of converted and new buildings of the nursing home.

Buster had never been to Manteno before but he grew up aware of it as the place where they took the crazy people on the blue bus with barred windows that sometimes went past on the Dixie. As he drove out of the VA lot, he saw the grounds fading in the truck mirror and they couldn't fade fast enough to suit him. The world didn't look quite right, didn't feel right. Buster never talked about it, but he knew there was just enough strangeness in the world to keep a man on his toes and prevent him from thinking he knows it all. Maybe it was Memory's crazy talk about wandering ghosts or maybe it was Rose Lahae's visit the day before, but the feeling he had was the one he first felt back in the spring of 1960 when he and Ellen were newlyweds. Being the youngest on the force, he got lots of night and weekend duty, but when he finally got a Saturday night off so they could go to the show, the projector broke down at the Lorraine during the Mr. Magoo cartoon. Ellen was disappointed but Buster said there was still time to get down to Damascus and they'd see whatever was on at the Egyptian. The movies down there always started a half hour later. Maybe they'd miss the first few minutes, but at least they'd see a movie.

They had no idea what was on, but they just took off, driving at a quick clip, hitting eighty south of Milton. He knew the county boys that worked that stretch. They hit the Damascus lights just right, rolled up and found a parking place right out front of the show. The ticket girl was just about to pull the curtains on the round booth when Buster rushed up with money in his hand. The girl said the show had started ten minutes ago, but he didn't care. He only glanced at the title of the movie on the poster—something about beaches. Probably a California bikini movie, maybe *Gidget*, exactly the kind of movie he was trying to avoid, but it was for Ellen. Being the wife of a seventy-dollar-a-week cop probably wasn't much fun, even if she never complained. An usher with a flashlight led them down toward the front where there were still seats. Buster was halfway down the aisle into the dark theater when he felt fear all around him. If he had been armed he would have had a finger on the snap of his holster. He looked at the faces in the flickering light of the black and white film and understood that the fear was from the people—all of them sitting dead still, all scared—but until he was seated and focused on the movie, he didn't understand. It wasn't *Gidget.* It was about the end of the world with Gregory Peck and Eva Gardner and even Fred Astaire.

He didn't see the title of the movie until they left the theater. *On the Beach.*

He wondered if Ellen had noticed anything strange when they started down the dark aisle that night, but he never asked her. It was not the kind of thing Buster talked about, but he never forgot that feeling of fear all around him, fear and dead quiet except for the big voices of the actors. Now, driving away from the VA Hospital through the grounds of the old insane asylum, he saw that old strangeness again in the colors of the darkness, heard the same queerness in the deep silence all around him. Like at the Egyptian the night of the end of the world.

Memory hadn't told him anything he hadn't heard before, but he made it sound true. Buster remembered hearing stories about Manteno when he was a kid. They said back when the old insane asylum was still running, farmers used to find escaped lunatics wandering in the fields. There was even the story of a farmer who sold good land that bordered the asylum walls for less than it was worth because he took up a runaway woman onto the heads of his combine during field corn harvest. The coroner said the woman was probably dead when the combine took her up, but the farmer sold the field. Good, black, prime farmland, and the farmer sold it cheap.

He didn't know if any of that was true, but driving in the night down the country blacktop that ran east from Manteno, never another car to be seen, he just didn't feel right until he jogged over and caught the Dixie Highway, and, after a mile or so, the look of the darkness and the sound of the engine and the tires humming on the road were right again.

Once he was back on Route 1 and heading for home, he turned on the radio and got the news and sports on WGN, and twenty miles later he picked up the Yonders station and rode it home, but he found himself thinking about Rose Lahae. What would she have seen at Manteno? Dick Trevino was singing "Bobbie Ann Mason" as he came up from under the viaduct and back into town, and there was Shucks grinning down from his billboard. Welcome to Harvester Country, said the giant ear of corn.

He saw Murdock parked in the gravel forecourt of the old Gas & Go! sitting back in the shadows watching the intersection. Murdock flashed his lights and Buster waved. Downtown was quiet, just a few cars out front of Snider's. Pabst sign flashing blue in the window. He turned down Fifth for home and he couldn't help looking both ways to make sure some ghost Nickel Plate freight wasn't barreling down on him at the crossing where nothing crossed anymore. A man taking a quick look up a railroad line that wasn't there might imagine anything if he wasn't careful and Buster was glad he didn't see a murdered girl in a yellow dress.

Chapter 24

Columbus Day

As soon as he got to the station the morning after his talk with Memory, Buster called Sheriff McIntyre and asked him to see what was in the evidence box of the Crawford murder file. McIntyre, in spite of being in the midst of preparations for the bust, called back an hour later. "Nothing but a busted pair of glasses. Other than that, empty as a banker's heart, as my old man used to say, and that makes the Jack Crawford murder about the coldest cold case I've ever seen," he said.

"The way Cockrell remembers it, Lane came in the door as a suspect in the Crawford case and went out as the defendant in the Wyatt murders. Wouldn't there be any record of that somewhere, of Lane being questioned about the Crawford Murder?" said Buster.

"That was back in 1960, Chief. How's your records from 1960?" said McIntyre, and he went on, "Cockrell says you got a man down there you like for your old Wyatt case, but even if you got a confession, which you haven't got or you would have said so, you'd need an eyewitness or something pretty damned compelling to get anybody to drag that case out again no matter what Lane decides to confess to. I ran that past the D.A. and he said in order to get an indictment, you'd just about need the victim to rise up out of his grave and stump in and point to the accused and yell to the grand jury, 'That's the one who killed me sitting right over there.'"

Or run into the court room in a yellow dress and scream his name. It was time to let it go. But he couldn't.

A few days later, on Columbus Day just before noon, Buster was cruising slowly down Hamilton and saw Keelan walking along, coming from one of his southside handyman jobs. He looked Buster right in the eye with just the faintest wrinkle of a grin. It was the grin that did it. Buster didn't know for sure what he was doing when he eased to a stop, snubbing the Interceptor up to the curb beside Keelan. They were out front of the Stratton house. Lyla Stratton watched from a chair on her high porch.

"Morning," said Buster. "I been meaning to ask you a question. What brought you back to town after all these many years?"

Keelan didn't bend down toward the window. He stood his height. "Greyhound as far as Damascus and then I stuck out my thumb."

"Thought maybe you were back to take some flowers out to the graveyard. For your dad's grave I mean, unless there are some other souls out there you might want to pay your respects to. I was just out there the other day. A walk around out there now and then helps you to not forget. If you'd thought to plant some flowers for your dad's grave when you first got home, some black-eyed Susans or the like, they'd be in their fall glory. It's too late now, though."

Keelan, no longer grinning, took a step closer to the window of the Interceptor and bent down, looking Buster in the eye. "I've never had much of a green thumb. Whatever I plant tends to stay down in the ground."

Mrs. Stratton was up from her chair, watching over the banister. Enough of this, thought Buster, but as he started to pull away, Keelan's grin was back. Buster hit the brakes just hard enough to make the front of the Interceptor dip and bring a little chirp from the Goodyears. He reversed slowly until he was beside Keelan again.

"You strike me as a man with an interest in the law, Putnam. Did you know that just because one man is convicted of a crime, even capital murder, that doesn't prevent the law from deciding somebody else did it after all and starting all over again and convicting a second suspect for the same crime? It's not double jeopardy, because it's not the same suspect. I had to look it up and, even then, I needed to check with the DA's office. Surprised me to learn that."

Keelan, standing straight now and still with that faint trace of a smile again, said, "You learn something new every day, don't you? But surely you got something better to do, criminals to catch. Looks like you got a house full of them over on Swisher."

Buster knew he should have driven away, but he didn't. "I know exactly what you did back in '59, Putnam. The only thing I don't know is why you made the mistake of coming back to our town. But what I do know is that your luck is running out and you're about this close to getting what you deserve." He held his forefinger and thumb as close as he could without contact and squinted with one eye through the tiny opening. He hadn't raised his voice, but he had said too much. He knew no such thing. He pulled away slowly, angry with himself.

Mrs. Stratton was watching it all, and a few other people had come out on their porches or were standing in the front windows of the big houses on Hamilton to get a better look at a police car stopped on their quiet street.

Buster saw Keelan's eyes in the mirror and he was mad at himself for having given in to stopping in the first place and more for slamming on the brakes in front of Mrs. Stratton, but most of all for a threat based on nothing he could ever prove. Maybe he had nudged him a step closer to getting in that canary-yellow truck of his and getting the hell out of town. But that would just be kicking the can down the road. You read about it now and then. Every reason to suspect that a man was likely to commit some heinous crime—they always called them heinous—but not a scrap of cause to make an arrest. And then when what happened happened, everybody knew what should have been done but what the law would not allow. You don't just run mad dogs out of town so they can bite somebody in the next town. You shoot them, but you couldn't even do that anymore, not even with mad dogs, and Keelan wasn't mad and he wasn't a dog. That's what made it all the worse.

▪▪▪

Keelan was smiling mad when he got to the Two Spot. There were a couple of high school kids, a boy and a girl, sitting at his window table thanks to Columbus and his three goddamn boats. Columbus sailed the ocean blue in fourteen hundred and ninety-two. That was about all they had time to teach him before they kicked him out of high school his senior year for stealing money out of the desk drawer of a teacher who was too stupid to keep his billfold in his back pocket.

He had to sit on a damn stool at the counter. Only a few people in the place and Dandy was taking forever. He finally got around to taking his order, but Keelan was still mad. He wondered if what Lawton told him was true. Could the law be so screwed up that they could hang as many folks as they pleased for the same murder? If there was a law like that, it was a double-cross, but what did he expect? They send one poor bastard to jail for the rest of his natural life and then just start all over again. They get as many chances as they want, and a poor man's lucky if he even gets one. But they still got to have at least one short hair of proof in their fine-tooth comb to hang a man. This still wasn't Russia just yet.

No, it wasn't the USA law he was worried about. It was Buster's law. He was taking it all personal. Our town, he said, like he had the right to say whose town it was and whose it wasn't. He ought to be protecting folks from that house full of drug dealers over on Swisher, not harassing him on the sidewalk in front of all the old ladies who might be planning to hire him for raking leaves and putting up birdhouses. Just thinking about that got him mad again, thinking about Buster quacking at him over on Hamilton Street, hounding him at the curb, squawking his tires and talking crazy talk about planting some kind of flowers, dead-eyed Susans or some such shit as that.

The high school kids were taking up his table just for a couple of cokes. Keelan drank his coffee and ate his burger and fries in a hurry and got up to pay at the register. His mind was full of cussing and he was halfway home when it started to sprinkle. Wouldn't you know it! He'd left his damn jacket on the hook at the Two Spot, but he wasn't giving Dandy the satisfaction of seeing him come back for it. He'd get it tomorrow. And then, of course, it started raining harder when he was still a block from his door, but he wasn't running. He wasn't giving folks the satisfaction of seeing him running in a rainstorm with no jacket.

As soon as he was in his living room, he took off his wet shoes and his wet jeans and shirt and grabbed a towel from the bathroom to dry his hair. He started for the bedroom to get some dry clothes, but he was more thirsty than chilly so he went in the kitchen in his socks and underwear, and poured himself an inch of whisky. The bottle was getting down to empty and if it didn't let up he'd have to walk all the way back downtown in the rain to get another one. And since he'd left his jacket at the Two Spot, he'd have to break out his brand-new black parka.

He turned on the radio and they were playing an oldie, a man singing, "I used up my last tomorrow today." He took a swallow of Old Crow, lit a cigarette and carried the glass into the living room, stopping in the hall to look at himself in the long mirror. Looked like sockfooted Death in his underwear, drinking a whisky and smoking a Camel.

"The only thing the matter with you is you're just no damn good," he said to the man in the mirror. And they both laughed.

He put on some dry clothes and sat on the davenport studying the whisky in the bottom of the glass, calm as a judge, thinking about justice. If he'd learned one thing in Nevada it was that once they smelled the slightest stink of guilty-scared on you, they had you, but even the cops, with all their tricks and threats and pleas and double-crossing laws, had to have at least one pointing finger to sit a man down in the hot seat, and, if he was reading Buster right, the old cop thought he had something. He's feeling his oats, thought Keelan, harassing me on the public streets, threatening me. Whatever happens now is Buster's own damn fault.

Old Harold must be in his eighties and, from the looks of him, walking around after dark, even talking to himself sometimes, he might be a little off, but if he remembered the car that put him into the gate that night, that'd give Buster what he was looking for. They'd believe him too. Nothing trumped an eye witness even if the eye witness was off his rocker. All they need is the barest excuse to haul you in, and the next thing you know they're telling you to confess or they'll tack on a dozen years. Except this would be murder, and the only choice they offer on first-degree murder is to plead guilty and rot slow or go to trial and get sent up to death row to wait for your day.

He didn't want to do it. He hadn't come home to kill more folks. At least this one lived alone. So be it. Buster left him no choice because he wasn't running. After this was settled once and for all, he'd just relax and enjoy his days. Maybe he'd get himself a dog, one he'd take better care of than the last one. Hell, maybe he'd make himself a friend. Fred Myers seemed friendly enough to shoot the shit with. Maybe he'd even make up with his sister, except she was too proud and carried a grudge. Jezzie couldn't see the funny side of nothing…no real harm done.

His mom knew everything and she had called him by his name again, after all those years. "You don't need me to tell you what to do," she said, and he didn't. He wasn't even mad at Harold. Buster was the problem. There was no call to be talking to him like that out the window of the police car on a quiet street and on Columbus Day to boot. That was the first time he could ever remember talking to Buster. Ever. One time too many.

When Keelan talked to the Devil it was in dreams, but it'd seemed just as real as talking to Buster over on Hamilton. Maybe, when he'd done what he had to do, he'd start in going to some church now and then. Worse sons of bitches than him went to church. He'd seen them walking on Sunday morning, wearing ties and stepping high. Keelan smiled, imaging himself trying to tie a tie. Why sure, he'd even go to church and pray and go to the library and read a goddamn book about something or other and somebody would say to somebody else, "See that fellow over there reading that book. I seen him praying at church the other week." Maybe come Christmas his mom would have him and Jezzie over for supper and everything would be just fine and dandy.

He raised his glass to the jug on the shelf. "Well, old girl," he said "I guess we know now what we got to do."

Part Four

Late Fall 1998

Chapter 25

KILLER FROST AND INDIAN SUMMER

Buster heard the doorbell just after nightfall. *Martial Law*, the show with the tough little Chinese cop, Sammo Law, had begun, but it was a talking scene and Buster could never understand anything Sammo said. Ellen was doing the supper dishes, so Buster went to the door.

Rachel Wyatt, in her bloody yellow dress, stood on the porch between Caspar the Friendly Ghost and Cinderella.

"Trick or treat!" said Rachel.

"Trick or treat!" said the other two.

"Cat got your tongue, Buster?" It was Ellen at his side. She gave him a look, squinting and smiling, before handing out two little trick-or-treat-sized Mars bars to Caspar and two more to Cinderella. She hesitated and asked, "Who are you supposed to be, Linda?"

"I'm Running Rachel, the ghost of the train tracks," Linda said in a perky voice, and Ellen handed over the treats.

Buster recognized them all now, the three Colliers kids from down the block, Bud and Brenda's kids. Linda, the oldest, must be ten or eleven. Nothing much surprised him anymore, but one second he was trying to figure out what Sammo Law was talking about and the next he was facing somebody who'd been on his mind lately, but not on his porch. Maybe it was catsup or maybe it was paint, but on that yellow dress, it was blood. He saw Rachel in his mind's eye, flopped back dead against the davenport.

Linda and Bobby said thank you and the littlest one, Cinderella—Buster could almost remember her name too—opened one of her candy bars and started to eat it. Ellen went back in but Buster stayed on the porch a moment longer watching the three kids walk single file out to the sidewalk. They were all alone, like in the old days, with no parents following along at fifteen yards. When he saw them turn east, the opposite direction from Keelan's house, he went back in. He wondered if Bailey, the Joliet kid and O were getting any trick-or-treaters and he wondered if, when he was a trick-or-treating little kid, he and his buddies ever knocked on the door of a murderer. Buster remembered being the Lone Ranger one year.

He went into the kitchen and joined Ellen at the sink. "I'll dry," he said.

"Running Rachel!" said Ellen. "The old women up on Waylon Avenue must be telling the old stories again."

"Every town has its ghost," Buster said. It was back during the winter after the murders that some folks got the notion of Running Rachel. Some said she ran barefoot in the snow. It was almost always somebody talking about somebody else who claimed to have seen her, rumors and snowed-in winter ghost stories, but there was one old widow lady living out at the north end of Front Street along the C&EI tracks—Mrs. Lockhart was her name—who said she saw her running once at twilight, just a glimpse and a trace of gold, gone before she could get a good look. In those days, back before Vietnam and all, when people said they saw things, most folks just let it be, as long as it wasn't too crazy. Seeing ghosts now and then was tolerable as long as you didn't make a habit of it.

"Don't put those in with the good silverware," said Ellen. The good silverware was from Ellen's grandmother and was kept in the back of the drawer. He knew that. Ellen stopped for a moment, looking at Buster's reflection in the kitchen window. "I guess it doesn't do any harm to dress her up like that poor girl—woman really, poor thing," said Ellen. "There're no relations of the Wyatts left in town to take offense, but I'm a little surprised at Brenda letting her girl dress up that way, like a real ghost, I mean."

Buster wondered if Rose Lahae could see ghosts.

When the dishes were done and put away, Ellen took two beers from the fridge, handed one to Buster and went to her desk to grade papers. Buster stopped in the living room to watch Sammo karate chopping his way through an alley full of bad guys. In real life somebody would just shoot him. He turned off the TV and carried his beer out into the front yard.

Draco the Dragon was just over the trees on Wilhelm Avenue across from the football field and there was the North Star to find his way home by and the W of Cassiopeia. It had been a while since he had done any star gazing.

The Scorpion was his favorite as a kid, but he remembered you had to go out to the tracks in back to see it because of the trees. His mom knew about the moon and stars. Tonight it was a waxing moon. It would be full in a few days. His dad wanted to plant shade trees out front but his mom wouldn't have it. They'd take away the stars, she said. With no tall trees out front and the old football field across the street, only the clouds could take away his mom's front-porch stars. The night was still mild but Carl Dun had been on Radio Yonders saying a cold snap was on the way. Carl had a backyard full of thermometers, wind socks, a lumpy-looking revolving thing with spinning balls and propellers and a garage bench full of instruments and gizmos, some of them inherited from his dad, others ordered, he said, from weather laboratories. If Carl said it was turning cold, it was. He said the kids were lucky Halloween wasn't a day later.

Buster walked around the house and out back to the vacant Nickel Plate right of way and up the bank to where the tracks used to run. The Scorpion wasn't out, but he remembered that it was always summer when he saw it. He didn't know the names of the other constellations in the southern sky, but they were familiar. The stars twinkled but the planets didn't. A lightyear is six trillion miles. Mr. Kennedy told them that in grade school. He said when you look to the heavens you are looking into the past and the past is always farther away but it's never gone.

He heard the doorbell and then the piping voices of kids calling out trick-or-treat, and then Ellen's voice. She knew them all. Mrs. Lawton, fifth grade. The last of the kids came to the door a little after nine but Buster left the porch light on till ten before turning in.

The weatherman was right and so was his mom. She always said Indian summer came only a few days after that first killer frost, and it did. After a chilly Sunday night, the day after Halloween, there were three cold days and three freezing early November nights before sweet Indian summer brought ten days of spring-like reprieve.

It was at the beginning of the last warm week of '98 that the call finally came. The DEA was set to spring Operation Marigold North at dawn on Sunday. Sheriff McIntyre said Houston had an intercept confirming that O would pick up the shipment somewhere in the area. Springfield wanted to make the seizure and arrests on the premises of the stash house.

"We don't know who's transporting or where O meets to take possession, but Houston picked up a call. Somebody in Chicago used the wrong phone. Mattoon has orders now and so do we," said McIntyre. "I'll give you the exact hour as soon as they tell me, but have your men ready."

Busy weekend. The big basketball game with Damascus was set for Friday, and the big raid was set for just before dawn on Sunday. Buster decided he'd better carry a second gun in addition to his .357 Magnum. Most of his men carried Glock semiautomatics now, foreign guns—safe but without a real safety. This time, just in case he needed more than six shots, he decided to carry his old .38 Police Special, the revolver he´d carried in training and during his first years on the job. He'd never fired a weapon in the line of duty in thirty-nine years as a cop or in his time as an MP in Korea, but he kept sharp at the shooting range in Damascus a couple of times a year. Yonders police would just be back-up. The boys from Mattoon would be carrying Glock 22s and assault rifles. If all hell broke loose at dawn at Bailey's house, it would probably be enough to wake up the town and maybe even old man Vigas next door to the stash house that still looked like the old corner grocery store to Buster.

He couldn't help thinking that it shouldn't have come to this. What he should have done when he first heard Mike Bailey was selling pot was to just go over there with Murdock and turn the place inside out, haul Bailey in for possession and let him know what was waiting for him if the charge was ever trafficking. Warry would have done that without batting an eye. An unwarranted search they'd call it now. He'd made a few, but not anymore.

Wednesday, two days before the Damascus game and moving up on the raid, Cockrell called with the news he'd been waiting for, and Buster wasn't surprised. Nothing was going to come of Freeman Lane's confession to the Crawford murder or any of the rest of it. Nobody in Damascus or Springfield was of a mind to overturn such an old conviction on the basis of a convicted murderer's attempt to swap one murder for three, especially if it meant digging up, maybe even literally, old skeletons.

"It's dead as a door nail, Buster. All disallowed and put in the nevermore file and don't expect to read another word about it in the paper either," said Cockrell.

"Did Wolfden get run over?"

"Just the opposite," said Cockrell. "He got made assistant sports editor and probably with a raise."

"How did all that fortunate shit come about?"

"Well, one way of looking at it would be to say Mrs. Crawford couldn't keep her man home when he was alive but ever since he died she's kept him deep down in his hole. Wolfden will be at your game on Friday writing about how the Bulldogs stomped your Harvesters instead of annoying folks in high places about how young Jack wandered up the wrong alley and into the path of a switchblade back in the Eisenhower days. I believe Wolfden's Twilight Zone Murderer story is as buried as your farmers and Jack Crawford."

"About what I expected," Buster said. He sat for a moment with the phone in his hand after Cockrell hung up. Like Memory said, you got to either forget it or become the avenging angel. He thought of Rachel trick-or-treating at his door.

That evening at home he took the old .38 out of the case and cleaned and loaded it. The idea of needing all that firepower caused him to shake his head. He'd have to go with holsters on both hips. Maybe he should go cross-draw. Two-gun Lawton! It made him smile. The last two-gun lawman he'd heard of in the general area was old Clyde Lovellette, the six-foot-nine NBA basketball player from the old days who got himself elected Sheriff over in Vigo County, Indiana, after he retired. He wore Justin roper boots and a Stetson and carried two six-shooters. Lovellette applied to be a state trooper but they turned him down because of his height. Same thing happened to Buster when he got discharged from the service. Clyde was too tall for Indiana and Buster too short for Illinois. Rejects the both of them. Lovellette closed down half the whorehouses over in Terre Haute, but they voted him out of office just in time to save the other half.

It was still early after supper, so Buster said, "Want to go to the show tonight?"

"Sure, but you don't," said Ellen. "You don't even know what's on."

"What is?"

"*Deep Impact*," she said. "It's about an asteroid or a comet headed for earth."

"Didn't we already see that?"

"No, we saw *Armageddon*. This one is about a different asteroid."

He wondered if worrying about asteroids and comets was what people in Hollywood did since their weather was always so nice. Folks who live under tornadoes and blizzards worry about things closer to home. He was hoping the warm spell would hang on a little longer, through the weekend anyway, through the basketball game and the bust.

During those last, lingering Indian summer days, Keelan still scowled out from his morning table at the Two Spot. Buster knew that what he told Keelan had put doubt and worry in his mind. At first he'd hoped Keelan might spook and just leave town. He was in the clear, if he only knew it, with no more need to worry about old murder charges than folks needed to worry about asteroids plowing into the Phillmore Building.

Buster was still waiting, but it wasn't for the bust. That would happen or it wouldn't. He was waiting for he didn't know what, but waiting all the same. The Thursday night before the big game he and Ellen were reading the papers and listening to Yonders Radio when Carl Dun broke in with a weather warning. He sounded excited and almost happy. "I'm not saying it will be anything like the Great Blue Norther of 1911, and we can thank our lucky stars for that, because on the eleventh day of the eleventh month of 1911 the temperature dropped sixty-three degrees from one day to the next and, according to my dad's records, twenty-five degrees in less than half an hour. I can't see that happening but we've got a winter storm warning, first one of the year, for Friday evening."

"Lord," said Ellen. "I haven't heard Carl that wound up since he recorded twenty-seven below that time. He was disappointed that he didn't get it confirmed. Maybe we ought to take a walk while it's still warm and nice. It'll be a long winter."

They walked out Iroquois all the way to Johnson Avenue and then back up the other side of Iroquois to Swisher and back toward home on Fifth. Ellen took Buster's hand the last two blocks and it was like walking home from high school or from the show.

Kids were playing in the twilight, in shorts for the last time till May. Buster and Ellen could hear the TVs through the open windows, and there were folks sitting out on their porches talking quietly, cigarettes glowing and fading. Indian summer passes slowly, but there's never quite enough of it.

It was a sweet night, the kind of night for remembering and hoping and scheming.

▪▪▪

Jezzie: Leaving work the other day, I was about to pull out onto the Dixie and I saw him coming. Clive, sitting back behind the wheel of that black Merc. Same leather jacket, same eyes. My foot slipped off the clutch and I killed the engine. But I knew better even before I saw the big bumper sticker that said Peoria Vintage Car Club. He turned west on Indiana road and I heard those straight pipes heading for California, one last time.

▪▪▪

Harold: Don't know what's getting into the weather these days. Must be something the government is doing. I love a warm stretch in the fall, before the bite of Old Man Winter, and, crazy as it sounds, lately I sort of miss the Devil, whether there is one or not.

▪▪▪

Whizdom: The coach came running, blowing his whistle, but it was Cory who got between us. "Come on, you guys," he yelled. "We're all Harvesters." Zeke's still got that little rebel flag stuck on the back window of his truck but, like Cory said, we're all Harvesters.

■■■

Ed: "What's all these cameras for?" Buster asked me. If I said what I was really looking for he'd think I was nuts. Maybe I'm as touched as old Harold, but it's no skin off nobody's nose but ours if one of us talks to nobody and the other one sits up here all night ready and watching for nobody to come walking up the walk.

■■■

Etna: Only yesterday he stood not much higher than my knee, running scared to me to save him from the Indians in the alley, but now he's beyond any saving I can do.

■■■

Keelan: They can't convict a man or even put out a warrant on him without court evidence, without somebody pointing the finger and saying, "It was him. He's the one!" Well, dead fingers can't point.

■■■

Buster: Mrs. Lahae didn't say unsolved. She said unavenged. Maybe the only difference between justice and vengeance is whether it's a judge or a witch who's doing the talking.

■ ■ ■

Midnight quiet came down over Yonders. The town slept the last warm night of the year in a deep silence broken only now and then by a dog barking up on Fugate Hill, a train whistle, a car trailing music or the soft hush of an airliner, coming from far away and going far off, passing over at thirty thousand feet.

Chapter 26

Game Night

The cold snap set in overnight and a chill wind whistled down from the north. "Looks like our weatherman knows his stuff," said Ellen at breakfast.

WGN Morning News predicted strong winds out of the northwest gusting to over fifty miles per hour in the evening and as much as three or four inches of snowfall by midnight with temperatures dropping below freezing. Buster got his fur-lined parka from the back of the closet.

A light snow flurry fell as he drove to work. The sun wasn't even a speck in the gray-white dome over Yonders Booster Club signs were up downtown, some hand-made by high school kids and others printed at the *Chronicle*. There were Go Harvesters! and Beat the Bulldogs! posters pasted to store windows and some taped to boarded-up storefronts. The first snow always brought Buster some sadness. High school football was done and it was a long time till baseball. Maybe if he had played basketball the winters wouldn't have seemed so long, especially after the respite of Christmas and

New Year's. And there was something else too. Maybe just the lonesome feeling of passing time. There'd really be a year 2000. Driving alone through the light snow on the first really cold November morning, Buster said quietly but aloud, "That'll just about do it." He'd retire before they started a new century.

McIntyre called twice during the morning to go over the drug bust details. Weather wouldn't be an issue, the sheriff said. The Mattoon Humvee and the support SUVs were all four-wheel-drive. The sheriff's department would send two 4x4 Yukons. Buster imagined a black caravan winding across town in the dead of the night, bearing down on the old corner grocery store where he and his grade school friends used to sit out front under the shade tree chugging bottles of Royal Crown Cola and Dad's Old Fashioned Root Beer and have belching contests after hours of pick up baseball games on hot summer afternoons.

By lunch time there was a half inch of snow over the town. He was late getting out and Ellen would already be back at school so Buster grabbed a quick lunch at the Two Spot, and he was glad Keelan wasn't there. Everybody was talking about how cold it was and how much colder it was supposed to get. Dandy was telling about seeing frozen crows fall out of the sky during the blizzard of '67. Nobody asked him anything about his crows. Folks knew better.

Buster spent the afternoon doing some paperwork in his office. He had another talk with McIntyre about where to post his officers as backup to cut off alley escapes for the bust. He called all six of his men into his office at the hour of the shift change for a full briefing on the raid and told them when it was coming and not to breathe a word even to the family.

It was nearly dark at six when he started home. After spending the afternoon cooped up in his windowless office, he was surprised at how much more snow had fallen, maybe four inches. The winds were swirling up the fresh snow beneath the streetlights. Some of the gusts hit the Interceptor hard enough to shake the steering wheel.

Ellen was home and looking out the front window when he walked up on the porch. The thermometer was down to twenty-nine. He could see his breath.

"Good thing it's Friday," she said. "Tomorrow'd be a bad day for bussing in the farm kids."

WGN Evening News opened with the weatherman in front of a map talking excitedly about white out conditions in Moline and Galesburg and "increasing winds and heavy snowfall out of the northwest sweeping down from South Dakota over Iowa." The map was in three colors that Buster knew well: Red was blizzard warning, green was blizzard advisory but the color for the Yonders area was the mild blue for winter storm advisory. "Be alert," the weatherman said, "for any changes in the forecast."

Buster and Ellen sat down to a quick kitchen-table supper. "I checked before I came home and Dornfeld says the game is still on," he said. "In fact, the Damascus bus ought to be getting here about now. Want to see the game?"

The wind was whistling in the eaves and rattling the mailbox. "Not in this weather," said Ellen. "I have a pile of papers to grade anyway. You can tell me all about it."

The reserved parking lot behind the gym was nearly full when Buster pulled in. It was snowing heavily and the freshly fallen snow was whipping up in the wind. The bare limbs of the giant oak back of the Happ Hopkins writhed like black skeleton hands and a fresh mantle of frozen snow cleaved to the trunk of the century-old tree veiling the carved initials, names and nicknames of high school sweethearts from the old days. True Love. Forever. No new carving was allowed, but Buster knew that

T W

+

B H

stood for Tom Wellington and Becky Hall, his girlfriend, class of '59, who ending up marrying a flyboy from Chanute Air Force Base. That, Ellen told Buster one day when she noticed it, is the trouble with carving on trees.

Buster hurried up the steps and into the sudden warmth of the dim corridor that led from the back entrance past the Clorox-smelling dressing rooms to the court. Before stepping out into the light of the gym, he heard the familiar chirping of the shoes, the varied cadences of dribbling, the swish of the net and the shouts of the players.

The Happ was half full and filling fast as folks came in shedding coats, stocking caps and scarves. The Harvesters weren't on the floor yet, but the Bulldogs, a dozen players, seven white and five Black, were running cross-over layup drills, yelling out to each other—big boys, fast and loose, almost wild. Each boy had the snout of a snarling bulldog on the back of his red and black warm-up jersey. Buster joined Mayor Tom standing courtside near the Yonders bench and Mayor Tom said softly what Buster was thinking: "Holy shit!"

"Six-foot-six is taller when you see it in the flesh than on television," said Buster, and Mayor Wellington seemed to stand a little taller.

"I'm surprised to see so many folks here what with this storm," said Buster.

"Blizzard, more likely," said the mayor. "We got Streets and Alleys on standby."

A big cheer came up and Buster looked toward the players entrance. The Harvesters, in blue and white, broke onto the floor. They were led by big Zeke Grandey and Butch Dawson. The co-captains ran side by side with the rest of the players zippering into single file behind. There were nine boys the whole town knew and one most had caught a glimpse of and all had heard about. Whizdom Lahae had three qualities that no one on the team could match: He was from Chicago, he was Black and his mom was a witch.

After the warm-up drills, the Harvesters went into a shootaround. The gym was filling and the cheerleaders were warming up the chilled fans with some of the same chants Buster remembered from his high school days. He looked along the front rows and saw Rose Lahae, dressed all in black but for a blue Harvesters stocking cap.

"See that guy sitting just back of our bench?" said the mayor. "The guy with the orange and blue jacket. I'll bet you five bucks he's a scout."

"Couldn't make it more obvious if he was dressed as Chief Illiniwek. You figure he's here to see their guy or Whizdom?"

"It's got to be for Whizdom. Word gets around. Otherwise, why come here for a preseason game with a Single A school?"

At the buzzer the teams went to their benches for last-minute instructions. The lights over the seating sections went dim leaving the powerful overheads to cast their glow onto the golden hardwood. And then there was a surprise. Five white players in Damascus colors broke from their pregame huddle and took their places at the middle of the floor.

▪▪▪

The Yonders players were about to take the floor, but Dornfeld called them back. "See that? That's what they think of us. They're starting their subs."

Whizdom looked to Dornfeld, "They're dissing us. We should jump them before they get their feet under them. I'll bet not one of them ever started a varsity game before."

Dornfeld was quiet for a split second and then he said, "Yeah. OK. Hit them hard right from the start. Go to the last twenty-second offense and full court press on defense. Bring it in! On three. One, two, three!"

The boys yelled, "Harvesters!" and ran out onto the court. Whizdom looked over the five Damascus players as he took his place for the tipoff. Nervous kids, trying to look tough. He'd never started a varsity game before either, but it was different. He'd played for Oak Park and on this very night, if his mom weren't a witch, he knew he'd have been making his first start as a Husky against Hinsdale only a little over one hundred miles away but in another world.

Grandey got the tip to Cory and the Harvesters broke downcourt. Cory, with two defenders running at his heels, fired a pass to Whizdom in the corner. He had to step forward to catch it and then he stepped back behind the line and went up for a high, arching, slow-spinning three that was perfect. Yonders 3 - Visitors 0. The Harvesters then went into a full-court press. The kid making the inbound saw no one open. Coach Campbell, off the Damascus bench, was yelling for a timeout but the flustered inbounder tried a long sideline pass that went wide and was caught in the first row by Stanley Ferris, a foreman at American Pride and once a Harvester forward, class of '79. Everyone cheered him and he flipped the ball to the referee and took a little bow.

Damascus took time. The crowd was so loud the cheerleaders didn't even try to lead a cheer. Whizdom saw the fire in his teammates' eyes, in Coach Dornfeld's eyes too. "We got just three or four minutes at most before he sends in his big boys. We got to make hay while the sun shines," Dornfeld yelled. Whizdom had never heard a coach say that at Oak Park.

For the next three minutes the Yonders starters dominated the Damascus subs who never settled in after that frantic start. The score was Yonders 10 – Visitors 2 when Damascus called another time. The Bulldogs looked stunned and embarrassed, but their coach had his clipboard and was drawing up plays, looking from player to player. The five regular Bulldog starters were bunched together on the bench, leaning forward, raring to go. Whizdom knew they'd be coming in soon. He took a quick glance at Wendell Truman. Truman was watching him.

"Just get me the ball," Whizdom said to Cory as they went back onto the floor. Cory did. Whizdom hit a short jumper and was fouled in the act. It was Yonders 12 – Visitors 2 with Whizdom at the free throw line when the buzzer sounded and Wendell Truman came off the bench.

"Thought you'd never get here," said Whizdom, smiling as Truman nearly brushed him, walking past to take his place on the lane.

Buddy Bowman, who always watched every detail, told everyone later that Truman put himself in the game. If he did, Coach Campbell didn't stop him, and he sent in the other four regulars next chance he had. The game changed with Damascus at full strength, but Yonders, urged on by the crowd, fought hard and that ten-point lead was only down to five at the half.

At the start of the second half, Damascus scored first—Truman on a tip-in—but Whizdom, double-teamed, fired a no-look, bounce pass off to Grandey all alone under the basket and the lead was back to five.

“The kid is more than just a shooter,” said Larrivee, and Whizdom liked hearing that and winked at his mom in her blue stocking cap as he ran back on defense.

▪▪▪

The cheering, as the teams continued to swap the lead, was so loud that no one heard the huge, ice-laden limb of the ancient oak crash to the ground. Yonders was under a blizzard, but no one in the gym knew except Buster who more felt than heard the crackling of Sally’s voice from the walkie-talkie speaker on his epaulet. He went out into the hall and stood in front of the trophy case. “Say again, Sally.”

“Buster, you hear me? Chief? We’re getting hammered. You looked outside?”

He walked down the dimly lit hall to the main doorway and looked out through the wind-blown snow, so thick he could barely see the streetlight on the corner. The street wasn’t so bad, but there were drifts in the parking lot that were up to the doors on many of the cars.

“You hearing this, Bruno?” said Buster. “Where you at?”

“Sitting out at Four Corners watching it come down,” said Murdock. “You need me?”

“Yeah, I’ll meet you out front of the gym. This is a hell of a lot more than three inches, more like five,” said Buster. “No way that bus goes back to Damascus tonight, but what worries me more is how we get these cars out of the lot so folks can go home. I’m gonna get Tom to get Streets and Alleys over here. I’ll meet you out front.”

Buster went back into the raucous gym just as one of the Damascus guards stole the ball from Cory Wilson and Damascus scored on a fast break. Buster glanced at the scoreboard. Tied. "You don't want to be missing this," said Mayor Tom.

"Afraid I'll have to and I need you to miss a bit too. We got some weather out there. I need you to get on one of the school phones and call Ralph and have him get over here fast with the plow and a load of gravel or salt, whatever Ralph thinks. Otherwise, we got more than five hundred people stranded out here."

Murdock joined Buster and the janitor in the school parking lot after the slick, slow drive from Four Corners, and the three, carrying flashlights, walked the parking area, raising their voices to talk over the wind.

"I think Ralph can clear the way to the street if it doesn't get much worse," said Buster.

"How's the game going?" said Murdock.

"We were still right in it last I saw," said Buster. "Whatever happens, this is going to be a night to remember."

While Damascus and Yonders battled and the cheers from the gym were muffled by the winds, Ralph, with the big Streets and Alleys Freightliner, plowed a path out of the over-filled parking lot as Buster, Murdock and the janitor shoveled snow from the steps and the walk. Once the drifts were cleared, Ralph got down from the cab and gave Murdock a bucket of rock salt to spread on the stairs. They were done just in time and Ralph was salting the driveway out to Main when the gym doors swung open and the first of the crowd came out shielding their eyes from the wind and snow.

Mayor Tom, his stocking cap pulled down almost over his eyes, was among the first out the door and found his way to Buster and Murdock. He shouted to Buster over the wind, "We almost did it! They beat us by three, but, by God, we made them sweat for it."

He would have said more but it was then that the wind-whipped power lines back of the power substation between Iroquois and the tracks tangled, snarled, broke and fell sparking to the ground, leaving Yonders blind in a rogue blizzard.

Chapter 27

Red Squirrel

The first big blast came just before seven. The north wind rattled the glass in Keelan's windows and howled around the corners of the house. He thought at once that this might be just the weather he had been waiting for.

If Buster had just said, I know you did it, Keelan could have said, but you can't prove it, and the two could have gone about their business, but no, Buster tells him that the law can hang two men for something even a damn fool knows only one of them could have done. If that was a lie, Keelan thought, he was just trying to fluster me, maybe run me out of town so he didn't have to know what he thinks he knows and not be able to do nothing about it.

If the law was as cockeyed as Buster said, Harold Dresher was the only witness he had call to fear. A judge might let a man like Dresher up on the witness stand and a jury would believe him, and now he'd not only seen Dresher's Chevy parked right out front of the police station and Buster's truck in front of Harold's house, he also had the Devil's word as to what the two of them were scheming about. It was hard to keep straight what he actually knew for a fact and the craziness of the Devil romping on the Nickel Plate, and then there was talk he overheard at the Two Spot about somebody seeing a ghost in a yellow dress running the tracks out by the graveyard. If all Buster's talk about the law was only bullshit meant to perturb him, then he'd be killing a man for nothing and that would be on Buster, not him.

His plan had been to wait for a big mid-winter storm and take to the alleys at two or three in the morning, but why wait and give them more time? Maybe this storm was just what he needed. He remembered hearing somebody on the radio say it was Friday the thirteenth, the lucky day for losers.

His Colt was loaded and the silencer fitted, but he wasn't going to rush it. It would have to get a lot worse outside. He sat watching the end of Candid Camera. They were about to tell some bastard that he had made a fool of himself for all the world to see and—wouldn't you know it!—the TV went out along with the lights. Still he sat, waiting to see if they came back on. Minutes passed. He went to the window. Not a light out there, not a car in the street and the wind was screaming over his roof. He felt his way along the wall to the kitchen and fumbled in the cabinet drawer for his flashlight. It was dim, but he gave it a knock and it came on stronger. He went to the bedroom closet and got out his parka and boots. Paul, down at the hardware store, tried to sell him a heavy, fur-lined yellow one. He didn't want to come right out and say he preferred something that would be hard to see in the night, so he said it didn't fit right. Paul was happy to sell him a black parka the same size that cost ten bucks more. It had deep pockets, deep enough for his gun with the silencer. He'd wear his thin gloves, piano player gloves he called them. He'd need touch to pick the lock and thin gloves for the trigger.

Was he really going? The flashlight dimmed again and he gave it another knock. He took the Colt from under the mattress and fetched his lock-picking kit from the dresser drawer. When he put on the boots he got the feeling he was probably going and when he put on the parka and his black stocking cap, he knew. He snugged the automatic into his right pocket. He'd had it all planned out as carefully as when he carried those two double aught shells jammed between his knuckles. Yes, he was going. It made him feel young again to be going out to do what he had to do. They'd play hell getting a power crew out fast on a night like this.

No more than ten minutes had passed since the power went off and the wind was still fierce. The flashlight went dim again and when he gave it a knock it went out. He threw it on the bed. As long as he could see his hand in front of his face, he'd know the way.

It took both hands to close the door behind him. It was pitch black at first, but his eyes reconciled with the night and he set out. In places the drifts were up to his boot tops. The wind jostled him as he walked and twice he stopped and widened his stance to steady himself against a hard gust. Not a headlight anywhere, only the faint glow of a

Coleman lamp or candles or a flashlight behind a window now and then.

He turned up the side street of Harold's block, cut down the alley and made his way past three back gates, halfway to where he reckoned Harold's house to be. He stood still for a moment recombobulating. He knew he had to pass back of a vacant lot and the backyards of three or four more houses, but was it three or four? He had never walked that alley. He had run it once, chased, the night he was treed. He began walking again, carefully now, leaning into the wind. Almost there, but he just wasn't sure which back walk was the right one, and then, suddenly, he saw the giant watching him from behind a trash can—that same Indian with his feather sticking up, the one who showed him the way to run the night he got treed, still standing there by the narrow walk that ran between a line of bushes and a long outbuilding up to the back of a house that might be Harold's. He ought to thank that Indian, stepping up to help him every forty years or so.

He could just make out the house at the end of the walk, but was that Dresher's house? He'd know once he got close enough, and he did. It was the wrong house. The back door flung open and he caught a glimpse of the man with a shotgun just before he felt the hot wallop of death and, for an instant, he saw the curse in Rachel's eyes.

That first jolt of pain that came with the blast faded fast and was gone and he was feeling warm and looking up at the most beautiful summer sky he'd ever seen. The air was fresh and sweet and hopeful and he could hear birds singing and the shrill, throbbing cry of summertime cicadas, and then the red squirrel, tail in the air, spoke up. "That's Keelan. Etna's little boy is dead."

Chapter 28

The Cold Ground

The last of the cars and pickups were slowly rolling east on Main. Ralph, at the wheel of the big Streets and Alleys plow truck, had hauled the last car, Holly Ann Butcher's old Buick, out of the back of the lot. It was quiet again except for the wind. The only lights still glowing through the wind-tumbled snow were the flashers on the radio antennas at Four Corners and the red cherry atop the water tower.

After Buster and Murdock put chains on the two police cars, Buster radioed Sally for news of the weather. "The Dixie Highway is still OK," she said. "County says it could get a lot worse unless the storm lets up. Illiana Power says we'll be in the dark till dawn."

Coach Dornfeld came out of the gym and told Buster they had booked the Bulldogs into the Four Corners Motel, but the driver needed to be led out there. Dornfeld was leaning down, talking to Buster through the half open window of the Interceptor.

"I'll get Bruno here to lead them out there," said Buster. "Hey, Coach, I didn't get to see much of the second half, but Tom said your boys gave them a game."

"You never seen the like," yelled Dornfeld over the wind. "That was the best game we ever lost."

The chief sat in the Interceptor with Murdock waiting for the Damascus players, cheerleaders and coaches to board the bus. When the bus driver flashed his lights, Murdock said, "What do you want me to do after I deliver this bunch?"

"Well, you can start by warming yourself up and getting a cup of coffee out of the machine at the motel. I think we've had about enough excitement for one night." Buster watched Murdock lead the bus out onto Main until he saw the flashing lights of the police car disappear into the night. He sat for a moment at the wheel. Another year. Yeah, that'd just about do it.

He was crossing the tracks on the way home when the radio crackled and Sally said, "Buster, I just got the strangest call from Ed Goodman over on Swisher. He said to tell you he just killed somebody, but he doesn't know who. Then he hung up."

"That's all he said?" As he spoke, he accelerated on the slick, empty street.

"That's all. He either got cut off or hung up. Should I call him back? The phones are still up and running."

"No, I'm on my way, and you better call Charlie to get the ambulance over to Ed's. You hearing all this, Bruno?"

"What we got, Chief?" Murdock answered over the static.

"Possible homicide," said Buster. "Come on over after you get the bus to the motel."

Maybe he just shot some old ghost that he brought back from Korea in his mind, but Buster knew Ed wouldn't make something like that up or imagine it. Ed might have shot something out of a nightmare, but only if it walked up to him on two feet and made tracks, and it wouldn't be an armed Brownie Scout cookie girl in a blizzard. If he used that 12 gauge at close range, they'd need a hearse, not an ambulance. He knew it would take Charlie a few minutes to get himself organized and he'd need to take it easy on the snowy streets. Murdock was coming in from Four Corners, two miles of icy roads away, so Buster would have a little time with Ed before they got there. He decided against using the siren and lights.

Swisher Avenue was so dark and the snow so thick that, if he hadn't known where Ed's place was, he would have had to turn his spotlight on the house numbers. He pulled to a stop and turned on the red and blue flashing roof lights to guide the others in. Snow pelted his face as he walked against the wind to the house, flashlight in hand. He kept the beam down and stopped just short of the glass storm door. He was able to make out the figure of Ed, white hair long and tousled, sitting erect on the coaster, his face lit in the dim glow of the screens. He remembered Ed had battery backup for his cameras and monitors. Buster, standing rock still, spoke loudly over the wind, but in a calm tone. "Ed, it's me."

Ed gestured for him to come in and Buster, flashlight beam at his feet, stepped inside holding tight against the wind to close the door behind him. He could make out Ed's pistol at his side and the shotgun on the table. It was quiet inside.

"There's a man dead out back," said Ed. "I don't know him."

"Show me," said Buster.

Ed stood and opened the door to the living room, letting the cold wind rush through from the back of the house. The kitchen door was wide open to the inside and the storm door was opened out, banging against the aluminum siding. He pointed and Buster cast the beam of his flashlight onto the body of a man in black, dusted in fresh snow, splayed out on his back no more than twenty feet from the stoop.

Ed stayed back as Buster went to the body and turned his light to the dead man's face, eyes open, staring up at nothing. If Ed had aimed a foot higher, Buster wouldn't have recognized Keelan Putnam, dead with his empty hands thrown out to both sides like Jesus on Golgotha, or like the thieves crucified at his side. His face was almost calm. Below that face was what a 12 gauge loaded with double aught buckshot does to a human being from twenty feet—close enough to keep the pattern tight. He thought of Rose Lahae. "I saw a man looking up in the night with frozen eyes and there was someone bending over him. It was you."

Buster knelt beside the body and was glad to find the Colt fitted with a silencer in the deep pocket of Keelan's parka. Ed hadn't killed an unarmed man. A judge might consider the silencer as proof of intent, but Ed would have had no way of knowing the man was armed.

"Do your cameras record?" he said over his shoulder.

"They do if you put tape in them. I just use them for eyes," said Ed.

Faintly in the distance, coming from way out by Four Corners, Buster heard Murdock's familiar siren. It would still take him three or four minutes. A long moment passed with Buster crouched by the body. Ed watched from behind. From halfway across town, they heard a second siren, the higher-pitched, old-fashioned whining of Charlie's ambulance.

Buster, with gloved hands, carefully removed the gun from Keelan's parka pocket. It was cocked and locked with the thumb safety on, the way men who carried guns carried guns. He doubted for only for a few seconds before releasing the safety and placing the gun just beyond Keelan's fingertips. Ed's eyes were on the black pistol in the snow. Buster walked back to Ed, turned him with his hand on his elbow, and they reentered the house. The flashlight shone on the old, cracked wallpaper. Pink roses and green leaves. They walked through to the enclosed front porch. Buster shut the door behind them and it was almost still.

"Who did I kill?" said Ed.

The first siren was very close, just down the block, and then it ceased as Murdock stopped at the curb out front, red and blue lights flashing. The ambulance was louder now and closing.

"You killed Keelan Putnam."

"Vernon and Etna's boy?" said Ed, and he put his hand to his forehead.

Buster studied Ed's face in the dim light. A war hero. A good man. Looking the old Marine in the eye, Buster said slowly, "I know you shot him when you saw him point that gun at you. I'd have done just the same."

Murdock was coming up the walk now. As he reached the door, Charlie drove up in the ambulance, stopped and cut the siren. The flashing blue and red lights of the two police cars and the flashing red of the ambulance tinted the wind-riled snow and the skeletal trees.

Buster accompanied the two men through the house and out the kitchen door. Buster and Murdock went through their forensics checklist as Charlie looked on.

"Safety was off," said Murdock when they finished.

"Yeah," said Buster. "I need you to witness while I take down Ed's statement."

They rejoined Ed, sitting on the coaster in the light of the flickering monitors. Charlie followed.

Buster sat down by Ed. "I want you to tell us what happened here. Just take your time and don't leave anything out."

Murdock held the flashlight and Buster wrote Ed's slowly spoken words in his notebook.

"I was sitting here watching it storm and I saw something on the backyard monitor. I could just make out a man coming out of the dark. I took the shotgun to the back door and there he was coming slow up the back walk." He stopped talking and looked down at his hands and then looked to Buster, but Buster's eyes were on the notebook page. Ed looked away from Buster and at the monitors. The night pulsed faintly with the flashing lights from the vehicles out front.

"He was holding a gun," said Ed, still looking away. "He aimed it at me…" He looked at Buster. "And I shot him dead."

Buster met his eyes. "Did you know him?"

"I do now that you told me. It's Keelan Putnam. But I didn't know before." Buster wrote Ed's last words, set his jaw and looked to Murdock who nodded. There was no need now to even take Ed down to the station.

Buster tried Ed's phone and it worked. Sally answered, and he asked her to call Coroner Crosby in Damascus. "Tell him we got a homicide and the body hasn't been moved and we'll keep it that way till he can get himself up here." He hung up and turned to Charlie. "Coroner needs to see him as he fell but we can't have him uncovered out there like that," said Buster.

"I got a tarp and some pegs but the wind'll get under it," said Charlie.

"I got five or six concrete blocks in the garage," said Ed.

After the tarp was secured over Keelan, Buster told Charlie he could go. Murdock, Ed and Buster returned to the porch where Ed sat looking at the three screens that showed snow and writhing black branches. The shape in the foreground of the third screen was the body. "For just a second there I was back in the war, but I knew better."

Buster nodded. "It's over and done with."

But Ed shook his head. "It's not right. He wasn't coming for me. It makes no sense him coming to rob a poor man. Where do you reckon he was really headed, or coming back from?"

Yes, thought Buster suddenly, what if Keelan had already been where he was really going? Just looking to see how many rounds in the magazine wouldn't tell him anything; he needed to check on Harold. That's who Keelan was gunning for. Of course.

"You stay here with Ed a bit. I need to check on something," said Buster to Murdock. "You OK for now, Ed?"

"Yeah," Ed said, "I reckon I am," and then he said, "Thank you."

Buster hurried through the cold wind to Harold's house and was glad to find the door closed and intact, but there was still the backdoor. He knocked.

Harold, half asleep, wondered at first if it was the Devil wanting in out of the storm. He tried the lights and then got his flashlight off the dresser and put on his robe and slippers. He pulled back the front door window curtain. Buster thought about shining his flashlight on his own face, but he was afraid that would scare the old man. It was Harold who shined his light on Buster's face and then he hurried to unlock the door and let him in, closing the door quickly against the cold. The two, their flashlights beams on each other's chests, talked in the dark living room, but just seeing Harold told Buster all he needed to know.

"Did you hear the commotion a while back?" said Buster.

"When the lights and the TV went off, I turned in. Slept like a log till I heard sirens. They sounded close, but I knew they weren't coming for me so I went back to sleep."

But a Mexican named O just a few houses away might have jumped to another conclusion, thought Buster. He looked at his watch. Getting onto an hour now since the sirens came wailing down Swisher. "Just checking. Everything is fine now."

"What wasn't?" said Harold, but Buster was on his way, leaving Harold standing puzzled in his living room.

He turned the Interceptor around and drove to the old corner grocery store. All three vehicles, the black Ram, the yellow Mustang and Bailey's old truck, were gone. He'd seen them when he passed on the way to Ed's, the Ram backed into the drive and Bailey's truck parked out front along with the Mustang. All three of them were gone and the front door was standing wide open.

He needed to call McIntyre, and then he needed to think how to go about telling Mrs. Putnam her boy was dead. Do you wake someone up in the black of the night, or do you wait and grant the mercy of breaking bad news in the morning light? He drove by her house. It was only a block out of his way. No lights inside. No one would go by to tell her. No one knew, just Ed and Charlie and Murdock and the coroner down in Damascus and Harold. No, he hadn't told Harold. It'd keep till morning.

Sally had the emergency generator working and a few lights on at the station. He checked the time before he called; it was going on eleven. He could tell from how McIntyre said "Yeah, what?" that he had a hunch the call had something to do with the big bust.

"Your Mexican and your Joliet boy are gone. We had a homicide just down the block from the house and, what with all the sirens and lights, it looks like your boys got spooked and cleared out. No vehicles there and the front door's wide open."

McIntyre asked one question and Buster answered, "Getting onto an hour and a quarter ago."

"Damn!" said the sheriff. "I'll call you back later." But Buster knew there was no way the Mattoon army would be coming to town. Not this time and probably not for a while, but there was no turning things back. He'd seen it come to Damascus and even to Blunt. The day would come, sooner or later. Mattoon commandos in battle gear armed to fight Arabs, and a dog named Gonzo.

He called Ellen and she answered on the first ring. She had heard the sirens and was worried, she said. He told her everything was under control, no danger. He'd be working another hour or so, but she should go back to sleep. He radioed Murdock. "Stay with Ed till your shift ends. I'll be in the office for a while yet filling out reports and I'll be by in the morning but, if I know the coroner, he'll be there before I am."

It was one-thirty when Buster left for home. The snow had stopped, the wind was starting to die and the streets were like Christmas. There was a Beat the Bulldogs poster in the window of the barber shop. He didn't realize how tired he was until he got to his front door. Just before he put his key in the slot, he heard the phone ringing inside but he couldn't get to it before it woke Ellen.

"It's Pete Bailey," she said in a sleepy voice, holding the phone out to Buster. The power was still off, but he had his pocket flashlight.

Buster remembered Pete as a northside hood back in the sixties, a hellraiser as a kid, but he came back from Nam quieter. He'd seen combat. "Buster, my boy says he's in big trouble."

"Well, he's not, but he is in a little trouble. You tell your boy to stay right there with you and not to go anywhere or talk to anybody until he talks to me, and make sure he does what you tell him."

"What did Pete want at this hour?" said Ellen.

"Same thing lots of folks want. A second chance for his boy."

"You going to tell me what happened and what you're talking about?"

"It was a homicide. Keelan Putnam was prowling out back of Ed Goodman's carrying a gun and Ed shot him, killed him."

"Good Lord!" Then she stopped and said, "You can tell me all about it in the morning. You look like a ghost. You get to bed."

"I'm getting up at six," he said.

He checked his watch and put back the lost minutes on his mom's ticking clock, wound it and set the alarm, but he awoke a few minutes before it would have rung. He had been dreaming he was a kid again, helping his mom gather a little bunch of black-eyed Susans from around the graves on the Lawton plot out at Floral Hill. It was a warm morning a long time ago. The sun was starting to climb the sky, making long shadows to the west and a lot of old folks were up and walking around, looking just like they did when they were alive. They were visiting with one another, familiar voices from when he was a kid, and he heard his dad's laugh coming from high on the hill. He was about to go looking for his dad when a train whistled, loud and close, and everybody looked down to the point where the tracks appeared at the base of Floral Hill. It was a streamliner, blue and gold, streaking south and whistling for the Double Aught crossing, crying its way past the old Wyatt place, and he heard his mother's voice. "Dixie Flyer, right on time."

But the dream was quickly lost behind the fresh memory of Keelan Putnam, dead in the snow, and there was another mother only a few blocks away who needed word of her boy.

Buster told Ellen all that had happened over a quick breakfast. "Does Mrs. Putnam know?" she asked.

"No. I'm going over there right now."

On the way to Etna's, Buster drove past the stash house, the front door still standing open. He'd go by and see Bailey after the coroner's jury. He'd bring the kid in for possession as a first-time offender and the most they could get out of him would be phone numbers of throwaway phones that would never ring again. No way O told him anything. They'd catch the kid in the Mustang whenever they took a mind to but those five or six hundred pounds of Mexican marijuana were long gone and with it the only one they ever really cared about catching. It was strictly a Yonders matter now.

Etna was at the door seconds after he knocked. She opened the door and stepped back and Buster entered. The radio in the kitchen was playing an old familiar song. He thought about asking her to sit, but Etna Putnam was not a woman to faint. She already knew it was awful, whatever it was, as soon she saw him at her door.

"Your boy Keelan was shot and killed last night. It was quick. He didn't suffer." He was about to say more, but she raised her hand to stop him.

Standing tall, she asked, "Was there call?"

Buster didn't say what they both knew, although Buster didn't know she knew that Keelan had been on his way to kill an old man for remembering a black car.

"There was call," Buster said. "It was Ed Goodman. He saw your boy coming up his back walk with a gun."

She closed her eyes for a moment and then, looking firmly at Buster, she asked, "Is he up off the cold ground?"

He was glad he didn't have to lie. He couldn't have her see her boy frozen in the snow, not even in her mind. Keelan's body was at Fisher's Funeral Home, he told her. She could see him in the afternoon after the coroner's jury.

"Don't go telling Jezzie. I'll tend to that," she said.

"I'll call you when you can go by the funeral home. I'm awful sorry, Mrs. Putnam."

"I know you are and I thank you," she said, looking now toward the door.

Buster followed her eyes and left. He didn't ask if there was anything he could do because there wasn't. The door closed softly behind him. He stepped down from the stoop and walked to the car listening to the morning, so crisp and quiet, but still a touch breezy after the blizzard. Some sunlight had broken through.

Just before he closed the door of the Interceptor, he thought he heard a faraway whistling, so faint he couldn't be sure where it was coming from. Sometimes, toward the end, his dad used to look up and say he thought he heard trains way out in the country on the Nickel Plate long after they'd taken up the tracks, trains that never got to town. It worried Buster that his dad was hearing things, but his mom just smiled her smile and he recalled that smile and her words. "It's just his ears remembering, hearing ghost trains running on moonbeams." And there it was again, far off. He smiled. Getting to be like his dad.

But as he drove toward town on Iroquois, he heard it closer, a real one, coming up from behind him on the C&EI. When he turned onto Main he saw it, a fast southbound freight cutting him off from the station. But there was no hurry. As far as he knew, there was not a single murderer walking the streets of our town, at least for now.

Chapter 29

The Winds of Regret

Etna stood behind the door until she heard Buster drive away and then she went to the kitchen and turned off the radio and walked to the window and looked out over the clean blanket of snow.

It all made sense. Keelan must have got his houses mixed up. Just like him. Whatever Buster Lawton and old man Dresher thought they knew didn't count for nothing now, and that was a final blessing. Nobody would ever really know the awful thing her boy did all those many years ago, nobody who was above ground anyway. Just her and Buster. She turned from the window and picked up the phone. It was Jezzie's weekend off. She answered with a sleepy voice.

"Can you get your car out, Honey? I need you to come by."

"Are you OK, Mom? What is it? Are you OK?"

"I'm fine. We just need to talk."

"I'll be over soon as I can shovel out."

"Drive careful, Honey. There's no hurry."

She hung up and looked again out the back window.

Seemed like only yesterday, as folks say, that those little kids were running in and out, playing cowboys and Indians, shooting toy guns and whooping it up out back in the alley. Jezzie knew Keelan when he was still little and good, before he turned. She needed to hear it from family, not from some loudmouth at the grocery store. He was still her big brother and he always would be, in spite of it all. The sun was out and, my, wouldn't they have had fun romping in all that snow.

She left the window and sat down in her chair at the kitchen table. Vernon had wanted to buy a new, bigger one, but it was a good solid oak table and plenty big enough, a wedding present from Amos and Unity, bought new down in Damascus. She could see them all sitting in their places over the many years: Vernon at the head with his back to the window, Jezzie on her side and Keelan on his, and she, when everybody was served, sitting across from Vernon and with an eye to the cookstove and a view of the backyard. There's nothing wrong with this table, she told him. It'll outlast us all.

When all's said and done, as bad as it was, it was better to have a good man like old Dresher walking the streets for another couple of years than to have another death chalked up to a Tucker. Buster would have figured it out anyhow.

It hurt her heart to think there wasn't another soul on Earth who cared that her boy was dead except, in her way, sister Spite, who had as much Tucker in her as any of them but with a Tucker woman's good sense to save her. She'd call Spite later.

Jezzie would come around to caring too, but she didn't know it yet. Etna'd lost track of little Mae, married again somewhere down in Kentucky or wherever she was, and it would be a mercy if her girl never knew what became of her father.

Not a living soul who'd care a whit, nor a dead one neither, except poor Vernon who was too good a man to see the bad in the world even if it walked up to him on the street and said hello. Not another single soul who cared, she thought, unless you count that jug of dirt he told her about. That was all her boy had to show for his days on Earth. Still, she thought, a body don't bring nothing with them into the world so anything at all is better than nothing at the end. Well, that'd be one more reason for her and Jezzie to make that drive down home come summer. She'd show Jezzie the old woods. And they'd mix the ashes and scatter them to the winds of Regret.

And, for all she knew, there might be some big, bright heaven waiting back of the stars above and maybe a big old God stomping around up there to make a lost soul feel at home. She wasn't counting on it, but for his sake, for Keelan, she dearly hoped there could be such a thing, that there'd be some forgiveness, that room would be made for him so he could be, which is about all anybody could ever ask because you start out knowing nothing and you look to others to guide you, and all they have for you is some old sayings that you can't make heads nor tails of.

The cold slowly came over her as she sat there, cold to the bone, but it didn't matter. Keelan would never feel any cold or any pain again. He'd never again feel lonesome misery. That of itself was a blessing, all the blessing he'd ever know, but a blessing all the same. She was glad they'd had that last visit the day he did forty years of talking over a couple cups of coffee. She was glad she had listened to him tell all he had to tell and glad she'd put her hand to his cheek that evening.

Her pa said life was too short for bellyaching. He told her that when the foxes killed the little chicks. She wished she could remember more of what the old folks said when she was a girl, things you pay no mind to as a child because you want to get out in the sunshine and run and play. Then, when you're old and trying to remember what to say to the ones coming along after you, you recollect so little that could be of comfort.

When she was a little girl just up from Regret, there was a saying among the Yonders old folks that she'd never heard down home. It made no sense to her then and it even scared her, but now, on this day, it sounded almost hopeful. God's in his heaven and the Devil's in the corn.

And for our little while, thought Etna, we're making do here in between.

Epilogue

1999
Independence Day

The Fourth of July came on Sunday and Harold had been up with the birds, listening to the early morning news. After breakfast, he sat looking at the phone on the dining room wall. Hard to remember the last time it had rung. He'd been on one end or the other of that wire all his life, calling from San Francisco, California, the day the troop ship brought him back home from the war, and he'd been standing behind his mom years later listening to her laugh and gab and waiting to get on the phone himself to hear about the marriages of his brothers and sisters, their good luck and bad, and weights and times of birth of new nephews and nieces in Kentucky, in Indiana and out in Washington state and California. And there was the dying too. There wouldn't be much more of that. Years and years of news had come over that wire, but the calls he most remembered and missed were the ones that weren't about much of anything, just kidding and laughing, shooting the breeze back when everybody was alive.

The Fourth of July wasn't like Christmas or a birthday, but still, it would be nice to call somebody. What would he say? Happy Fourth of July? Maybe he'd call his brother down in Louisville a little later. After lunch he did call, but nobody answered and a recorded voice came on. He didn't know what to say so he hung up. They were probably all out at a park for a picnic or maybe a ballgame. Harold read the *Tribune* at the dining room table and stepped out on the front porch around one o'clock, but it was too hot even in the shade, so he went back in, turned on the electric fan and picked up the book he was reading. *Crusade in Europe* by General Dwight David Eisenhower. Thick as a brick. His bookmark was halfway, but there were another three hundred pages to read and the book was due on Wednesday. He'd read it before, many years back, but he'd seen it on a library shelf when he was poking around the history section and he checked it out again. It'd been maybe forty years since he read it the first time, but nothing had changed and it made him feel, just for a minute now and then, like he was a young Seabee halfway around the world and feeling his oats. He'd have to walk over to the library and renew it or they'd fine him. Maybe he could finish it in three days. He settled into his big chair and listened to Ike talking slowly off the pages, telling all about the war.

It was twilight out when he woke, the book fallen closed in his lap—he'd lost his place—and he looked at his watch. Just after seven, past time to be hungry, but he figured he'd roust up something for supper. He had a bologna sandwich with mustard and a glass of milk and watched the WGN news. He thought about maybe driving out to the park later for the fireworks. He used to drive out there with his mom, but he wasn't seeing as well as he used to for night driving. Besides, from the porch swing he could see the sky out over the park.

They usually started around nine-thirty, so a little after nine Harold was sitting in the swing when he heard footsteps on the porch stairs. He spoke before he looked up. "I sorta been expecting you."

But the man standing before him was not the one he'd imagined.

"Expecting me?" said Ed.

"Who else would I be expecting?" said Harold, and he was not really surprised to see his neighbor. Since that blizzard night of November last, Ed had changed his ways and his hours. He was turning on lights in the living room and the rest of the house about the same time as Harold and turning them off about the same time too. In the days immediately after that night, Harold had seen a police car parked out front of Ed's a couple of times and had seen Buster and Ed sitting on the coaster, heard their voices when Ed walked Buster out to the Interceptor. Buster was retired now, turning the town over to the Murdock boy, but the old chief still dropped by now and then to sit a spell with Ed on the porch. Harold thought of walking over to visit, but after what happened to Putnam, he decided maybe he'd best wait for Ed to make his own way over.

He hadn't talked to Ed since Keelan Putnam got himself killed. Terrible thing. But now Harold and Ed sat in the swing talking as if Ed hadn't shot anybody and as if Harold didn't know he had. Neither had done much recent talking to anyone and they both enjoyed the opportunity to share stories. Ed never mentioned the war and Harold didn't speak of the Devil. They talked about old times, about when they were kids, each in his own day, robbing roastin' ears off the corn wagons and running the alleys with their friends and their dogs. Harold told Ed about seeing Cassius Clay, back when he was still called that, jogging in the park down in Louisville, and Ed told Harold about hunting deer with his dad and about how he made Nighthawk to watch over his folks when he went off to fight in Korea.

Ed sat up straight and startled when he heard the first of the fireworks. They always started with a big bang that rattled the whole town, quieted the birds and set the dogs to barking.

"For a minute there I almost forgot it was Independence Day," said Harold.

"They don't never let you forget it," said Ed, gazing out over the trees where the first of the screeching rockets flickered the sky to the west. Harold and Ed kept swinging slowly and occasionally one of them spoke. "That was a whopper." "Lord!" And they were both smiling by the time the display reached its crescendo. As always, there was one big, final blast and then the quiet, broken only by a couple of howling dogs.

They sat a while longer, each lost in his own thoughts until Ed stretched his arms over his head and yawned.

Harold yawned a moment later. "Now you got me started. Time to hit the rack, I guess."

Harold, just a bit portly and still wearing a long sleeve white shirt on the warm July night, his slicked-back hair as black as the day he joined the Navy, got up when Ed did and accompanied his neighbor down from the porch.

"Don't be a stranger," he said from the concrete slab at the foot of the stairs, and Ed waved back over his shoulder.

▪▪▪

Yonders, twinkling through the leaves of the summer trees, lay quiet and at peace from Indiana Road out to the graveyard and from Four Corners to the crest of Fugate Hill.

ACKNOWLEDGEMENTS

Thank you to my grandmother, to whom this book is dedicated. From her deathbed she said, "No reason you hanging around here. Go on, git! Go over to Europe and race your motorcycle, but you'll come home and tell your stories to us in the end," and to Heidi, my wife of more than 50 years, who believed in me even when I didn't.

And a heartfelt thank-you to many people who helped me over many years with this book:
...to the great team at Trebol Editions led by Iana Petrova for the decision to publish and promote the book.

...to my sons Kenny and Dennis...each one for his invaluable help.

...to three novelists who guided and encouraged me: Lisa Reardon, Russell Rowland and Carter Sickles.

...to careful readers: my high school classmate and town historian, Carol Johnson Hicks, the late Ken Hebson, Ruth

Gore (who *demanded* that I publish this book), Roger and Mary Steffens, Amy Hunke, Bruce Howard, Dwight Howard.

...to the late Jean Minick for her insights and memories shared over a couple of coffees at Henning's on the Dixie.

...to editor Matthew Miles for his skill and patience with every comma and semicolon.

...to David Christian for advice on ballistics.

...to two inspiring professors at Monmouth College back in the sixties, both of whom changed my life: Grace Boswell and Dave Roberts.

...to the editors-in-chief who taught me the Who? What?, Where? and When? of professional journalism: Clem Cohen (*Caracas Daily Journal*), Javier Herrero (*Motociclismo*, Madrid) and Jaime Alguersuari (*Solo Moto*, Barcelona).

...to two distinguished lawmen: Hoopeston Police Chief Mark Drollinger (deceased) and former Vermilion County Chief Sheriff's Investigator Rodney Kaag, both of whom gave me important encouragement and professional perspective on the now and then of police procedures.

...to a distinguished novelist who told me at a long-ago Bread Loaf Writers Conference, "Don't write your novel until you have more life experience." (I certainly followed that advice!).

...to the Chicago & Eastern Illinois and the Nickel Plate Road for those long, lonesome train whistles, and to my son Arthur who still pulls that whistle cord in Nebraska.

...and to my deceased parents Helen Swisher Carlson and Arthur Alfred Noyes for instilling in me the love of the sound of the written word.